MATED BY THE WOLF

SHADOW SHIFTERS SERIES

MILA YOUNG

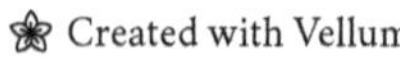 Created with Vellum

CONTENTS

MATED BY THE WOLF

She's forced to marry the enemy... but he's the wolf shifter who broke her heart years ago.

Selena Kurt agrees to an arranged wulfkin mating to protect her sister from a dangerous alpha wanting to claim her. To Selena's surprise, her match is Marcin Ulf, the next in line for the Hungarian throne...and the wulfkin who broke her heart years ago. He's seductive, dominant, and dangerous. She might give herself to the enemy, but he'll never own her heart.

Taking the enemy's daughter will only be the beginning. Marcin knows the neighboring alpha comes with plans to start war, stopping at nothing until he destroys the Hungarian pack. But Marcin has every intention to take back what belongs to him. He'll stop at nothing to win over Selena.

GLOSSARY

Moonwulf – Wolf shifters who will transform from human to wolf form only during the full moon

Wulfkin – Moonwulves who have gone through the Lunar Eutine rite of passage and are now able to change at will into their wolf form

Dracwulf – Unstoppable berserker-like creature that is half wolf, half wulfkin and will kill anything in its path

Lunar Eutine – A rite of passage for a moonwulf to permanently transform into a wulfkin. It takes place beneath a blood moon. Eutine means true of heart and draws on a moonwulf's connection to his or her inner wolf. When the moon is completely shrouded in black, a new wulfkin will be delivered.

Alpha – The leader of a pack of wulfkin/moonwulves who rules only over his or her claimed territory

Varlac – A reigning wulfkin clan who rule and set laws for all alphas living under their territory jurisdiction (e.g. Europe, Africa, etc.)

Varlac Emperor Alpha – Varlac leader who rules over every alpha and pack in Europe

Varlac Sultan Alpha – Varlac leader who rules over every alpha and pack in the Middle East and Asia

Venery – A sport engaged in by Varlac leaders whereby they hunt wild animals

Battle of Innocence – A challenge whereby a worthy champion will engage in a tournament or task on behalf of another wulfkin facing charges. If the champion succeeds, the wulfkin he or she is representing will be found innocent and freed. If the champion fails, the wulfkin will be found guilty and punished accordingly.

Boon – On the completion of a battle of innocence, if the champion succeeds, he or she will be granted a boon, allowing him or her to claim any prize he or she desires. Within reason of course.

CHAPTER 1

MARCIN

The inner wolf nipped at my insides, promising speed and stealth to track our opponent exceptionally fast if I shifted. Except we weren't playing by those rules today.

Remain human and hunt.

Staring at the snow blanketing the terrain didn't reveal my enemy. But standing out in the open in daylight made me an easy target, so I sprinted into the deciduous forest stripped of its color.

The earlier crispness of the day—pine, fresh, and clean—was overpowered by the distant fireplace smoke in the air, burning my nostrils and making my throat itch.

Underlying it all was that earthy scent of wet fur. It called me straight ahead.

A growl reverberated in my chest, and I summoned my wolf's strength, embracing his fire. An invigorating energy zapped through me, and my flesh prickled. This was the closest I'd ever come to harnessing the wolf without shifting, and I longed for the full transformation.

I rushed ahead, dodging trees, leaping over dead logs ... each step precise with minimal sound. About fifty yards away, I picked up the repetitive hop of a rabbit scurrying for cover. The breeze brought no new scents but shook the dry leaves that cascaded around me.

Where are you?

A crunch of twigs snapped from behind. I jerked around.

The gray wolf I'd been hunting lunged toward me.

My breath froze in my lungs. I threw a punch, connecting with the side of his head, but I held my ground.

The wolf's stunned body crashed into me. He whimpered. Still, his fangs grazed my shoulder, snagging fabric and flesh on the way down.

I recoiled, grasping my wound.

He collapsed with a thud but quickly scrambled back onto large paws. His dark fur bristled. His lips peeled back.

The scratch would heal, but my leather jacket ... hell, it had been a gift from an alpha in Norway, specifically made to be fireproof and with multiple secret pockets in the lining.

"Today's training was a seek-and-find mission, not seek and attack." My words boomed, sending birds fluttering out of the nearby trees.

Aron's ears flattened against his head, and he lowered his belly to the ground. "Draw on your wolf's strength and remain in human form. Those were my instructions."

"For months, I'd trained new pack members, and they still didn't get it. We couldn't hide who we were from humans forever. We had to learn to adapt. Controlling our wolf side was the answer. Damn it, we were wulfkin—half wolf, half man— and the moon didn't control our wild side, so we sure as hell should be able to control it ourselves.

A whine resonated from Aron's chest.

I dusted foliage and snow off my jeans. "We're doing this again."

The crunch of snow sounded, and I turned to find Vincent, my second-in-command, striding closer with two other initiates alongside him, both in their pants and bomber jackets. Maybe the training wasn't a complete loss.

"The weather's turning for the worse." Vincent drew the collar of his black coat tight and wrapped his arms across his chest. Snow dotted his dark brown, cropped hair, and his cheeks were weather burned.

Despite the lack of strong winds, the arctic cold sunk its teeth into my bones, just like Aron's bite.

Vincent's gaze shifted to Aron, who now crouched naked in human form—hugging his knees, teeth chattering.

I took off my jacket and tossed it to Aron. "Go put some clothes on and come back.

We're going another round."

"You heard him, wulfkin," Vincent called out. "Another round."

Aron slipped into the jacket, nodded, and bolted toward the castle. The other initiates ran off into the woods behind us.

Vincent stepped closer, his voice low and brittle. "Six mock hunts and he still shifts. Is he suited for our pack? We're wasting our time."

I stared at my second-in-command, my friend and a wulfkin I considered a brother.

The look in his deep-set eyes was pure trust. His honesty was refreshing and unrelenting. I'd grown up in a world surrounded by power-hungry wolves, and Vincent was a blessing.

"He'll pull through. Give him time." I needed a loyal, strong, and large pack behind me. They had to trust in me and the direction I chose. So if it took twenty practice hunts to help initiates find their strength and curb the desire to turn, then twenty they'd get. If after that they showed no improvement, then they could return to Father's pack.

When I was sixteen, Father had encouraged me to become an alpha by taking over a neighboring pack because no son of his would simply inherit an alpha status. *You must earn it.* I followed his instructions in hope that it would make him proud of me, but I couldn't have been more wrong. Months later, I stopped taking his advice on how to rule over my pack members. Fear never built loyalty—only gutless, selfish wulfkin who'd slit your throat at the first opportunity. Now, both my and Father's packs lived in the Hungarian castle, and lucky for everyone, the place was large enough to avoid stepping on each other's toes.

Foliage snapped deeper in the woods. I stiffened; my gaze

swept the woodland. A figure ran toward us from the direction of the castle.

Father's personal servant, an eighteen-year-old wulfkin with a red nose, emerged, his breaths labored. "Marcin." He took a deep inhale, and his words rattled. "Varlac Emperor Levin is home and demands your immediate presence."

A quiet chill limped up my spine. Good ol' cold and calculating Father caused panic the moment he'd arrived back home. "I'll see him later."

"No. Please, he'll beat me if you don't show up." The young wulfkin's wide eyes pleaded with me.

I gritted my teeth. When had my father ever created anything but chaos? Never. Vincent patted my arm. "Go. I'll finish here."

I rubbed my eyes with frosty fingers. My instincts screamed at me to stay out in the woods all day and night, not giving my father the satisfaction of obedience.

"The alpha ..." The young wulfkin's voice cracked. "Is holding an urgent council meeting. Everyone's in the great hall, waiting for you."

"Council meeting? What for?" The only time Father called urgent assembly was when he sprang yet another law change on all the wulfkin in his territories. As a Varlac emperor who ruled over every alpha and pack in Europe, it gave him the freedom to do so. But perhaps his arrival back home from Transylvania came with news about my brother, Enre, who lived with a pack in Romania. At the age of fourteen, he had run away from home, but I couldn't blame him, not with the way Father used to beat him. Distance was his safest option. It didn't make it any easier to swallow the fact that I'd lost a brother at such a young age.

The young wulfkin in front of me shrugged, his large coat giving the impression he was taller than he was. "Come. He's impatient today."

"My father's middle name is Impatient," I responded with no exaggeration.

Vincent broke into a deep chuckle. "Don't think you have a choice. We'll regroup later."

"Yep." My voice strained. "Guess I don't get to change my

clothes either." Blood stained the shoulder of my white shirt, the fabric shredded above the torn flesh that stung each time the wind brushed across the wound.

Vincent retreated in the same direction as the initiates. I headed toward the castle.

My steps echoed off the stone walls, and shadows flickered across the dimly lit corridor like spies tracking my movements. Candelabras lined every inch of the castle. We didn't live in medieval times, but Father insisted on the ambiance they created.

Ahead, the ten-foot, double oak doors leading into the great hall were closed. The cast- iron door knockers, formed in the shape of a wolf's head with a deer leg in its jaws, mocked me. This room was Father's stage. The one location where he gathered his fearful minions and dished out punishments to flaunt his power. Whatever sadistic decisions Father intended to showcase today would end up affecting me somehow.

Always did.

I pushed open the creaking doors, drawing everyone's attention. Seventy or so wulfkin stood around in a large circle: Father's pack, a handful of mine, and council members.

The arched windows on one side of the room showed only the white sloping mountains behind the castle. No furniture filled this room since it was a place of business, as Father often said. The only sign of hospitality was the blazing fire roaring in the hearth centered on the back wall, but it did little to warm the large space.

Wulfkin parted, and I stormed forward, my sights set on Father's throne at this end of the circle of people. A bear's pelt, complete with head and glassy eyes, hung from the back of his tall seat. Father's trophy and bragging rights to anyone who'd listen.

The moment I emerged from the crowd, my gaze fastened on two figures at the other end of the court. Ice filled my veins.

Enre, my younger brother whom I hadn't seen for the last twelve years, was on his knees, hands bound behind his back, mouth gagged, and chained with an iron chain tethered to the floor. Blood streaked his cheek. A welcome back hug from Father no doubt. A dark-haired beauty kneeling next to Enre was in the same plight. Who was she?

"What the fuck is this?" The words tore past my throat.

"Such language." Father gave me a smarmy response. "Come take my side, son."

When Enre met my gaze, his features twisted into a grimace. Sure, we didn't have the brotherly relationship I'd dreamed of. I didn't blame him for loathing me. When we were growing up, Father had been unstoppable in his torment of Enre. The most I could do was divert him long enough for Enre to run away. Two broken ribs had been worth the knowledge that my younger brother would no longer be a punching bag.

My thoughts numbed, bludgeoned to death by the sight in front of me. What the hell was going on? I lunged toward Enre and pulled on his restraints, the clangs a lonely song in the deathly silent room.

"Someone give me the keys." My voice thundered and echoed throughout the hall. "Enough of your theatrics, Marcin. Take your place next to me." Father's underlying

tone carried venom, the kind promising repercussions.

I stepped between the prisoners and the supposedly greatest leader of Europe. The solid wulfkin sat stiff in his ruling chair, silver strands above his temples giving the impression he had horns. Wouldn't be far from the truth.

"Is this how you welcome your son back home, with chains and gags? What message are you sending to your packs?"

Father shifted in his seat, tightness capturing his thin lips. "If anyone crosses me— even my own blood—they'll pay."

I moved closer, hands curled into fists. "How exactly has Enre crossed you? He's your son, for moon's sake. Weren't you the one who taught me to check all my facts before making accusations?"

He huffed. "I have the facts, and you'd better steady that sharp tongue."

My muscles flexed, urging me closer, and the inner wolf prodded my chest, ready to show Father a thing or two. "I won't let you treat Enre like an animal ever again."

The rigid posture Father took, the way his fingers crushed the seat's arm, were all warning signs of a volcanic eruption, punishment for defying him in public. But the explosion of fire in my chest would shadow his venting, leaving him choking on his own toxic cloud.

Control yourself. Don't destroy the trust you've built with him for years. I softened my expression.

Father lifted himself out of his seat with the swiftness of a predator.

While challenging my alpha to a fight would bring me the ultimate satisfaction, his guards would step in before I laid a hand on him. And my pack wasn't large enough yet to take on his entire army. Killing him had crossed my mind, but with the council aware I intended to overthrow him, I'd be the number one suspect, meaning I'd be punished by death. The usual law of killing alphas to replace them didn't apply to Varlac leaders.

They had their own set of rules involving natural death, handing over the position to another, or having hard evidence proving he or she had broken a rule. A crafty Varlac in the past had made sure of these changes to the rules.

The only reason I still lived in this hell of a castle with my pack was to keep my enemy close and plot his downfall.

"Marcin. Either sit by my side or leave." The coldness of Father's words was a blade to my heart, but I couldn't force my legs to move. Not when my brother remained chained, and I had a lifetime of atonement to make up for his treatment. I should have done more to protect him, should have taken the hits. Fear had been a crippling cancer.

"At least unchain them. They aren't going anywhere." I approached and stood at Father's side to show him I could play the game too.

He sat back down and folded one leg over the other. A quick

wave to someone in the crowd brought a tall wulfkin with more muscles than sense strutting toward Enre and his companion. Father's minion removed the gags and ties from Enre and the female.

When Father gave another wave, a second servant scurried over with a silver wine goblet. He handed it to Father, who sighed and backhanded the drink. The goblet clattered to the stone floor, and red liquid splashed across several spectators nearby. Father snatched the young wulfkin's wrist. "How many times have I told you to always hand me blood wine in my right hand?" He raised his hand into a fist.

The wulfkin shrank beneath Father's iron grip.

I seized Father's arm. "Let's focus on the topic at hand."

He tore free from my grasp and released the young wulfkin, who cowered and retreated into the crowd.

Across from us, Enre rubbed his wrists. When he looked my way, his hooded gaze and arched eyebrow yelled confusion.

Enre cut our staring match and turned his attention to Father. "You said the council would give us consent for Daciana"—he glanced at the dark-haired female next to him and back—"to hand over her pack and land to me. You agreed that Daciana and I would come here of our own free will to present our case to the council. Not to be sentenced." His voice deepened. "I should have expected you wouldn't hold true to your word."

So, that was Daciana? She was also a pack member from Transylvania. I'd heard many tales about her warrior-like skills along with her beauty. Well, the stories hadn't been lying about her attractiveness, so I suspected she could hold her own in a battle. But I had no idea Daciana had taken over the Transylvanian pack from their now ex-alpha, Sandulf.

I glanced at Enre, but his glare locked onto Father. A transfer of pack and land was acceptable under our rules as long as both alphas were of sound mind. So what was the issue?

"Before the council can review such a request, you and Daciana must prostrate yourselves and beg forgiveness for the rules you have broken. My rules."

I cringed and glanced across at Father on his throne, smirking. I'd been born to the devil. Father would twist anything to serve his own purpose, but what exactly did he need from Enre?

"What are you talking about?" Daciana's posture stiffened, and a snarl hung off her last word.

Father's harsh voice bounced around the room. "Daciana, you are held accused of the creation of a dracwulf."

Dracwulves were banned for a good reason—they were unstoppable berserker-like wolves that killed everything in their path. Why would anyone willingly breed one?

"That was Sandulf, not me."

"Tsk, tsk." Father wiggled a finger at the brunette. "You know the rules. You took over the pack, and that includes your previous alpha's burdens and responsibilities.

Sandulf is dead, so you will now face the council on his behalf." A few murmurs rolled out from the crowd.

I crouched next to Father and whispered, "We already spoke about eliminating this law."

He waved me away as if I were no more than a gnat and leaned forward in his seat, a smile creeping across his mouth.

"Enre, with your recent acquisition of the Bulgarian pack, you will now face charges for the dead humans found at every location their pack had traveled. If found guilty, you'll both face death."

The audience broke into a clamor, and the horrific reality of the situation curdled my insides.

Enre's face paled. He never said a word but took the accusation as he used to take Father's punches and strikes—without emotion or reaction.

"This is ridiculous," I said. Wulfkin had to obey their leader; it was inbred in us and came with deadly consequences if we refused. But to hold someone accountable for his or her alpha's actions was ludicrous.

"Your accusations are barbaric." Daciana's voice was strong and piercing. "Blaming us will prove nothing."

"Release Daciana and punish me." Enre's deep voice sliced through the room. "That's what this is about. It's what you've always wanted, isn't it? And to get your grubby fingers on Transylvania for Marcin."

Why would he think that? "That's not true. I don't—"

"Shut the hell up, both of you," Father said. "These are my rules, and both Enre and Daciana will face the council for their alpha's actions. End of story."

My blood congealed to ice. Going against Father would only push him into finding Enre guilty. Father's insistence to punish him and Daciana meant one thing—he wanted Enre dead.

I leaned closer to his ear. "Too much emotion is being thrown around here. Don't let the council be unfairly influenced. Let's regroup in a few days, after everyone has cooled down."

"No! We do this now." Father faced the crowd. "I call the council." One good thing I'd instigated was getting Father to agree to setting up a council who had to give their approval on all major rules and decisions, alongside him.

The pulsing urgency made my head spin. I had to shut Father down this very second.

He couldn't keep getting his way.

Tibor, the eldest of the council, emerged from the crowd. We exchanged glances, my stare imploring him to fight the proposal.

"Emperor Levin." Tibor crept toward Father, his gaze lowered. "Perhaps there are other ways to conduct such a hearing."

Father's face reddened. His lips parted, but his words were stolen by the loud creak of the doors opening to the great hall.

A servant rushed into the room, directly to Father, and whispered a message in his ear.

The only word I overheard was *arrived*. Whom was he referring to? "Now? Already?" Father asked.

The servant nodded. "I'll be there shortly."

The young wulfkin darted from the room, leaving the door slightly ajar.

"Well, seems a break is being forced upon us after all. I have a small distraction to attend to. Nobody leave until I return." Father glanced my way. "Marcin, you're with me."

I didn't move at first. "What's going on?"

He gave no response but glanced at the guards. "Tie them back up." Father took long strides toward the exit. Around me, the crowd's voices escalated and two guards approached Enre and Daciana. I jogged out of the room after Father, curiosity burning a hole through my gut.

"We need to talk," I said. "You've been gone for over a week and never left a word with anyone as to what you were doing, and then you return, acting like a madman. Enre is your son!"

Without stopping his wild rush around a corner, his response was swift. "The only reason I'm ignoring your insolence is because today is a special day. Quickly, now." He picked up his pace.

For 137 years old, he showed no sign of slowing down. For the sake of all packs, I prayed to the moon he would soon, especially since a few wulfkin have been known to live to 180.

And his version of a special day was probably a twisted, demented new torture device he'd ordered to use on Enre.

Maybe I should have visited Enre before now and made peace with him, but the time had never seemed right. Today, it looked like I would never get that chance.

"Where are we going?"

"Patience." Father smiled as he marched.

He pushed through another entrance that led us past the marble staircase curling upward. Sunlight from the window on the second floor reflected off its black banisters. The bronze wolf statues on the newel posts at the base of the stairs seemed to watch us rush past.

We headed directly to the welcoming room, reserved only for guests.

"Who's here?" I asked. Father's secrecy meant it was most likely someone I didn't want anywhere near our home.

He halted a few steps in front of me and swung around just as the winter gale rattled the tall windows around us and snow fell at an angle outside. "I hadn't intended for him to arrive this early. I had planned to tell you about it, but it's—"

"Him?" Father had made an enemy of everyone he crossed, and he had no close friends, so who got him this worked up?

"The Varlac sultan has arrived." Father's eyes creased at the corners, the complete opposite reaction he'd ever worn when speaking of the Turkish Varlac leader we considered the enemy.

"What the fuck for?" A month earlier, we'd received a warning from the sultan, who'd insisted we killed two of their kind. I had nothing to do with the murders, but last week, I'd scouted the sultan's territory without Father's orders. I had to uncover what kind of army we were dealing with before the situation escalated. I was convinced no one had spotted me, but my trespassing could be considered an act of war and confirmation of the recent killings.

Maybe they were here for payback. Except, why the hell was Father grinning wildly?

"Your language is so vulgar sometimes. You don't need to always swear." Father shook his head as if that annoyed him more than the bullshit going on in the great hall.

"The Turkish clan has threatened to attack in the past," I said, trying to convince myself more than Father. "Is the sultan here for a final warning?"

"Quit your worrying. You sound like a female." Father placed a hand on my arm, his cold leeching through my clothes. "We have never seen eye to eye with the Turks, but their alpha negotiated a resolution to stop our constant fighting. Neither side will lose any additional wulfkin."

"Where is my real father, and what have you done with him?"

"It will now end," he continued. "But it all lies with you, son. Make me proud."

The world spun beneath me. "What are you talking about?" Father must be sending me off with them as a prisoner of war. It wouldn't be unlike him.

"Quickly, we can't keep our guests waiting." He whirled around and hurried down the corridor.

Guests? What had he gotten me into?

CHAPTER 2

My family and I had been shoved into this waiting room from the moment we arrived at the oldest castle in the Őrség region of Hungary. Stone walls, dark wooden cabinets, soaring windows, tall ceilings, and wrought iron candelabras. Smells of coffee and jasmine wafted through the place, with a hint of earthy soil and wolf. Even the cobblestone fireplace, its mantel carved with wolves howling at a moon, screamed medieval times. At home, we had flat screen televisions in every room. Only so many reruns one can watch.

I fidgeted in my frozen, unforgiving seat. Even my inner wolf trembled inside. Bad enough the snow had iced my toes and fingers the moment we arrived in the country, but—

"Selena, if you've changed your mind—"

I offered Father a short smile and ironed out my posture as he paced from the arched window to the semicircle of empty chairs in front of me.

"No, I'm fine." Yeah, change and it would be my younger sister thrown into this pit of bloodthirsty wolves. Not happening.

Before coming here, I had two options: be sold to a mad alpha in Turkey whose last two wives had mysteriously vanished, or mate into the wulfkin family who had tried to have me killed. I was convinced assassins were more likely to negotiate than a demented alpha, so I chose the latter. The small fact that I knew Marcin would be my arranged mate in Hungary factored into my decision. How could it not when we had a history? I fell for him big time when I was sixteen. Back then, I believed he was my true mate, so we ran away from our families to start a new life, leaving behind the rules, drama, and constant threat of war. But we were discovered, and after a targeted arrow struck my shoulder, Father accused Levin. The Hungarian alpha insisted the arrow was meant for his son and blamed my family. I had seen a Hungarian archer release the arrow, but Marcin never leapt to my defense or supported my argument. Either way, Marcin and I were torn apart. I didn't want to believe he'd side with his father, but then again, he never returned to Turkey to whisk me away like he'd promised. For years, I hated him, and I still had no idea if I would ever get over his deceit.

I glanced up to watch Father pacing. "Baba, if you don't stop, you'll wear out that rug.

What is that on the rug anyway?" I leaned forward for a better look. "Animals ripping each other apart? Charming. Anyway, I doubt Levin would be happy."

Rumors about the great Varlac Emperor of Europe depicted him as a wulfkin short on patience. Wrong him and he'd kill you before asking questions. I had every reason to believe the stories. All the Varlac leaders around the world might be painted with the same stroke, but none were feared as much as Levin. "Those poor creatures on the carpet might end up being us." The knot in my stomach coiled at the idea.

The captain of our guards, Zeki, cleared his throat and set his hand on the hilt of his sword.

A few paces away, Father reprimanded me with an intrusive glare. "Don't shame me by calling the emperor by his first name."

I squared my shoulders but swallowed my complaint. The time for protesting had been back in Turkey, along with my dignity and whatever life I'd created for myself. Aside from sparing my sister from a forced mating, the union of our clans would stop the imminent war. Our packs had been feuding for generations, but lately the situation had escalated threefold. Two of our pack members were murdered last month, and Father insisted it was the Hungarians. Except, a week later, three of Levin's pack members were found butchered near the Turkish border, and we were blamed. Without listening to reason, Levin declared that he'd flatten our pack and rip out the hearts of every last family member. The waiting was over. War was happening. My father swore he had never issued a killings order and suspected Levin lied, but there was no way to prove it.

Father panicked. Our pack wasn't big enough to fight Levin's, so he struck a deal. Mate me to his son and offer Levin a patch of Turkish land as a dowry to mend the troubles between our packs. Yeah, I was a bargaining chip for peace, and it sucked big time.

On my feet, I patted down my dress. This black velvet kaftan was useless in a freezing cold medieval castle. My wide belt had shifted sideways, and I tugged down on the wide sleeves that kept riding up for the millionth time. The seamstress who'd sewn this dress specifically for today should've spent a day in it to see it needed more layers. A chill crept up my spine, and I blew warmth into my cupped hands while sidling next to the fireplace. Father's attire appeared warmer than mine with his long red coat with fox fur lining along the edging.

"I can hear you all the way from the toilets." Aisha's footsteps ricocheted behind me, and I turned to find my younger sister hurrying in from a corridor dimly lit by chandeliers, her focus on her cell phone, her fingers tapping away. Her Bohemian-style white with floral prints kaftan fluttered around her legs.

My sister radiated childhood innocence. She believed in the goodness of wulfkin and enjoyed each day as if it were her first. At sixteen, Aisha had her life ahead of her.

Apparently, it was too late for me. At twenty-five, any well-respected wulfkin female should have been mated by now, or so Father kept reminding me. What was so great about being well respected anyway? Zilch.

"Aisha." Father pointed at her phone. "I've told you before. No more chirping—"

"It's called tweeting, and I'm not. This castle is in a black vortex where Internet connection is non-existent." She dropped a hand to her side, still clutching the cell, and smiled at Father.

Aisha should have gone into acting, or espionage, since she lied so convincingly. When I'd glanced at her phone this morning, she'd had reception. Her insistence on sharing photos of her henna body art was bordering on an obsession, despite Father's fits of rage each time he caught her in the act. But damn, the girl had close to a hundred thousand followers, and I guessed her fans expected footage of her art. My hands and legs might have made the occasional appearance.

"See, why can't you smile a bit too?" Father stared at me with eyebrows pulled together into a flat line.

"Just because I agreed to this arrangement, doesn't mean I have to like it." I dragged myself to the icy chair, my hip stiffening. I rubbed the old injury that didn't agree with the cold.

Father attempted to laugh, but it came across forced. "I never thought that after finding out you ran away with Marcin, we'd be arranging this reunion."

Yeah, the irony of it all.

Father's servant Ela rushed across the room, her breath racing, her pregnancy weighing on her every move. She handed Father a drink. He gulped it down and pushed the empty goblet back into her hands. "Get my clothes ironed and hung in my closet immediately."

She nodded, one hand pressed to her lower back as she retreated. I couldn't help myself. "Surely you can ask someone else to do that. Ela's been sick from our travel."

Father's narrow gaze might have scared off his guards, but I stood my ground. "She'll be more productive after resting."

He shook his head and looked away, flicking a hand at his servant. "Fine."

Ela, a woman in her late twenties, offered me a tiny nod of appreciation before leaving.

Then the doors at the rear of the room scraped open. I fell in alongside Father, with Aisha by my side, just as we'd been instructed.

Levin, the Hungarian Varlac emperor, stepped inside. The hefty wulfkin whisked closer, his chest puffed out and pride oozing from every inch of his austere posture. I'd seen Father wear the same mask all too often.

"Sultan Boran, you're early." Levin took Father's hands into his. "Welcome, welcome. My home is yours."

Father pulled back, his voice loud and sharp. "You are most gracious, Emperor." Then another wulfkin entered the room behind him. Solid, tall, and all shoulders. And suddenly my heart hammered so hard the walls seemed to be thumping too. *Marcin.*

Windblown hair draped over his shoulders, tawny brown strands reaching halfway down his chest. His shirt was torn across his shoulder. Blood stained the fabric, worn as a badge of honor for whatever heroic deeds he'd accomplished.

Our gazes locked, and he stopped midstride. It was like a sucker punch to the gut. All the air left my lungs, leaving me light-headed.

Sea-spray blue eyes, darker than I remembered them, searched my face. Shock crammed behind his gaze as his cheeks blanched. He'd had no idea I was coming here— it was written all over his frozen expression, the way his mouth fell open, his breath hitched.

My wolf prodded me, stirring inside, well aware of who stood before us. Marcin had grown into even more of a wulfkin god: muscular, strong cheekbones, and a chest broad enough for me to sleep across. All I could think about was touching him to make sure he was real and not in my imagination.

Move closer. Take him.

I shouldn't, yet every molecule in my body fought against the logic that said stay away.

Sure, I'd planned for this very moment and even practiced my nonchalant response in front of the mirror. Except now, my voice was wedged somewhere between my toes and head. My body shook with the desperate urge to be pressed up against him, feel his hungry kisses, listen to his wicked whispers. I struggled with the charge in my veins screaming that I should run to him, throw my arms around his neck, and forget the past nine years. Forget that he tore out my soul. Forget that I mistook him as my mate because he'd lied to me. Abandoned me.

Father touched my arm, and I flinched. "Did you hear me?" "No, sorry."

"Emperor Levin, this is my eldest."

I lowered my gaze. Blood dotted the tips of Levin's boots. Wulfkin blood. He'd probably returned from flogging a poor wulfkin who dared speak against him.

"Yes, I know you. Lift your head so I can look at you properly," Levin said, amusement woven beneath his words.

The moment I did, my gaze swept across the room and landed on Marcin. The pressure inside me deepened. Why wasn't he saying anything? It killed me to stand there and stare at him without moving closer. He might as well pull out a blade and carve up what was left of my heart.

Our history was meaningless. Now, he was nothing more than the one I had to mate with for this peace treaty. I doubted he'd welcome even a hug from me. Levin, on the other hand, seemed ready to drag me into his private chamber. The vision made me ill.

Marcin strode closer, his arms tight, a hooded gaze hooked into his father. When Marcin finally glanced my way, my insides iced.

"Selena?" The sound of his voice was soft, almost desperate.

I trembled. For a wild moment, I was certain he'd take me into his arms, his hands digging into my back as he kissed me, but it didn't happen. Just like he'd never come looking for me when my father locked me up for weeks after we were caught running away together in Turkey, threatening to sell me off to another alpha. Marcin and I had known each other for years, but we spent a few wonderful weeks together in Turkey when I was sixteen years old. At the time it felt as if we'd known each other for a lifetime.

Levin shifted toward me, blocking my view of Marcin, his heavy breaths gliding across my face and stinking of blood. Next he circled me, and my primitive instinct screamed to attack him, rip his jugular out. Instead, I sensed his footsteps around me, his fingers grazing my arm, lifting my hand to his nose. Then he peeled back my upper lip with a thumb.

Fire raced through my veins, and I smacked his hand away. Levin's brow twisted, but he grinned.

"Selena." My father's voice was poison. He snatched my wrist and squeezed. "Apologize." He always asked me to back down, to let others walk over me, and it jabbed me like an angry wasp each time anyone spoke to me that way.

"I agreed to this of my own volition, not—"

Father's frown chased away my words. Turkish Varlac rules insisted females had no standing until they were mated.

"Don't worry, Boran." Levin patted Father's shoulder. "Young ones these days have lost their respect. Selena will perfectly match my sharp-tongued son. Marcin, you remember Selena Kurt, don't you? She's your future mate, just like you wanted all those years ago."

"What's going on?" Marcin said, his words piercing and direct, shadows dancing beneath his eyes. "What's she doing here?"

An invisible fist struck my stomach, and with every instinct in my body, every wisp of my being, I fought the urge to scream at Marcin, force him to admit we had a past, a caring one at that, and not react as if he'd just discovered his future mate was a hideous mutant monster. I had to remind myself I wasn't facing the Marcin from years ago. He'd been a young boy then. Now he was an adult wulfkin, leading his own pack and ruling by his father's side.

And at once, it became too much to handle. The rage I'd used to cover the pain of Marcin's deceit shoved forward. I clamped down the emotions shredding my insides to shards because those kind of feelings only led to hurt.

"Come." Levin threaded an arm around Father's, his voice toneless because our emotions didn't matter, only his transaction had merit. "Join me by the fire to warm yourself while they get reacquainted."

Aisha retreated to stand near the captain of the guards.

Marcin said nothing at first, but stared at me as if I'd grown two heads. A scorching fire penetrated my skin, and my face burned.

I swallowed past the boulder in my throat. "It's been a while. Nine years, right?"

The corded muscles in his neck tensed. "It's been too long." He averted his gaze when he spoke as if I meant so little to him. "Excuse me, please." He swung toward his father and, in a few long strides, reached the Varlac leaders. At least the repulsive Turkish alpha would have been excited to see me.

But I had to remember—my mission here was only to protect my sister and help ease the war between the clans, like any dutiful Varlac daughter. Still ... if I had to spend the rest of my life with him, how could I live with this changed Marcin, when the one I loved no longer existed?

"Why didn't you talk to me about this first?" Despite Marcin's attempted whisper, his words bounced around the room.

Levin shook his head and refused to face him. "So you can run away again and make the situation between our clans worse? Trust me. In a few days, you two will be inseparable."

"Father. This—"

"Enough!" Levin faced his son and took a deep breath, obviously calming himself. "Marcin, I will only ask you once to accept this." The harshness underlying his tone had me retreating a few steps. He refocused on my father and broke into a theoretical discussion about our merger.

Marcin stood there for a few moments, his chest heaving, his posture curled forward, and hands fisted. Only then did he return to me.

I contemplated turning away from him. If I did, would I be any better than him? I managed to lift my chin with a smile.

"Selena," he said, his voice low and brittle. "We're in the middle of a council meeting right now. I'll organize for someone to show you to your rooms."

A softness swept across his expression. For that short pause, I stared at the young Marcin who longed for peace between all wulfkin, whose reassuring words injected me with the confidence to strive for anything in life and reminded me of his pledge to take me away from my father. They'd been lies. All the things he'd said were fabrications. My permanent hip injury attested to that.

Levin's words sliced my thoughts. "Sultan, join our council meeting and see how we deal with those who break rules." His tone darkened.

"Wonderful." Father turned toward Aisha and me. "Come along." He then accompanied Levin out of the room with Marcin storming out the door behind them.

Aisha rushed to my side, weaving an arm around mine. "That wasn't too bad."

I exchanged glances with my sister, offering her a frown. "Were we in the same room?"

"I think he's just shocked."

Except how could I ever fully trust Marcin again after I got injured and he ditched me?

"Ladies, this way." Zeki, our guard, stood near the doorway. "You don't want to fall behind your father."

We hurried out and soon emerged into an enormous courtyard, the length and width of four train carriages. The cold was worse than inside, if that was even possible. Father vanished through another set of doors ahead. The castle's cobblestone walls encircled the area, casting shadows over the empty yard. No plants or flowers or much else except snow, which had recently been shoveled into heaps against the walls. Farther ahead, an old-fashioned well sat in the center like an ancient relic that had watched the world pass it by.

Colored lanterns, cushions, and music would transform the place into a welcoming sight. Though I doubted the Hungarian clan did happiness.

Aisha's hand squeezed mine. "Everything will be fine. You'll see."

"Thanks." I leaned against her shoulder. We hadn't been separated since her birth, and missing her would be an understatement. I'd be left in this place with Levin leering at me and

Marcin ignoring me. Running away would be interpreted as an insult and would lead Levin to attack our home in Turkey. Nope, I'd make this work, somehow. We entered a dark corridor with more candelabras and tapestries lining the walls. Our boot heels clicked loudly as we rushed to catch up with the alphas.

"I have a proposal to make." Marcin strolled alongside his father, standing taller than him. "Drop the charges against Enre and Daciana, and I'll go through with the mating."

He might as well have shot an arrow into my heart. It shouldn't surprise me that Marcin used me as a bargaining chip when my father had done the exact same thing. It must be an alpha thing.

"No. You'll be mated, and your brother will face charges."

Marcin fell back a few steps and glanced over his shoulder at me for a split second.

We were both trapped in the same forced mating. Words pressed against my mind, willing Marcin to ignore his frustration about the unfairness of it all and about dishonest parents. But what difference would it make? When Father first broached the topic with me, it had taken me a week to speak to him again. But his threats of mating Aisha were oh so convincing ... and manipulative.

Before us, two grand doors opened. Inside, several hundred candles against the walls and in the overhead chandeliers wavered from the draft. Arched windows lined three walls, overlooking a snowy landscape of mountains. Perched on the back wall, above the fireplace, was a flag with an image of a wolf wearing armor ... the Hungarian Varlac symbol of the iron wolf, always ready for battle.

A large group of wulfkin waited for us inside. Wolf scents— timber, earthy, flowery— struck at once, reminding me of a stuffy room that hadn't seen the light of day for months.

The sea of wulfkin parted, and we strolled through, the hairs on the nape of my neck rising.

Once in the center, the crowd closed in behind us. Across the other end were two wulfkin, a male and female, their mouths taped and their hands chained.

I bit my lower lip, staring at the blood dribbling down their faces. The male had the same blue eyes as Marcin, but unlike Marcin who was fair skinned with light-colored hair, Enre was tanned with black hair and obviously took after his father. I recognized Marcin's brother instantly. What had Enre done?

My gaze shifted to the female kneeling next to him, her dark hair pulled into a ponytail, shoulders thrust back, and gaze wide.

Aisha nudged me to my seat and slipped down alongside me, Father on my other side. "Today." Levin broke the stilted silence. "Two alphas, Enre and Daciana, stand

accused in place of their deceased leaders for breaking our Varlac laws."

I slid to the edge of my chair, my insides tight. I'd seen Father punish wulfkin for committing deadly crimes, yet these two were being punished for someone else's acts. Savagery. Father always used a strong fist, but he was fair most of the time, putting wulfkin first. Except when it came to me, apparently.

And a female alpha? Unheard of at home, yet here she was. Maybe I still stood a chance of Father bestowing the same status on me without a mate.

Levin's voice rumbled as he explained the reasons for punishment and how, if found guilty, Enre and Daciana would die. I gripped the arms of the chair. Senseless killings. Aisha gasped beside me, and judging by her pale complexion, she agreed.

Levin rattled on. I leaned closer to Father and lowered my voice. "This is unjust." He patted my hand. "We don't interfere with another pack's rules."

Levin's gravelly voice made my skin crawl. "I call the council to hear your verdict."

"They don't stand a chance," I whispered. "I ... I won't marry into this pack if they are killed." If this was a normal occurrence here, I wanted no part of it. Mating contract or no.

His scowl did little to alter my determination.

"Father, please." I racked my mind for a solution, for a way to help the two wulfkin who looked as if they'd been in a marathon, running for their lives—worn down and beaten.

Then it hit me, and I whispered, "Stop this. Call for a battle of innocence." Each inhale quickened, and I readied to jump to my feet with my proposal, to defend these poor wulfkin.

But Marcin was on his feet and striding halfway across the room. "If you punish them, I demand the same fate."

"So dramatic, Marcin. Sit down."

"No." An electric charge spilled through the room, the kind before a wulfkin transformed—Marcin's. Mine stirred inside too, responding to his, and he glanced over to me for a second. Did he feel it too?

Levin flicked his hand, and two guards closed in on Marcin. More wulfkin entered the great hall, all stocky and obvious fighters, exchanging a knowing nod with Marcin.

This situation would end in bloodshed. What family was I getting myself into?

"Levin, Marcin." My father stepped steadily, his hands resting across his belly. "What about a traditional trial that will truly show us if the accused are guilty?"

My gaze was glued on Levin, and I prayed he accepted.

His lips pinched, and if ever anyone was about to self-combust, it was him. Instead, his ballooning rage morphed into a fake smirk. "Whatever do you have in mind?"

"A battle of innocence. Two worthy champions are selected to represent Enre and Daciana in a challenge decided by you, as it is your territory. If a champion wins, the wulfkin they represent will be innocent and released. If they fail, the wulfkin will be guilty and punished accordingly. One champion will battle on behalf of Enre, the other for Daciana. And as an extra incentive to attract the best warriors, the first of the champions to win the challenge may claim a boon."

A cacophony of voices and howls from the crowd swept through the room, their feet stomping against the wooden floorboards with their approval. Enre nodded.

Marcin approached my father and bowed approvingly. "I give my consent to the quest." He faced the audience. "Does any council member here have reason as to why we shouldn't proceed with the redeeming quest to prove Enre and Daciana's innocence?"

Levin's loathing was on full display from his warped lips to his creased nose. He gazed over the cheering mob that might just as well turn violent if their entertainment was now snuffed away.

"I generously appreciate your contribution, Sultan, but we deal with rule breakers differently in Hungary. We don't reward them."

Marcin gestured for his pack members to retreat into the audience with a nod of his head. "It's what the pack wants."

The crowd roared in agreement as if Marcin had them eating out of his hand. No doubt who the wulfkin preferred. Marcin slid into his seat, as did my father, leaving Levin standing alone. Every eye was on the Hungarian Varlac emperor, and I couldn't help but wonder how someone on such a power trip would react to not getting his way.

He pushed his jaw forward as an anaconda might do before devouring its prey. "Sultan, thank you for your suggestion." Levin's words were clipped and strangled, clearly disapproving of our interference. "In honor of having you in my home, I give my consent to the quest."

An explosion of cheers burst out from the surrounding crowd. Would they have had the same reaction if Levin sentenced Enre and Daciana to death?

"But I call for a venery," Levin continued and the excitement flatlined at the mention of the word that took its origins from Varlac leaders hunting wild animals for sport. "A venery will be held for all to enter and to find the two worthiest of champions to take on such a trial. As is tradition."

Maybe it was the elevated tension in the room, the mounting egos, or simply that I wondered if the wulfkin in Turkey would have made a safer choice. I questioned my decision to willingly throw myself into the devil's den.

CHAPTER 3

MARCIN

The day was fucked up, and it wasn't even lunchtime yet.

Father attempting to kill my brother under the pretense of his made-up bullshit rules and arranging for me to be mated to our enemy's daughter was just the beginning. The Turkish clan had attempted to kill me at the age of nineteen, and now I was being thrown to the slaughter. Why else would Father dredge up my past again? And to top it off, we were now running an ancient battle of innocence, including a goddamn venery. Yeah, every wulfkin would jump in for a chance at the boon the sultan had suggested. A bloodbath was a guarantee, assuming my father didn't kill the Turkish alpha first for stepping on his toes.

My father wore a permanent smile as he strolled alongside the sultan down a stone corridor barely lit by the wrought iron sconces mounted to the wall. If it were up to me, I'd have the whole place wired up with recessed lighting.

The group swung left toward the marble steps leading up to the guest chambers, and I trailed behind them, my mind drowning.

Selena walked arm in arm with Aisha. I couldn't help noticing she now walked with a slight limp, favoring her left leg. Nine years ago, I had accompanied my father to Turkey so the two power Varlacs could discuss a resolution for the raging war between our clans. But from the moment I spotted Selena in Turkey with a cropped hairstyle, reminding me of a pixie with her green eyes, I was lost. My wolf had claimed her that very second. We both had controlling fathers, and we thought running away was the answer.

Unfortunately, neither of us had seen the archer. Selena had stepped in my path and taken the blow. It struck her shoulder, and the momentum took her down a gorge, breaking her hip. We'd made the decision together, but she'd paid the price. That incident tore our clans further apart.

And still, I lived with the guilt of her injury. I never expected to see her again. After the arrow incident, Father told me I'd be killed by the sultan if I ever stepped foot in Turkey again. Of course, I had ignored the threat and went back for her, but guards drove me away, insisting Selena wanted nothing more to do with me and that she was being mated to someone else. My father told me to forget her and that he would kill her himself if I took her as my mate. Now she was thrown back into my life, stirring emotions I had tried to ignore for years. All that remained between us was a raging river of uncertainty, blame, and regret. My wolf wasn't helping matters, pining to connect with her wolf like a damn love-struck teenager. For years, I'd convinced myself she was the past. Now confusion muddled my head. Sure, my wolf insisted she was ours, but I wasn't convinced of her motives, who the real Selena was anymore, or whether she still carried any emotions for me. Only after I sorted out my crap with Father and Enre would I entertain the thought of uncovering where Selena stood. Mating was a whole different beast I wasn't ready to tackle.

Today, larger problems existed, like saving Enre and Daciana and removing Father from power. Then again, if this mating ensured a peaceful union between our two clans, I was all for it.

But Selena refused to leave my thoughts, like a recurring wave, crashing into me, grabbing at my heart, then sliding away. I had to get my head together. *This reaction wasn't supposed to happen.*

On the second floor, Father opened the door to our visitors' quarters: a compact living area with six bedrooms, two living areas, three bathrooms, and a kitchen. The Turkish alpha, his guards, and his daughters trailed inside.

"Sultan, please enjoy your stay," Father said, his voice dripping with noxious honey. "I'll arrange for lunch to be sent to your room and will personally collect you for dinner."

The sultan bowed and accepted my father's hand. "Thank you." He receded into the room and shut the door.

Father jerked around, a frown morphing his expression into a scowl, and he brushed past me toward the stairs. "Marcin, with me."

"I'm going to see Enre."

He halted halfway down the steps and offered me the kind of look that could scare off a slew of bears. "What for? You got what you wanted. He's safe for now. We have another problem to handle."

He huffed and continued his hike down the curved steps, his hand gripping the banister for support.

I took a long, slow breath to calm my spiking pulse. What I really wanted was to punch a wall. How many more problems could there possibly be in one day?

Once we were inside his quarters, he slammed the door shut and pounded the floorboards in his rapid march from the window aglow with snow-capped mountains to the door leading to his bedroom. Father had no need for furniture in the main living area. It would only get in the way of his deadly pacing ritual.

The crackling fire threw shadows across walls covered in tapestries, a menacing puppet show.

I strolled toward the window and leaned a hip against the frame, the outside cold chilling my back.

"I'll strangle that Turk." Father's hands throttled an invisible foe. "No, better yet, I'm going to throw him off a cliff. Or tear him limb from limb."

"I liked his suggestion."

"You would." He paused and glared my way. "Next time you defy me in public like that, I'll cut your tongue out."

With Enre gone, I'd be the only heir to Father's legacy, and even though he showed no intention of dying by natural causes, it was pretty late for him to mate and start over with another son. I'd bet that was the only reason he hadn't yet cut out my tongue.

Father sighed, his lips drawn into a thin line. "That Turk is here barely a second, and he gives me orders. I'll make this work our way." He tapped the side of his temple and nodded. "You enter the tournament, win, then claim a boon to take over Transylvania for your pack. Enre and Daciana's packs will merge under yours, giving you the largest pack in Europe. We ... you'll be invincible."

The hairs on my neck bristled. I was too tired for all this crap. "No. That's not going to happen."

His eyes narrowed. "Don't upset me now with your righteousness. You'll mate with that Turkish bitch and gain land into Turkey through her dowry. We'll finally make inroads there."

The seething beneath my skin bubbled to boiling point, but defending Selena would only aggravate him further. "Is that all I am to you? Your pawn for taking over territory?"

He strode over to the fire and rubbed his hands. "I won't expect you to understand. It's a wolf-eat-wolf world. Either we make the first move, or the Turks will finish us off."

"Fuck that. Have you thought that maybe the Turkish are honest about desiring peace between our clans?"

The way he stared at me, his cocked eyebrow and tilted head, said it all. A peaceful solution hadn't even entered his mind. He was a cloak and dagger, stab you in the back kind of wulfkin.

I crossed the room in a few quick strides. Enough of this conversation. "This ends now. I'm telling the sultan things have changed. They should leave. The deal is off."

"You do that and Enre and Daciana will die. Whether it's now or later, death will come swiftly to them if you go against me on the boon in any way."

I froze in the doorway, rage burning a hole through my chest, and responded without turning around. "Do you ever do anything with good intentions?"

"Ha. What use would that be?" He broke into a chuckle. "You can go."

I left the raving lunatic behind. The sooner I pushed Father aside, the quicker we'd end his antics. I raced down the steps to the ground floor. At the moment, with Enre, Father had my balls in a vice. But if I convinced the council to back me, we stood a good chance of overruling him, stripping him of his power and his pack—the only way to stop his savagery. My own pack had grown to a strong twenty-four, not yet outmatching Father's, but considering each of my warriors could take two of his, we weren't far away.

First, I'd pay my brother a visit, then the council, and see where we stood. Surely, after witnessing Father's earlier madness in the great hall, they'd be eager to replace him.

I shoved my hands into the pockets of my jeans and stepped out into the snow-covered courtyard, taking a sharp right toward the dungeon's entrance. First order of business was getting my brother and Daciana transferred to comfortable quarters.

A rasping sound from behind me sliced through my thoughts, and I glanced over my shoulder.

Selena was across the yard, dragging a plant in a terra-cotta pot to who knows where. The scraping sound raised the hairs on my arms. A red line tarnished the concrete from the door to her position, bleeding into the melted snow, looking like a trail of blood.

I was convinced that plant had once belonged in the front foyer. Now snow dusted its green leaves and white bell-shaped flowers.

"Need a hand?" I asked as I strolled closer, the tightness in my gut returning threefold. How was I supposed to get anything done if I acted like a puppy dog each time I bumped into her?

"Nope." She didn't turn, but continued dragging the plant. "You're really determined to get that plant out here, aren't you?"

She shoved the pot into a snowy corner, protected by an overhanging ledge several feet above, and dusted her hands. "Did you know these are snowdrops and survive better outdoors, rather than choking to death inside?" When she faced me, her cheeks were blushing. Movement stirred behind her eyes. Maybe we were strangers after all. My hands tingled to reach out and take her into my arms; my wolf demanded we run free in the woods, but I had no idea where I stood with her.

"So you're doing the plant a favor?" I asked. Only Selena would care for something like a potted plant when anyone else considered it insignificant.

"Figured if I'm going to live here, I've got to make it feel more like home." Her voice sharpened as if challenging me.

But I wasn't my father and preferred a less aggressive approach. "Would you like me to show you around the place?"

"Thanks." She tucked a loose lock of long, dark hair behind her ear and approached to stand beneath a window awning where the light scattering of snowflakes didn't reach her. "But I promised Aisha we'd go exploring together."

"Fair enough."

A wall of silence jutted up between us as the quiet closed in around me. Any other woman, and I'd have no trouble striking up a conversation, but right then, my mouth refused to work. I couldn't get enough of staring at how different Selena had become. She was more attractive than I could have imagined, from her long, slender neck to her delicious full lips, and those almond-shaped sexy eyes framed by black makeup that curved upward at the corners. When we were in Turkey, we expressed our attraction through long, passionate kisses, bodies pressed together, but we'd never had sex. She wanted to wait until we were officially together, and I respected her decision.

I reminded myself that Selena was in the same position as me, probably forced into this arrangement.

A breeze fluttered past, sweeping long hair off her face. I glanced around the empty yard, but her gaze didn't leave me. It burned into me.

"Funny how things have turned out. When we wanted to be together, our parents tore us apart, and now we're being forced together—" My voice died. Heat scorched up my neck and cheeks. *Damn*, that came out wrong.

Her eyes squinted, and her shoulders stiffened. "I voluntarily agreed to this mating."

"I didn't mean—"

"It's okay, Marcin. I understand exactly what you meant. Look, I'd better head inside." A disgruntled mien slid across her expression.

Was she sulking? Would she have preferred if I took her into my arms and stated I'd make a perfect mate for her and everything would turn out all right? I wasn't sure I had that much arrogance or the confidence to spin such a lie.

"Selena." I reached for her, but she brushed past my hand and hurried toward the door before vanishing inside.

Idiot.

As much as my instincts craved chasing after her, I headed in the opposite direction, my head hanging low. Nothing I could say would alter our situation. That we'd known each other before didn't mean shit. Nine years was a long time. Especially after I'd tried so hard to explain the misunderstanding about the arrow that struck her shoulder, yet she outright accused my family of trying to assassinate her. Somehow, because I didn't leap to her defense, I was in on the whole thing? Bullshit. How could she ever think I'd harm her? Obviously, she wasn't the wulfkin I thought she was, but now, so much time had passed between us that I had no idea if we were a good match anymore. And I had no intention of spending a lifetime with someone who didn't trust m.

Damn, even two of my pack members had sworn they witnessed a Turk release the arrow targeting me. It was a long time ago and maybe we'd never find out the truth, but a lot had changed for me—I'd gained a pack and more responsibility. We were different wulfkin, led different lives, and held different beliefs. For all I knew, she supported my father's dictatorial approach, though I somehow doubted anyone could stoop that low.

Over my shoulder, I caught a glimpse of the potted plant that lit up the dingy corner, giving the place a new look. It was somehow inviting. I pushed on.

Snowflakes melted against my skin, and the cold winds tugged on my shirt. At the other side of the courtyard, I pushed open the doors and greeted the two burly guards, who jumped to their feet from slouching positions.

"At ease," I said.

The bearded one smiled and settled heavily back in his seat. Father made them work grueling, long shifts, so all the guards were exhausted most of the time.

I stepped around a corner and descended a curved stairwell, the smell growing mustier. Torches on the walls created pools of light across the flagstone steps. At the bottom, I reached an iron door protected by a wulfkin I recognized all too well.

Sanyi's hooked nose creased when he looked up. He'd broken it so many times that even with wulfkin healing, it refused to mend properly. A few months ago, the guard had requested to join my pack, but he didn't cut the grade after getting into a brawl with me, then Vincent. No one should get on Vincent's bad side. My second-in-command was the strongest fighter I'd ever come across. Sanyi got his nose smashed in, again, and ended up as Father's prison guard instead.

"Open the door."

His lips curled upward, flashing a smile of black decay. "Can't do. Your father gave instructions that no one was allowed inside." He squared his heavy shoulders and shifted to stand in front of the door, his coat pulling across his wide girth.

I stepped closer, my wolf shoving against my insides, well aware of how much this wulfkin needed a lesson in manners. "Open up or I'll deliver on that promise I made when I caught you cornering the kitchen helper last week."

His cheeks paled. "I ain't risking your father's anger."

My voice deepened. "If you don't open up, you won't have a life to risk."

Sanyi glanced over my shoulder and back, his chest rising and falling with each quickened inhale. Getting in trouble was only the start of what was coming for him if I ever caught him near a young girl again.

He reached for the keys at his hip and licked his lips.

It took every inch of strength not to smash his head against the stone wall. He just had to slip up once more, and I'd deliver the blow. I had eyes all over the castle.

"Open the door."

He hesitated at first but threaded the key into the hole, the clang resonating around us. "I will have to tell your father about this."

I refused to respond to his weak threat and walked through.

Once inside, the door smacked shut and a cloud of dust blew around me. *Bastard.*

Farther down a murky corridor that reeked of mold and urine, two guards nodded my direction.

"I'm looking for Enre and Daciana."

"Next level down," one said and handed me a flashlight.

Of course Father would put my brother in the worst pit. I shouldn't have expected anything less. "I need the keys to their cell."

The wulfkin handed them over, and I headed downstairs, into darkness. I switched on the light, noting the wooden beams covered in cobwebs overhead starting to rot at the corners. A squeak near my feet revealed a large rat scurrying across my boot and into a hole in the cracked masonry wall.

At the landing, I swept the light across the circular enclosure in the center of the room. Two layers of iron bars, as thick as my wrists, meant no wulfkin was ever breaking out of there. It had been built to house dracwulves—vicious and unstoppable wolf creatures that had been banned for good reason.

Inside, Enre and Daciana were on their knees, side by side, their wrists chained behind them to a boulder. My heart sank.

Mud squished beneath my boots as I hurried. Sweat, urine, and brackish water smells cloyed at the back of my throat.

I unlocked the first door and stepped inside to the next one, hinges groaning as I swung it open.

Every memory flooded back: the whippings Enre received, the time his pet fox was butchered in front of him, Father spreading vicious lies about Enre not being his legitimate son.

Not that anyone could prove or disprove it since we'd never known our mother. She had vanished soon after Enre's birth.

"Enre, Daciana, I'm so sorry you're in here. This should never have happened." I rushed closer, placed the flashlight on the ground, and released them from their iron manacles, which rattled and fell into a heap. The guilt of watching Father beat Enre as a child stuck to my insides like tar. I should have done more, should have suggested we run away together at a younger age, should have ... a shivery whisper of bitterness seethed in my gut. I should have taken Enre's side in front of Father and shown him his actions weren't acceptable.

But at seventeen, I was powerless and weak against a warlord. So, I did the only thing in my control. I aided Enre's escape, even if he didn't know it at the time. And now was my chance to help him once again.

"What's your game?" Enre asked, standing barely a few inches from me, his words sharp. The cuts and bruises on his face were already healing.

"No game. I'm doing what Father should have done the moment you arrived home." "This isn't my home." His tone dipped, and his eyes morphed into wolf eyes.

Daciana approached, her sharp gaze on me. The stories I'd heard of her beauty weren't exaggerated in the slightest. With the darkest of hair, pale skin, and a wild look, she could enslave any wulfkin.

"We appreciate your help, Marcin," Daciana said. "And it's nice to finally meet Enre's brother." She took me into an embrace, and I hugged her back.

My chest squeezed at the warm reception when I'd expected a slap or worse. "It's my honor. Honestly, if I knew you were coming, I would have made sure Father didn't get his way or treat you as he has."

Daciana's weak smile did little to conceal the concern crammed behind her eyes. Enre glowered at me. "I don't buy this. You want something."

The depth of his suspicions was fully given, except he didn't have all the facts about how I had previously helped him escape, the numerous times I stopped Father from beating him. Enre didn't know I generally took the brunt of it. "Everything I've ever done was to protect you from Father."

Enre released a long breath, accompanied by a low growl. "Sure you did."

I doubted it would make a difference to explain myself now. Enre wasn't ready to discuss the truth or believe me.

"I don't expect you to ever forgive me, but I will participate in the tournament quest. My second-in-command and I will represent both of you, win, and give you back your lives, your peace, and Transylvania. Father won't ever touch you again. Until then, I've arranged for you to stay in one of our guest quarters and be treated as visitors, not enemies."

Enre's lips pinched into a hard line, his gaze falling behind hooded eyes. That look was a warning that if I didn't tell him the truth, he was about to make sure I had a very bad day. Except, Father had already beaten him to it.

"I don't believe you," Enre said. "And just because we're going to stay in a nicer room, doesn't mean we aren't in prison."

Nothing I said would change this tune. I had to show my brother I meant every word.

Daciana finally broke the strained silence. "Thank you, Marcin. You're a true blessing."

"Come, let me show you to your quarters. I'll get you both new clothes, food, and anything else you need." I picked up the light and headed out of the prison cell.

"I want to return home," Enre said. "I'm working on it."

Daciana walked by my side, smiling, and the footsteps behind me confirmed Enre followed. I couldn't blame his cautiousness because I wasn't fooling myself into believing everything would turn out rosy. But unlike my younger days when fear dictated my actions, I refused to repeat my mistakes.

Sure, Father would explode after discovering what I'd done here, but I had no problem taking on his wrath for my brother. It was long overdue.

CHAPTER 4

"*Y*ou've been requested to dance for everyone during dinner." Father's words were stern, yet his averted gaze screamed hesitation.

"Baba, I won't do it." No way would I prance around for Levin and his minions. "Selena." Father's voice echoed through the guest room. "We don't have a choice."

I glanced at the scratches covering the door, wondering if the last guests here made those marks while being tortured by Levin. "My dance was meant to be a private one. Marcin and me. As part of our mating ritual. Not to the entire Hungarian pack. Levin delights in humiliating us."

Father, his white hair unruly, placed his hands on his belly. His purple kaftan with golden embroidery around the sleeves and neckline was in desperate need of an iron. His brow furrowed, and he nodded in agreement. "Levin's taken offense that he wasn't invited to the private dance."

"Because he isn't my future mate." My voice climbed.

"I know. Do you think I want you dancing for all those strangers? It's a slap in the face, an embarrassment for you to be up there like a common belly dancer. But Levin insists that if we don't comply, we're to leave tonight. Then there'd be no stopping him from attacking our home."

A ghostly finger traced the length of my spine, and my shoulder blades jutted together.

Was this a sign of my future in Hungary—jumping through hoops for Levin?

Father took my hands in his warm ones. "We have no choice. Give them a simple dance, nothing too extravagant. Quick and short. Let's show Levin we can cooperate."

My response stuck to the roof of my mouth. What could I possibly say when I was asked to deal with a bit of humiliation to protect my family from imminent war?

The sincerity in his eyes weakened my resolve. His heart was in the right place, always had been, which was why I'd agreed to this mating in the first place. It wasn't for me, or for him, but for Aisha and every other wulfkin back home who shouldn't live in terror of being attacked by the Hungarians.

Outside the window, snowflakes drifted from fat clouds, and the cold refused to leave my bones. I missed the warmth of home, the ocean views, and the banquets. But Hungary was my home now, and I had to make the best of it.

I sighed and dragged myself to the furry blankets. Dropping to my knees, I foolishly hoped that Marcin would, at least, welcome me. But his earlier comment had made it crystal clear where he stood—he had no interest in mating with me. I'd be stuck in the enemy's home with a mate who didn't want me.

Aisha opened her bedroom door, and Klaus, my pet dracwulf, squeezed between her and the doorframe, knocking her aside. The four-foot-tall wolf trotted toward me on all fours, head high, tongue dangling from his mouth, his nails click-clacking across the flooring. Sure, I couldn't keep him in Hungary, I accepted that, but I'd miss him insanely. In the woods back home, we'd found two dracwulf pups, barely larger than my hand, so we adopted and trained them. I'd never spent time away from them. Now, they were obedient and loyal like any ordinary dog, just larger.

"I'm joining Levin for afternoon coffee." Without another word, Father left the room.

I lifted myself to my feet and scratched Klaus's long ears,

loving how the tips were inky black, and the underside of his chin was white as if he wore a beard like Santa Claus. The rest of him was light gray. Dracwulves were banned under Hungarian law because in ancient times, wild dracwulves ate entire villages and hunted their prey for weeks on end. But under Turkish rules, they were seen as sacred animals, good omens sent to us from the moon goddess. It was believed that the spirits of our ancestors resided in dracwulves, and their lively, aggressive behavior was a reminder that we weren't untouchable. *Remain grounded and humble* were Father's words when we grew up.

But Father had agreed for us to bring our pets to Hungary with Levin's approval, and I suspected it had something to do with showing Levin that even the most feared creature had compassion if treated well. Whether an emperor who had his ego stuck up his ass, as Levin did, would recognize such subtleties was a different matter.

"That blows about the dance." Aisha's amethyst genie pants billowed with each step, and the golden coins around her ankles sounded the familiar chimes of home. "It sucks that you have to be their show pony tonight. Someone ought to teach Levin a lesson."

"Absolutely." I leaned against her shoulder and noticed the curved lines of henna swirling from her ankle down to each toe. Impressive. No one in all of Turkey had steadier hands than Aisha.

"Come, I'll do yours for tonight." She smiled. "You've got to impress Marcin." She wiggled her eyebrows.

I stroked Klaus's back. "Not in the mood to impress anyone." A part of me refused to play nice. Not when Levin thought he'd wear us down with humiliation. If it was a dance he wanted, then I'd show him one.

S till unable to shake away the cold since arriving at the castle, I pulled the winter surcoat tighter around my chest, the bells on my costume jangling underneath. With me needing to entertain the locals, changing outfits was out of the question.

I took a step through the parting grand doors and into the dining hall alone. Aisha insisted she was attending later.

Candelabras hung from the arched ceiling above the U-shaped seating arrangement in a room with close to thirty wulfkin inside. Nearly every chair was taken. Guards from both Varlac clans lined the walls, standing at attention; the musky wolf scents invaded my nostrils. The air was thick, as were the chattering voices. On the back wall, a display of swords was fanned out above the two Varlac clans' flags—the Hungarian iron wolf and our black wolf floating in a tangle of red smoke and howling to a crescent blood moon. Wisps of crimson mist floated upward from his mouth, representing our souls connecting with the moon goddess.

Back home, we rarely held large banquets. No females were ever invited to meals when guests arrived. But here things were different, with the female wulfkin being allowed complete freedom to go wherever they wanted. The notion was unnerving, yet exciting. Red tablecloths darkened the dim room while the red and white tiled patchwork across the floor was definitely a modern addition. I stepped deeper inside, spotting Father at the center of the table, alongside Levin. Then my sights landed on Marcin, who hadn't noticed me yet.

No one batted an eye at me.

A piercing scream from a woman at the dinner table penetrated the room, raising the hairs down my arms.

I froze.

Wulfkin jumped to their feet, recoiling against the back wall, several escaping out the side doors. Four guards stepped forward on either side of the tables. The electric charge of wulfkin about to transform crackled through the air. Every single eye focused in my direction.

What—

A long howl broke out behind me, and I jerked around.

White as snow, Aisha's dracwulf, Grit, stood in the doorway.

My sister gripped his leash as his muzzle lifted into the air with his song.

Was my sister insane?

She stepped closer with a nervous smile on her lips; violet fabric flowed down to her feet with a thick matching belt, showing off her tiny waist. Henna tattoos curled up her arms with wisps of the art stretching toward her collarbone. Her dark hair was pulled into a tight ponytail, striking against her dark eyes and bright red lips. A golden chain crossed her forehead. Grit trotted alongside her.

Oh, fuck.

I gripped her arm. "What are you doing? Father will murder you."

She broke my hold. "Someone has to show Levin he can't walk over us."

I nervously glanced around at Father. His forehead glowed red, the way it always did before he exploded. The guards behind him approached, probably waiting for an order to drag Aisha out.

Levin stood from his seat, while Marcin hurried toward us, a grim expression crossing his face, maybe to usher us out before we caused more pandemonium.

"We should leave," I said. "Quickly."

Before I could pull Aisha out of there, Marcin reached us, his gaze locked on Grit. "What are you doing with a dracwulf? They're illegal. Are you trying to get yourself killed?"

"They're our pets." Aisha's voice wavered, but when Levin and Father stepped up alongside Marcin, I lost all feeling in my legs.

"Aisha just got confused. We'll get rid of Grit." I nudged Aisha by her shoulder to retreat. But Father lurched past me and seized Aisha's arm. His face was on fire, and his lips bent out of shape into a snarl.

The pain his grip must be causing would hurt, but Aisha held her ground. "He's harmless; you know that."

Levin pushed past Marcin and said, "How dare you bring those abominations to my dining hall! I agreed to you bringing them into my home, but having them here where we eat is an offense." He halted the moment Grit looked up and released a growl. The kind that said, *come closer and I'll rip your arm off.*

Aisha snatched her arm free from Father's.

"Sultan, what's going on? I thought we agreed that you'd keep them locked up." Rage inflamed Levin's words.

Father stared at the Hungarian emperor and raised his voice. "Because we don't ban dracwulves, back home we welcome them into our lives, including joining us during our meals. They are creatures of the moon just like us. The moon goddess loves them.

Otherwise, she wouldn't have given them life. Grit has been trained from a pup. He's never hunted a thing in his life and is more obedient than my own daughter who should have known better."

"You share a meal with these disgraceful creatures?" Levin's response was a spear to my chest.

Father's posture stiffened as he inhaled loudly. "Your laws are no less disgraceful. Our embrace of the dracwulves is about nurturing life. Protecting animals."

Levin's face contorted in a disgusted expression as if Father's belief was beyond his comprehension. "Wulfkin are at the top of the food chain, or have you forgotten what your ancestors fought for?"

The two alphas eyed each other, neither blinking—egos, puffy chests, and creased noses on show.

Ice formed in my veins. The Varlac leaders were about to break out into war over Aisha's stupid stunt. I choked on the tension in the air.

"This was my idea, and if anyone is to be punished, it's me." Aisha lowered her gaze, attempting to show some remorse, though, in truth, I doubted she felt it. On the bright side, maybe if Levin saw that dracwulves could be trained, he might be more lenient toward Daciana.

No one said a word at first until Marcin spoke up. "No one is punishing anyone. It's a simple misunderstanding of cultures. Come, let's all sit back down and enjoy the blood wine that's flowing." His attempt at a jovial laugh came across strained, but I appreciated his attempt to cover for Aisha. He patted Levin's shoulder. "I'm sure some of our rules seem strange to them too."

Looking up, I studied Levin. He gave no smile or slip of emotion from his angry pose—furrowed brow, the corner of his mouth lifted slightly, fists pinned by his side.

Silence.

Was Levin going to sentence Aisha to death alongside Enre and Daciana?

Levin ran a hand down his face and pushed a tight smirk across his lips as if he'd just had the same realization. "That animal is not joining us for dinner." He faced Father with a snarl. "Boran, you need to teach your daughter to grow out of her childish ways.

Otherwise, I will."

"I had no idea she was bringing it to tonight's meal. For that, I must apologize." He glanced Aisha's way, and the promise of retribution and punishment was clear in his stony, cold eyes.

Where was he going to lock Aisha up after he finished with the belt? I wouldn't sit back and let him touch a hair on her head. Sure, Aisha was an idiot, but her actions came from a good place.

Father waved over several guards and instructed them to take Grit back to our rooms before turning to Aisha. "Return to your chamber with the guards. You don't deserve to be here after that show." He turned away. "Come, Emperor, let's return to our meals."

Levin's cheeks were bright red, and he shook his head before joining Father back at their seats. The majority of wulfkin also returned to their chairs.

Aisha pouted as she traipsed outside with Zeki, the captain of our guards. Well, that sure got Levin's attention. Maybe her stunt was my fault, and I should have made it clear she wasn't to pull one of her antics, especially since they weren't new to her. Half the pack in Turkey expected trouble when she was around.

"Shall we?" Marcin offered me his bent arm.

I draped mine over his, and a jolt passed through me from

the touch. The only other time that happened was the first time I had touched Marcin back in Turkey. All of a sudden, my wolf was shaking with need, with urgency to claim him, with the shattering realization that she identified Marcin as our soul wolf.

Marcin glanced over and smiled in that knowing way. Did he feel it too? Then he broke into a chuckle.

"What's so funny?"

"Don't think anyone can ever beat that entrance." Marcin leaned close as we skirted around the tables, his fresh kindling and musky scent weakening my knees. "Your sister's got spunk."

"Thanks for standing up for her."

"I know what it's like to be cornered." He winked.

He might as well have kissed me. Every molecule in my body liquefied as I stared at him striding alongside me, a permanent and delicious smirk splitting his lips.

The candlelight drew attention to the long scar lining his chin, an injury he didn't have the last time I'd seen him.

He stared at me with a hunger he hadn't held earlier in the day. My heart betrayed me as it twirled in an unruly prance.

He directed me to a seat right next to Father, who I swore was ready to pop. On the other side of Father sat Levin, chortling like a pig. Next to him, Marcin spoke with a handsome wulfkin that had tanned skin and short, cropped hair.

I eyed the plates of raw slices of meat on the table. The sweet smell tickled my nostrils, so I forked a small piece and ate it in one bite.

Settled in my chair, I grabbed a goblet and guzzled the water, ignoring the glances my way. Maybe I needed a full bucket of blood wine to forget what had just happened.

Instead, I focused on finishing my meal. Nothing like drowning my sorrows in food. Then I spotted a familiar face, even though it had been years since I'd last seen him. Irmak sat several seats away to my left. He had been appointed to live in Hungary under the care of Levin's pack as a way to forge a better alliance between our two clans, to keep a treaty, stating that neither clan was to cross the border of each other's territory. We also had a Hungarian ward living with us back in Turkey. Though in truth, I wasn't sure if it kept Levin in check as well as it should have. Hence, my proposed mating to Marcin.

I smiled at Irmak, and he responded with a polite nod before swinging back to a conversation with someone on his side. He seemed established and happy enough, so maybe all hope wasn't lost for me.

Levin pushed to his feet and clapped a few times, silencing the room. "That was quite the introduction, wouldn't you say? Since things have calmed down, we can all feel safe once again. Tonight is a special occasion for us all and hopefully one of many more to come. We are lucky enough to have the company of the Varlac alpha from Turkey, Sultan Boran, whose reign extends all the way to China. His blood carries the lineage of Sultan Mehmed the Conqueror, a true warrior of his time. Though"—he wiped his lips and smirked—"rumor has it that Mehmed had lost the Transylvanian land when he fought Vlad Ţepeş back in the 1400s." Levin thumped Father's back. "Those would have been the days."

Father broke into a forced grin, though the tightness around his mouth revealed his annoyance.

"We are also honored to announce that Marcin has found a mate. The young wulfkin is Selena Kurt, daughter to Boran." Levin swept a hand in my direction.

Fire hit my cheeks. Everyone in the room gawked at me. I smiled nervously and noticed Marcin was studying his goblet, obviously embarrassed.

"She'll make a nice addition to the family." Levin clucked his tongue, staring at me. "And don't forget, anyone interested in participating in the upcoming venery challenge, please place your name in the bucket. Everyone is welcome to join, but only the first twenty randomly selected will participate. Maybe I'll even join." He laughed, coaxing the crowd to join him like a pack of obedient hyenas. "All participants will be announced at first light tomorrow."

The boon on offer swept into my thoughts ... an opportunity for me to claim anything without question, though I suspected there would be limitations. But what would I claim? Freedom to choose my own mate, to leave Father's control, to end war between the clans? Like that would happen easily. My thoughts flew to Daciana and her punishment relating to her alpha who'd raised a dracwulf. Here we were with them as our pets, and that poor wulfkin was about to be put on trial for one. So, maybe me gunning for the boon wasn't such a bad idea, especially if I got to free Daciana from Levin's punishment, show Father that girls could be just as powerful on the field, and protect Aisha from any other forced mating proposals.

Levin's sharp voice carved through my fantasy. "We've been promised a unique style of entertainment tonight. Please put your hands together for Selena."

Right. Time to entertain the monkey—Levin. For a smidgen of a second, I recontemplated my dance. Then I pictured Marcin's wink and his words of encouragement. Yep. I was sticking to my original plan.

CHAPTER 5

MARCIN

*M*ore dishes with sliced venison shank were set on my end of the table, and the aroma had my stomach growling for more. My second-in-command, Vincent, drew one plate toward him. I gulped several mouthfuls of blood wine—three parts fresh deer blood, one part red wine to water down the thick consistency—a popular drink in Hungary among wulfkin. Then I dug into my gamey, almost sweet meat.

At the same time, my stomach spiraled with distaste at the idea of my brother sitting in an isolated wing of the castle, guarded by Father's wulfkin, not invited to the family meal. I had spent an hour of convincing Father not to force Enre and Daciana back into the dungeons, and while I'd won the argument, his deathly glare promised retribution for defying him. I didn't give a shit.

Voices around me grew to a mundane buzz. The smacking of lips and tearing of meat escalated, grating on my nerves. I shoved my plate away.

On my other side, Father had barely touched his food, deep in conversation with the sultan about the early onset of winter and game hunting as if the pair were best buddies now.

When I glanced over to the empty seat next to the sultan, the unsettling ache in my gut deepened. My wolf stretched inside me, whimpering for release, for a real chase, for Selena. Then he nudged me with a sense of an exciting memory. Selena and I in our wolf forms during the full moon, running wild in the forest, tracking our prey in Turkey. She had meant the world to me, but was that because I craved escape from Father's dictatorship and heavy-handed punishment? Back then, Selena had offered me a glimpse into a new life filled with freedom.

I gulped down the rest of the blood wine, and my bladder called for time out.

But the single drumbeat ringing through the room had me remaining in my seat. The tempo picked up, and Vincent slapped me on the back. "My friend, I do believe this performance is for you." He gulped back his wine.

I glanced up.

Selena strode toward the U-shaped table, barefoot and dressed in a black skirt sitting dangerously low on curvy hips. Her hands were tucked behind her back. With each step, the slits running from the top of her thighs to her ankles peeled back, revealing long, lean legs.

My pulse lunged into a competition against the quickening tune. The black bra did little to conceal her bust that bounced with each step. Tiny bells dangled from the bra and swayed across her trim belly.

I couldn't deny Selena's beauty. Ink-black hair fluttered behind gently sloped shoulders and draped behind her hourglass body. From halfway across the room, her green eyes, framed by dark eyelashes, called to me. And for a crazy moment, I imagined myself going to her, taking her into my arms, but it was my wolf's insatiable desire to claim Selena.

Her gaze met mine, and the corner of her mouth curled upward in that sneaky kind of way that told me she was up to something. I couldn't wait to see what she had in store.

Then the music morphed into a single violin piece, melancholic, thin in tone. It vibrated through me.

Selena halted in the middle of the room, tilting her head forward, but her hands remained behind her back. The nostalgic melody played by the bow, graciously gliding across strings, sang of subtle sadness mixed with hope.

Selena slid a leg forward, the fabric gliding aside to reveal her thigh, her toes poised toward the ground.

My stare fastened on every inch of the beauty I craved. She'd never danced for me before, and now with everyone's gazes lingering on her, a tinge of jealousy swept through me. My black-hearted father was to blame, stealing the private dance meant for me alone. Arguing with him had gotten me nothing but frustration, and when the sultan agreed, I had no leg to stand on. Didn't make this moment any easier to swallow.

Selena's hip lifted and dropped in slow motion, and my throat dried. She took several steps, her gaze still lowered. Undulations flowed through her body like a wave, rolling through her pelvis, along her waist and to her chest in a rhythmic pulse, mesmerizing me. I gulped more wine, almost choking in the process.

Then the music sped to a bassy tune, and her head shot up, gaze locked onto me. My insides tightened.

Her green eyes reminded me of the river in the woods. I'd fantasized about waking up next to her every morning for years ... but that was a long time ago, a memory. Then why did my wolf still demand she was ours?

Selena's hands pulled out from behind her back, and in her right hand, she gripped a sword the length of her arm. She raised the weapon above her head as she bounced into a crouched position and up again.

I glanced over to the sultan and noticed his grimace. The way his jawline hardened and his rigid posture indicated he was ready to stand up in protest. Was this not the dance he'd expected from his daughter?

The music climbed to a crescendo, and my attention fixed back on Selena, who now had the sword balanced across one shoulder, the hilt in front, the blade behind her. She broke into a spin, faster and faster, the jingle of her costume a constant chime in the background. Her long hair flung around her as a cape might do, her arms stretched outward. I swore her eyes were closed, and her spinning made me dizzy, but the weapon on her shoulder wasn't going anywhere. Now, this was the kind of control my pack members needed. She'd grown into an impressive wulfkin with outstanding abilities. But it was so much more than that. For years, I'd told myself she was the past, to be forgotten. Now, staring at her, my body betrayed me, my wolf refused to listen to reason, and even my heart pounded as if we'd just met for the first time.

She came to a dead stop, her eyes opening, the blade in place.

Goddess, how could I be so blind not to see how much I'd missed her before now? Admitting I actually missed her became imperative. Had I made a mistake to stay away from her this long?

The explosion of clapping that flared around the room was quickly overshadowed by a fast-paced number of hand drumming. Selena had the hilt in her grip now, whirling the weapon with a precision that sliced through the air, all the while her body shimmied on the spot. One slip and the flying sword would decapitate several spectators.

Her movement sped up until I couldn't decide between staring at the hypnotic jiggle of her breasts or the blade that now spun so fast, I could easily mistake it for two.

A clip-clopping tune started, and Selena swayed her hips in a figure eight. She headed toward my father, her eyes set on him, while twirling the blade without pause.

I slid to the corner of my seat, fearing the worst. If she killed my father, she'd be slaughtered on the spot. Surely she wasn't that insane?

Several guards stepped toward Father, but he simply brushed them away with a wave of his hand, smiling at Selena who now stood directly across the table from him. The sword spun above her head in one hand, her body shimmying and entrancing his attention.

The sultan sighed loudly.

Selena set a hand behind her back and withdrew a red silk scarf, which she waved in the air. She calmed the spinning of the blade and lowered the tip to the side of Father's cheek, never touching him, but I noticed the way his back flinched.

A few gasps came from the audience.

Selena hurled the silk scarf into the air above Father's head, and within the same second, she swept the sword upward and swiped it through the fabric.

Two halves of a scarf cascaded over Father's head. He chuckled and caught the fabric, inhaling its scent.

That small act made the hairs on my arms prickle. Wasn't this dance supposed to be for me? Was her focus on Father a little game to lure him into a false sense of security so she could kill him? She wouldn't be the first person who attempted to finish him off, but Father was too smart for that.

Now she was doing large circles with her hips while holding the sword at both ends, the music quickening.

Selena could handle weapons. Good to know.

She broke into a body wave, her smile playful yet sultry as she held my gaze. I wasn't sure how to take it—a threat or something else?

My bladder tightened worse. I'd be ultrafast. I pushed away from the table and hurried toward the side door before taking one last glance at Selena in a beautiful back arch with the sword balanced across her stomach. A thousand images slammed into my mind of her naked and in that position.

Once in the hallway, I rushed to the bathroom.

Tibor, the head councilman emerged. He was the last council member I needed to gain support from to go against Father.

I glanced behind me and spotted no one. "Tibor, I wanted to speak to you and—" "Listen, Marcin. I know what you're going to say, but I've spoken to the council, and

we've agreed not to take action at this point. Save your breath."

An invisible fist collided into my gut. "We've talked about this. You agreed his actions were affecting all wulfkin."

He laid a hand against my arm, his touch frosty. "We still agree, boy. But with the sultan here, this is the wrong time."

"It's the perfect time." I squared my shoulders and struggled to keep my voice low. "We strike now, show Boran the old ways are gone and that we are serious about a truce."

Tibor shook his head.

"This is our chance to show the sultan we are changing. The old threats are the past, and we plan to forget them for a better future."

"And does that include you forgiving the Turks for attempting to assassinate you?" The response wedged in my mind and refused to come out at first. "Of course."

Tibor stared at me, long and hard. He patted my arm. "Well, make sure you first convince yourself of that before you insist on a complete overthrow with the enemy in our midst." He pushed past me.

I snatched his elbow. "Now is the time. You're making a mistake."

He pulled free and brushed down the fabric of his coat. "The council will not back you."

I watched him disappear into the dining hall, along with my plans to guarantee Enre's and every other wulfkin's immediate safety. Sitting back and doing nothing wasn't an option. I had to take action and now.

The severity of the council's decision skewered into my chest, along with the dire consequences of not removing Father from his position ... sooner rather than later. That realization left me with one option—win the boon by any means possible. When the sultan went home, the council would have to back me. Then I'd correct Father's mistakes.

After a quick bathroom stop, I headed outside to enter my name in the well. Thoughts of Selena floated through my mind along with the emotions she'd reawakened, the urgency to touch her and spend time together like we had so long ago.

Maybe Father was right. My mating with Selena could be a blessing in disguise after all.

CHAPTER 6

SELENA

I dragged myself into the snowy courtyard, heat from my dance sizzling my insides. The lanterns above the doors painted the cobblestone walls in silhouettes, and for those few seconds, I could have sworn I'd stepped back in time.

Behind me, clapping and cheers from the dining hall still echoed, but my intention had never been to gain favor with the locals. Rather, I was making it clear to Levin that he shouldn't mess with me.

That backfired big time.

My skin crawled at the way he leered at me and sniffed my scarf. A normal wulfkin would have instantly seen the underlying threat and glowered at me with a death stare. Not Levin. Did I just give him extra reason to pay me the wrong kind of attention? My flesh rippled with goose bumps.

Considering no one ever said no to him, I might have just dug my own grave.

And Marcin ... he left the room halfway through my dance and never returned. I huffed and rubbed my arms as the cold now leeched through my performance clothes.

An icy wind blew. I'd left my coat in the dining hall, but I wasn't ready to return and face Father's wrath, Levin's creepy stares, or anything else.

Several feet away lay the stone well. White powder dusted

the circular wall and piled into small mounts along the base. A notebook and pen peeked out from beneath the swell of snow. Inside the well, I found a wooden bucket dangling from a chain, its lid sealed with nails. A slit had been roughly cut into it. Levin's words rushed forward in my mind, the ones about anyone participating in the venery having to submit their names in the bucket.

The *boon*. I could win it; then maybe Father would have to reward me with the position of alpha. If Daciana could hold the title, then why not me? I could use the boon to finally end the war between the two clans, though it wouldn't help Aisha and me to pick our own mates. But Father would never agree to that, as females were never made to be alphas, according to him.

Besides, the moment my name was found in the ballot, I'd be ridiculed, and Father would have a stroke. *Females don't fight or participate in male sports.* I cringed every time he said those words.

The more I stared at the bucket swaying in the breeze, the tighter my chest grew. *Put your name in already.*

I chewed on my lower lip. Should I? Father was pissed at me, but how much worse could it get? Well, a lot shittier—he could break off the agreement and still mate Aisha to the alpha in Turkey. He might even mate us both to him. I gagged at the thought. Besides, what message was I giving to the Hungarians if I entered? The main reason for my mating was to create peace. Competing could easily be misconstrued as a threat.

Coldness snapped around me, and I couldn't peel my gaze off the bucket. Only one solution if I won—I'd use it to free Aisha and, if possible, myself from Father's shackles. I crouched and wiped the snow off the notebook near the well.

Snow crunched in front of me.

I jerked up as a dark figure shifted in the shadows.

Marcin stepped into the light, his hands deep into the pockets of his pants, and his long, chestnut hair waving in the wind. How long had he been watching me? When the breeze changed directions, slapping me in the face, his scent filled my nostrils—musk and the freshness of newly chopped wood. My wolf rose inside me, insisting she say hello ... or maybe more than hello. She nudged me, yearning to come out and play.

Marcin always had this instant effect on me. Even in his smart-casual gear—blue-gray jeans that hugged those perfect hips, a white shirt, and dark-blue blazer dotted with snowflakes—my heart thrummed under my breastbone. Long, tawny strands draped over his shoulders, and his blue eyes sparkled against the light across from us.

"Have you put your name in?" he asked.

His directness stole my voice, and I hugged myself to help with the cold drilling into my bones. "N ... not sure if I w ... want to." I could hardly talk from my teeth chattering.

"Why not?" Sidestepping around the well, he slipped out of his jacket and draped it over my shoulders.

I slid my hands into the sleeves, his scent overwhelming me. My wolf *was* clambering for release. *Not now.* Shoving her back, I pulled the jacket tight around my neck and glanced at Marcin. "Thanks."

"Come, let's head in until you decide to put your name in the bucket. We haven't had a chance to properly talk." He brushed past me and toward a side door, not the one leading back to the dining hall.

Marcin strode alongside me and down a hall heading deeper into the building. "What would your father think of my entry into the venery?"

Behind us, the wind whistled beneath the door, and the torches on the walls flickered, giving the area an eerie ambiance.

Marcin didn't seem to notice as he dragged open a monstrous door. "I don't care what he says. If you want to enter, go ahead."

His response startled me at first. Marcin's voice wasn't layered with any underlying meaning. Sharp, convincing, and truthful. But also flat and lacking emotion. He truly didn't care what I did. In fact, his drifting gaze told me his thoughts were miles away and had little to do with me.

I hurried inside the room, instantly embraced by the warmth of a blazing fireplace against the back wall. Above it stood a stuffed bear, twice my size, in an attack posture, its head just shy of scraping the ceiling. I detested seeing animals treated as trophies but swallowed the protesting words. My gaze shifted to the side walls covered with weapons—parrying daggers, bows and arrows, swords, axes, and shields.

"Wow." I approached a curved, double-edged knife and reached out to touch the golden hilt. "Isn't this a jambiya?" I fingered the handle of the blade, a symbol of manhood in Yemen. "So glad to see this isn't made from rhinoceros horn."

"Father tracked it down from an old craftsman." Marcin's footsteps closed in behind me. "Figured after your dance earlier, you'd appreciate this room."

"If I had this room back home, I'd train with each weapon until I mastered them all." I glanced over my shoulder at Marcin, who studied me, unabashed at being caught. The corners of his mouth lifted slightly. Why was he smirking?

Dropping my gaze, I slipped past him, angled around the brown leather sofa cradling the fireplace, and warmed my frozen fingers.

"So, were you the first to put your name into the bucket outside?" I spoke with my back to him, though the light footfalls behind me told me he'd crossed the room.

"Haven't done it yet."

"Your father will enter you anyway. You're an automatic participant." I faced him ... all six foot three reclining on the couch, legs stretched and crossed at the ankles, arms by his side. His blue stormy eyes reminded me with whom I spoke. The emperor's son, the same family who tried to kill me. I now played in the devil's house and couldn't let my guard down. Levin's atrocious acts were notorious across every continent, and I'd need allies if I wanted any chance of surviving. Considering how Marcin stood up for Aisha in front of his father, I struggled to believe he might take after Levin when it came to leadership and manipulation.

So, I'd tread carefully with Marcin if I wanted him as an ally. Maybe I could also finally get to the bottom of what really happened back in Turkey that day we were caught escaping. And why he never came back for me.

I sat at the opposite end of the huge couch from Marcin, who wore a calm expression. My inner wolf snapped to full alert whenever we were in Marcin's company. No denying that fact.

Only the crackle and snap of the fire filled the space between us, and each time I attempted to ask a question, my throat seized. What would I say? *Oh, it's nice that we're getting mated now ... after your family tried to kill me.* But I was doing this for Aisha, for her safety, not my happiness. If I could barely strike up a conversation, I was in for a long, lonely future, but my need for an ally meant being extra nice. Doing what it took.

"I never knew you were into swords, but I was impressed by your technique during the dance." Marcin's voice was soft, obviously struggling for a comfortable conversation too.

Plastering a smile on my face, I twirled a long piece of hair around a finger, pushing aside my apprehensions and embracing my mission. I needed to get closer to Marcin to find out exactly what was going on in this place. "You should see me out on the field in fight mode."

He shifted in his seat to face me. "Your father doesn't mind? Last time we spoke, he barely allowed you to leave the house, let alone pick up a weapon."

I shrugged. "What can I say? Life's changed a lot since then. Father isn't exactly thrilled with the idea, but if he ignores it, he fools himself into thinking it doesn't happen."

Marcin broke into a chuckle, his deep voice caressing the length of my back, raising the hairs down my arms in all the right ways.

"Fantastic. I've got several female wulfkin in my pack who are stronger warriors than half the males. You're welcome to train with us anytime."

My shoulders shot back. "Really?" I'd jump at the chance. Especially if it meant training with a pack of real hunters, rather than just me alone behind the house or sneaking in training sessions with the captain of the guards when Father wasn't around.

"Why not? I'd love to see how you handle a sword in the field."

"You've got yourself a deal." The idea excited me more than it should, but for years, I'd wished for Father to extend such an invitation to me. He never had. Was this sudden kindness Marcin's way of easing me into our upcoming mating? I couldn't blame him for it, although his reaction earlier in the day disturbed me, so I had to ask. "Look, Marcin. I know you're not a fan of our mating, but—"

"Don't worry about that now." He sat up, elbows on his thighs while glancing sideways in my direction. "Father said our *mating* was being put aside until after the tournament."

The way Marcin said the word *mating* seemed to sting him, and he was dismissing the ritual as if he'd already ended it. Was that his intention if he won the boon?

Sure. He planned on breaking off the mating. Then I'd be forced back home, and Father would mate Aisha and me off. Much as I loathed the idea of a forced mating with Marcin, it served a real purpose. Aisha would be free, and it protected our family, not to mention hopefully stopping any more wulfkin from dying on either side.

But now that Marcin had come clean, I couldn't ignore the obvious answer whacking me in the face. He was placating me, pretending friendliness, when in fact he planned to push me away. So, why was he bothering to be nice at all?

"Well, don't worry. It's loud and clear." I stood, took his jacket off, and tossed it on the couch alongside him.

"What are you talking about?" He now stood next to me, so close I felt his exhale on my cheek, and my knees weakened.

Damn, he was fast.

His hand coasted into mine, and he lifted it to his chest just like he used to when we were younger. I didn't realize how much I missed those days when he'd reassure me with his sincere eyes. Couldn't he see what repercussions his actions had on both packs?

I had to face the cold, hard facts. Instead of playing a game that would only end in breaking my heart further, I slipped my hand free. This wasn't the Marcin I'd once loved. *Forget your foolish dreams.* And as much as faking it seemed like the answer, that wasn't me.

"Father will be wondering where I am." I swung around the couch and hurried toward the exit.

The door flapped open, and I froze. Mud and excrement invaded my nostrils.

A flurry of cold wind whooshed inside, throwing hair over my shoulder, my skirt billowing around my legs. The doorway stood empty, but I spotted the wisps of a shadow backing away.

At the same time, a faint whistle carved through the air coming from the hallway. Quick footsteps closed in behind me.

The moment I dove sideways, Marcin crashed into me, bringing us both to the ground hard. Air gushed from my lungs. Hardwood floor planks hit my face with a *thud.*

"Selena, are you all right?" Marcin jumped to his feet, stretching a hand out to me. "Are you hurt?"

"What was that?" I accepted his hand and was on my feet in a flash.

"Stay here. Lock the door." He spun and bolted from the room, heading right. The same direction I'd seen the shadow vanish.

I replayed the scene in my head. Someone was in the hallway all right, but why run away? Then I remembered the whistling sound ... an object being thrown. Maybe an arrow. I retraced the path from the door and back, scanned the floorboards, the couch. Nothing. Something felt wrong, and the mud and putrid smell was blocking out the wolf scent of the intruder.

I reached the fireplace and lifted my gaze. As I did, I caught a glimpse of something silver, shiny.

I gasped.

Impaled into the wooden fireplace frame was a small dagger with a metal end, engraved with a crescent moon. The weapon was the length of my hand.

Was I imagining this? I couldn't breathe.

The dagger protruding from the mantle said otherwise. Someone had tried to kill one of us.

My hand trembled as I reached out to run a finger across the moon pattern in the silver.

This wasn't any ordinary dagger. It belonged to my father.

I plucked it free and shoved it into my skirt's pocket, my heart threatening to break through my rib cage.

CHAPTER 7

MARCIN

"This is an outright insult." The sultan's voice boomed as he paced back and forth in front of the fireplace in the weapons room. "I thought you invited us here for a truce, not a slaughtering. But it's no surprise, considering how you treat your own son."

I cringed at his flippant remark and glanced over at my father who stood behind the couch, gripping the back of it. The flickering light from the fireplace turned his twisted expression into a sinister one.

"Sultan, there's no sign of the weapon, so—" I began, but he cut me off with a curt wave of his hand.

"Someone attempted to assassinate my daughter. You said you saw someone in the hallway, and something was flung toward Selena." His gaze settled on his daughter, who stood several paces away, hands folded in front of her stomach, then he refocused on me. "Someone from your pack—"

"Enough." Father pushed away from the couch, loosening his collar. "There was no evidence of an assassination attempt, just a shadow."

The sultan huffed, his lips flattened. "That's a lie. Someone attacked Selena, and it was only luck of the moon goddess they missed."

All eyes turned to Selena, who'd been too silent for my liking. "What did you see?" my father asked.

Selena glanced behind her at the closed door. Was she contemplating a quick exit? "It happened so fast." She turned to face us. "The door flung open and a gust of wind came in, then Marcin crashed into me and we both fell to the floor." Her words were calm, almost too serene as if she were reading a menu at a restaurant.

"See, it was just the wind," my father said.

I didn't believe them one bit and marched to the doorway, and then made a beeline back toward the fireplace—the same direction I'd seen a tiny object flung into the room, but found nothing. How could Selena not have seen something coming right for us? I turned to Father. "I heard something flying into the room. Whoever had thrown it had to have followed us from the courtyard," I said, with my back to both Varlac leaders. "They opened the door and shot at us before bolting." I studied the carved wooden frame along the mantel. If an object was flung into the room, it would have landed somewhere in this vicinity.

"Oh," Selena chirped. "Did I mention the smell of mud and crap? Did you sense it too, Marcin? Maybe someone left a window open out in the hallway." She strolled toward me and set a hand on my forearm, the slightest of quivers resonating from her touch. Her stoic expression gave little away, yet my instincts were on full alert. She hadn't openly touched me this way since arriving in Hungary, so what was she up to now? I couldn't work out her intention and stuck to the truth.

"Yeah, muddy footprints vanished out the back door into the woods. Someone was there, so I've got wulfkin searching for the culprit," I said.

"Doesn't prove a thing," the sultan blurted, his jaw set hard and his body angling away from me to face Father. "How can my daughters feel safe after this? You're blaming us to deflect attention from yourself." A slight growl hung off his last word as he shot Father with his glare.

"Right now," I said, "there's no way to know who was targeted. We don't even have a weapon." I didn't buy into my own bullshit, but the plan was to stop the Varlac leaders from killing each other. We almost had world war three back in the dining hall.

"It's probably nothing." Selena sidestepped me, our arms brushing. My inner wolf responded within a heartbeat, prodding me to get closer. But hell, talk about this being the wrong time.

Silence struck, the kind that came before a huge storm shredded the place to bits.

She approached the sultan in hasty, jerky steps, speaking ultrafast. "Let's not jump to conclusions, Baba."

My father hadn't moved from his position near the couch, though the tight muscles in his neck said it all. He was pissed. Who wouldn't be? But a new expression slid over his face as quickly as putting on a mask.

"Sultan, we don't want a repeat of what happened nine years ago. I'll put extra guards on duty for both our sides."

I stared at Father. Why was he so accommodating? My suspicions flew to his involvement, but until I had more facts, I refused to add to the fire.

"Excellent idea," I said. Anything to extinguish the growing tension.

The sultan shook his head, his gaze bouncing between Selena, my father, and the door. "This isn't over."

If the sultan still held a grudge for Selena's injury from years ago, then yeah, maybe he could be responsible. But he would have to know fingers would be pointed in his direction. Despite the cruelty my father was capable of, he was too calculating to simply bring the Turkish Varlac leader here, kill Selena, and start a war. It made no sense, especially since I recalled Father's excitement about gaining a foothold into Turkey with the dowry.

My father clapped, the sound resonating through the room, and approached the sultan. "Okay, I do believe we should return to our meal." The underlying tone of Father's voice rocked as if he too was desperate to move past the stalemate. I wasn't buying his laid- back reaction. I'd find out what he hid later.

On the other hand, the sultan hadn't quite settled down and still wore a grimace. His stare targeted Selena. "Mohammad," he bellowed.

A stocky, bald guard pushed open the door, a sword at his hip. He resembled a grizzly bear in size, with a jacket tight across his chest. How could he protect anyone when he could barely move his arms?

"Take Selena to her room." "What?" Her face paled.

"After this incident, you'll be guarded twenty-four hours, and you're not to go anywhere in the castle alone. End of discussion."

Selena's mouth dropped open. "Take her."

Mohammad marched toward Selena. She squared her posture and shoved past him on her way to the door. The guard chased after her. Well, at least I wasn't the only one with *father* issues.

"Come, let's return to the hall." Father said.

The sultan released a loud exhale. "You're lucky you only have boys." "Ha. They have their own set of problems, trust me."

The pair left the room without a glance my way. Fine by me. Time to get my head together and work out what the fuck had happened in this room.

Retracing my steps from where Selena was standing, I trod toward the fireplace, scanning the ground for anything out of place. If something was thrown at us and missed, it could have fallen anywhere in the room. I tossed the couch cushions aside. Nothing hidden underneath. I lifted the edge of the sofa off the floor to find a layer of dust. No surprise.

The fire crackled and spat as I studied the burning logs, figuring whatever was aimed at us might have fallen in. Not even moving them around with a poker helped.

I retreated to the entrance and angled myself to face the exact spot where Selena and I had been standing; just one foot left from the couch. Then I lowered myself as I assumed whatever was thrown would be aimed at our chest for maximum impact. My gaze lined up directly with the corner of the fireplace mantel.

I inspected the curves and floral patterns, running a finger over the wood. Something rough brushed under my finger, and I dropped my hand. A thin slit of a puncture was near the far corner. The kind caused by a small knife. I inhaled the faintest wisp of bitterness and a sickly scent. What was that? Taking another sniff, I was convinced I recognized the smell but couldn't place it. So familiar that the sourness stung my nostrils. Poison.

Did the sultan put a hit out on me, or had Father ordered someone to take out Selena? Was I approaching this wrong and perhaps the answer lay with another enemy? Goddess knows, Father had enough of those to fill a country.

But where was the weapon? Surveying the floorboards around me revealed nothing. I ran a hand down my face and sighed.

Selena was the only person alone in this room after the attack. If she'd taken the weapon, what was her reason and why hadn't she told anyone?

My chest tightened with dread.

***

A sonorous trumpeting echoed around me. I rolled over in bed and dragged a pillow over my head to block out the sound. It came again, louder. What the shit was going on? I shoved the pillow and blanket aside, then reached to the bedside table, tapping for my cell in the dark.

Six fuckin' o'clock?

The toot boomed from outside again, long and thudding. Wouldn't be the first time Father insisted on an ungodly catch-up, involving every wulfkin in the castle. I swore I'd find that blasted horn and destroy it.

Rubbing my eyes, I dragged myself to the window. The sun showed no sign of rising anytime soon. A silvery hue from the moonlight reflected off the snow-capped trees. This scenery was why I'd picked this room. Aside from it resembling a loft and being in the highest point of the castle, the view reminded me of my true nature—a wulfkin. Wild at heart, but feet planted squarely in the human world.

Ten minutes later, I stood in front of the mirror ... washed, and dressed in jeans, a long-sleeved shirt, and a coat. Strands of hair poked outward, but no matter how much I patted them down, they refused to flatten. The ends clumped over my shoulders.

Whatever. I could barely keep my eyes open. After yesterday's horrendous events, I had planned a full day of hunting after Father announced the participants in the initial challenge. My name had better be on the list.

After dinner last night, I had cornered Father about his relaxed state in the weapons room. He swore he wasn't involved but insisted if someone wanted to kill Selena, he wasn't going to rush to stop them. Then he doubled the guards watching over me. That was the closest he'd ever been to showing me he cared.

In the hallway, three guards stood to attention. I gritted my teeth. No one needed to protect me, and I somehow doubted they'd be able to keep up with me while I trained with my pack out in the woods.

I passed the sentries while heading toward the circular staircase.

Did the sultan have several guards following Selena around too? Although, after seeing Selena's dance, hinting of her fighting ability, I'd say she could more than handle herself. Images of her dancing in the skimpy costume came to the forefront of my memory, the way her breasts bounced, her curvy ass. Damn, she'd grown into a breathtaking wulfkin. She'd always been a stunning female with her large almond eyes, pouty lips, and a body to die for, but those memories were blown away by the real thing. Yet, considering how last night ended, with a weapon missing and her being potentially responsible for its disappearance, I had to get my head out of the gutter.

Outside, I pulled the collar around my neck and hurried along a worn path in the snow toward the courtyard

Ahead, a large crowd of fifty or so wulfkin huddled around the well, their whispers floating on the breeze. Several guards stomped their feet in the cold, while others were wrapped up in several layers of furs. Near the gate, two wulfkin were warming their hands in front of a brazier, sizzling with chestnuts. Tentacles of curling smoke wafted in the air. The rich and sweet aroma coaxed a growl from my stomach and put me back on the street corner of Vincent's hometown, deep in the woods of Lapland in Finland. His mother had been roasting them when I arrived there, scouting for recruits, and every sentence from her lips was a variation of, *"Would you like more food?"*

I pushed past the entrance to the courtyard. Torches lit the place, and snowflakes cascaded like a backdrop from a picturesque postcard. But this place was anything but a tourist attraction.

Father and the sultan stood to the side, talking about goddess-knows-what. But at least they weren't at each other's throats.

The moment Father spotted me, he waved me over, and the sultan vanished into the mass of wulfkin. Snow crunched underfoot as I approached him and scanned the area for Selena without success.

"Marcin." Father clapped a hand against my back. "Nice of you to finally join us.

Thought you might be with your brother, showering him with more luxuries." My hackles flared. It was too early for this bullshit.

The whiff of coffee caught my attention—strong and nutty. Behind him, I noticed a long table with coffee-filled thermoses. I nodded to the youngster manning the stand.

"Come. I'm about to call out participants in the venery. I need you by my side." Father's words dragged me back to the reality of being awakened at a ridiculous hour.

I offered him a look, the one clearly protesting my necessity to be there. He'd do what he wanted anyway, so what difference would it make?

He brushed past me and stood in front of the old stone well, waving a quick hand to someone behind me. The blare of the fuckin' horn had me cringing again. Oh, that instrument was going to be twisted into a pretzel shape soon.

The voices died, and when I spun around, my sight landed on Selena, at the edge of the group, shoulder to shoulder with her sister. The sultan stood guard nearby, along with several beefy men. I could only imagine how large those wulfkin were in their wolf form. They'd be a force to be reckoned with, but swiftness wouldn't be a trait they offered with so much weight behind them.

Selena met my stare—cold and empty. Maybe she wasn't a morning person either. But regardless of her hair pulled into a messy ponytail and bloodshot eyes from an obvious lack of sleep, the pout of her full lips called to me, begging to be kissed.

"Marcin," a disembodied voice came from my side, and I snapped around. Coffee boy handed me a cup. Best sight in the world.

"Thanks." The heat instantly warmed the back of my throat along with my frozen fingers wrapped around the mug.

"I appreciate everyone joining me so early this morning," Father began, though it wasn't as if he'd given anyone a choice with the blaring horn. "At the kind request of our guest, the great sultan, we are holding a venery to select two champions to prove the innocence of Enre and Daciana." He turned and pulled the chain, raising the bucket out of the well.

When prying off the lid, he said, "Sultan, if you'll join me, please."

I took another gulp of coffee, making everything all right for a short while. Selena kept staring at me. What was going through her mind? Was she picturing herself kissing me, both of us naked and locked in each other's arms, or quite the opposite and involving her sword? I preferred the first option. In all honestly, rekindling our relationship had played on my mind a lot since she'd arrived. My feelings for her still beat with ferocity, and my wolf reminded me about every moment we'd spent together, how much he missed her. But it seemed fate had other ideas. Maybe I was fooling myself to think anything was possible.

"Alex," Father's voice climbed with the first name plucked out of the bucket, then handed the note to the sultan for confirmation. Alex was one of Father's pack members, and I assumed he was a backup plan in case I didn't make it. Father would do anything to claim that boon and stop the sultan from winning the prize.

Father continued with the names; a dozen had passed, and with only eight positions left, a layer of sweat rolled down my back. I preferred handling my own problems and would hate to rely on anyone else winning the boon on my behalf.

But surprisingly, no guards from the Turkish clan had been pulled yet either. Perhaps they were trying to be on their best behavior, and I guessed that entering might give the wrong impression. I'd encouraged my pack to enter as it offered them an opportunity to join a good old-fashioned hunt.

When my name was finally called, I gulped down the coffee and set the mug down on the well behind me. Number eighteen. Better late than never.

"Selena." Father's voice held an uncertain tone as he stared at the next note he read out.

I snapped to attention, my gaze sailing across the crowd to Selena.

Her eyes widened, and if I hadn't known she might have removed evidence from the weapons room last night, I might actually believe the sincere shock on her face. And to think that last night she acted all shy as if she hadn't put her name into the bucket.

"This is a mistake." The sultan's voice inflamed, sending the crowd into murmurs. "I do not give my permission for Selena to enter. She isn't here to fight or participate in the venery." His words darkened, his glare targeting Selena.

She shook her head at her father in way that implied she had nothing to do with her name being in the ballot.

"Sultan, clearly this handwriting is feminine. No one else put her name in." Levin patted Boran's arm, smirking a bit too obviously. "So she must participate. Those are the rules."

Boran's nostrils flared, his chest rising and falling rapidly.

Father plucked another name and read it out as if he hadn't just openly caused tension between a daughter and her father. A case could be made for eavesdropping on that interesting conversation, but Selena's words came back about her having trained as a fighter since a young age. She'd make a strong competitor.

"Levin," the sultan said, interrupting Father. "I can't allow this to happen. First, I have to speak with my daughter, and then I will come see you."

Father said nothing, but watched as the corners of his mouth threatened to spread into a grin.

The sultan snatched Selena's elbow and dragged her inside, the door slamming shut behind them.

I pitied Selena. My first reaction urged me to chase after them and force her father to back off. Who was I to get involved in their family squabbles? I had enough of my own to drown in, especially after last night and the nagging suspicion that Selena was somehow involved in the assassination attempt against me.

CHAPTER 8

"What do you think you're doing?" Father shoved open the door to our suite, and I pulled my arm free from his grasp, rubbing the skin where his fingers had left vivid marks.

I stormed inside the room, and the first streams of sunlight stretched over the forest horizon outside the window. Down in the courtyard, all the wulfkin stood around, more than likely gossiping about me. Then I spotted Zeki darting through the crowd toward a door. Where was he going in such a rush?

"How could you?" Father's voice barked.

"I told you I didn't put my name in the bucket." I turned to face him. Sure, I had intended to put my name in the well, but Marcin interrupted me, and with the dagger incident, I'd completely forgotten. Obviously, someone wanted me to enter. The idea had sent a pestering shiver worming its way up the back of my legs. Wouldn't be the first time the Hungarian clan tried to finish me off, but it seemed like a lot of trouble to bring us here, then kill me. Surely Levin would target the great sultan first.

Aisha shut the door behind us.

Father's face reddened as he paced to the window and back, hands gripping his hips. "If we were back home, you wouldn't see the light of day for months. Maybe I should tell Levin to lock you in his dungeons. That might keep you in check." His glare held no hint of a joke.

I struggled to swallow past the boulder in my throat.

"You're here to seal a mating ritual with Marcin." Father's voice reminded me that I might have to beat Marcin in the venery, and he might not take too kindly to that.

He continued, "Not to act like a tomboy or give Levin any reason to consider us a threat to his family."

I huffed. "Baba, please. That's not—"

Father's scowl robbed my words. "Someone tried to kill you last night. What if the killer is in the tournament and targets you?"

My voice vanished when I tried to respond. Had the assassin put my name into the bucket? And is that why this person stole Father's dagger—to frame our family? I refused to believe Father was behind the assassination attempt. Only a fool would use his or her own weapon to strike the enemy, especially since the dagger would be left behind at the scene. Everything Father did was to protect his pack and family, so killing Marcin would not gain him anything but a quicker war.

I preferred to believe Marcin was responsible, especially since he genuinely seemed to have no problem with me entering the venery. Images from our past crept to the forefront of my mind—Marcin and me sneaking out of my house before dawn to run away and live as a couple forever. He brought chains in his backpack to tie us to trees during the full moon. We were still moonwulves back then, controlled by lunar events. At the time, I had gotten so angry at him for bringing them along that I refused to speak to him, but on our first night, it had saved our lives and stopped us from entering the city to gorge on humans. Was this another incident where he'd done something thinking it would help me?

"Selena, are you even listening?" Father's sharp tone cut through my thoughts. "Sorry."

"I said, you're not participating. That's final."

"It's not fair." Since I had been selected to participate, it irritated me to be told I couldn't enter.

"Nothing's fair in life, but we all make sacrifices for those we love." His gray eyebrows lowered.

Yeah, I'm making all the sacrifices. I glanced over at Aisha, who had her phone on her lap, tapping away, and I fully understood father's warning. Go against him, and the deal with protecting Aisha was off.

"When I was young," he continued, "I left everything to marry your mother. Now look at our empire and how far we've come."

I didn't have it in me to ask him how happy he really was, considering he spent most days and nights with his council and rarely had time for Mother or us. The only reason my mom knew we were going to Hungary was because I'd told her. Father had been too busy to mention it. I shook those thoughts away. No use opening up old wounds.

Last night's events steamrolled through my mind, and I had no reason to hold back my finding from Father now. If I'd told him last night, he wouldn't have been so convincing with Levin when arguing our side was innocent.

"I have something to show you." Once across the room, I dug a hand into my bag near the fireplace and plucked out a wad of tissues.

Father stood a few paces from me as I peeled back the paper. His nose creased. "What are you doing with my dagger?" Even Aisha strained to glance over our way.

"This is what was shot at Marcin and me last night. I found it in the fireplace mantle. I took it before anyone saw."

His shaky hand reached over.

"Careful, the tip has poison on it. I smelled the bitter scent on it."

Father's furrowed brow hooded his eyes as he pinched the dagger by the hilt and lifted it to his nose. His cheeks went pale.

"I don't recognize the poison." His back was stiff, and he set the dagger back into the tissues, rewrapping it. He took the bundle from me. "You did well to take it. Goddess, if they found this, Levin would have us butchered on the spot."

"So this wasn't your doing? You didn't try to assassinate Marcin?" I asked.

His head jerked up, worry lines deepening around the corners of his mouth. "And put us all in mortal danger? I brought the daggers in case things got out of hand."

"Then we were set up."

He nodded, though his eyes were miles away. "I will speak with the guards." "Didn't the Hungarian servants take our bags to our room the moment we arrived?"

Aisha padded closer.

Father turned to her, not saying a word. His face paled further. He crossed the room in a sprint and dashed into his bedroom.

Aisha and I followed him to a large duffle bag sitting on the king-sized poster bed covered in creamy silk covers. He retrieved short swords and several knives. Then he plucked out a black briefcase-style box and opened it. Inside was a line of silver daggers with the family emblem carved on them. Two empty slots stared back at me as if they were pistols to my temple.

"By the goddess," Father's words were barely a whisper. "There's still one missing."

My stomach churned, and if I'd eaten breakfast, it would have been projecting out right about then.

Father and I exchanged glances. If Father wasn't involved, whoever took the daggers wasn't interested in killing me directly. They were targeting Marcin to frame us.

As far as I was concerned, Levin had to be at the bottom of this, despite last night's act. He had lied all those years ago about his wulfkin shooting an arrow into my shoulder. Why not now?

I slouched on the edge of the bed. Surely, Levin wouldn't kill his son to frame us.

I couldn't stop the panic threading my chest. We were going to be murdered, and those back home wouldn't see it coming.

"We're in so much shit," I managed to say, barely louder than a whisper.

"Baba, take us home." Aisha's plea quivered, and she approached Father as a small child would do when frightened.

He shook his head. "The moment the assassin uses the second dagger and strikes Marcin, Levin will declare war. Even if it happens after we leave, he could easily claim my guards returned to finish the job, especially if we abruptly end the mating." His shoulders hunched forward as he spun the gold ring on his finger in a hypnotic motion. "We stay."

"We have to tell Marcin." The idea had inherent problems, but was it up to us to keep such information from him? I couldn't live if I did nothing and he got hurt.

"Are you insane?" Father asked. "You can't tell Marcin or anyone about this. Do you both hear me? He'll tell Levin, and we'll be dead. We can't trust them. You leave this to me."

"Marcin is the only person on the Hungarian side we *can* probably trust. I've got an in with him. I should use this to protect us."

Father shook his head. "You heard Levin last night. He's putting extra guards to watch over his son. We all keep our mouths shut about this. Understood?" His voice rumbled.

I didn't agree one bit, but going against Father could get us all in mortal danger if this got out to Levin.

"Then we need to find the missing dagger." Aisha sat on the bed, the mattress bouncing beneath me.

"And how do we do that when we have no suspects?" Father asked.

Maybe Aisha was onto something. "Simple," I said. "I'll have a private dinner tonight with Marcin and try to discover who his enemies are." A saner person would have taken slow steps to get Marcin on her side, get him to share. However, there was no time to play coy with the venery starting tomorrow. "It's as good a place to start as any. Until then, I'll try to spend as much time with him as possible and insist guards follow me for protection."

Father strode to the window. "Except for the venery."

I huffed. "Well then, there's only one solution. I remain in the challenge. How hard can it be? It's a venery, meaning we'll be hunting down some kind of animal."

Father faced me, the light of morning sunshine behind him giving him an orange glow, softening the worry lines beneath his eyes. "You're not entering."

I climbed off the bed and approached him. "The assassin isn't after me, but I can be an extra eye on Marcin, tracking other participants in the venery. If he's shot, we're all dead. And it's too late to get our guards to enter. But I'm already in."

Aisha was by my side, an arm wrapped around my waist, drawing me into her. "Besides, Selena is kick-ass when it comes to fighting."

Father's mouth opened, but no words came out at first. He scratched his ear. "We don't even know why or how your name ended up in the bucket. Someone's trying to trap you."

"Or they just wanted Selena to have a bit of fun," Aisha said.

I spun around toward her, watching her back away, a hand clasped to her mouth. "What did you do?"

"Aisha." Father's voice flared, and his whole face shook, hands clenched to his side. "You had no right. You—"

"I ... I wanted Selena to kick some Hungarian butt before the mating ritual. Zeki told me about the bucket when I wasn't invited to dinner, so I made a quick detour. I'm sorry. I didn't know this would happen."

"Do you know what you've done? The position you've put us in?" Father marched closer, but I jutted out an arm to stop him. After last night's screaming match, Father had grabbed his belt, but when I jumped in to defend Aisha, he had pulled away. Good thing because I wasn't sure I could ever raise my hand to my father, even if he was gripping a weapon against me.

"Selena, I'm sorry. I was hoping you'd think it was Marcin, and it might help you two bond. You were inseparable back in Turkey, and I know you still love him. I just want you to be happy." Tears glossed her eyes.

"You're so silly sometimes." I moved closer and took her into my arms, her head cradled against my neck.

"Moon Goddess, what have I done wrong to deserve an imbecile for a daughter?" Father stormed around the room. "As if we don't have enough problems. If we don't find the culprit who took my daggers, none of us will be going home."

The silence was deafening. Entering the tournament would have been fun, especially to have a female represent Daciana, but now the danger radar had just hit the moon.

A sudden knock had us shooting each other concerned looks.

Father flinched and headed out of the bedroom. He opened the door.

"Apologies for the interruption, Sultan Boran. Emperor Levin has asked me to fetch you for breakfast, after which you, Levin, and Marcin will spend the day in his meeting room."

"Give me a moment. I'll be right down."

Aisha and I emerged from the bedroom as Father shut the door, his expression turned into a grimace. Yep, we were wading in dangerous waters, the kind filled with piranhas.

"What do we do now?" I gnawed on my bottom lip.

He tugged down on his shirt and glanced my way. "You've got less than a day to brush up on your hunting skills. I'll go to Levin and see what I can uncover." Sighing, he opened the door again and planted a forced smile on his lips as he stepped out.

"We're so dead." Aisha brushed past and faced me, her arms wrapped around her stomach. "How else will this play out? The only thing on our side is that the assassin is obviously a terrible shot since they missed the first time. But what if you're not around the next time, then ..." She gasped. "Did you see how Levin treated his own son at the hearing? It'll be us, but worse."

"Calm down. That won't happen. Marcin is with Levin today, which means guards will be everywhere." I couldn't have Aisha panic, and I had to stay in control.

"Maybe you should tell Marcin."

"I really want to, but didn't you hear Father?" The more I thought about it, the more I believed Father was right.

Aisha's brow creased in the I-don't-buy-your-argument way. "But you and he ran away once. You told me you thought he loved you. Surely—"

"That was nine years ago. He's made it clear he doesn't want to be my mate." I rubbed a hand along my hip, the one I'd broken when I fell down the gorge during our attempted runaway escapade. No matter how much my insides tightened in Marcin's presence, I couldn't go there again.

Aisha paused for a moment, her shoulders stiff and her lips pinched. "Not all men are like Father or Levin. They don't all automatically assume everyone is out to stab them in the back. Marcin deserves the truth. He's the target."

I glanced out the window where the sun was in its full glory, bright against the cloudless sky. The mountain peaks glistened with snow, and despite the beauty, Aisha's terror leeched into me. Marcin had a right to know he was in danger, except every time I contemplated the idea, my gut turned, demanding we stick by Father's rule and not trust Marcin. My wolf instinctually protested, nudging my insides that it was the wrong decision and we should trust Marcin.

"We listen to Father," I said, focusing on the current threat, the dagger, and the upcoming venery. Then it hit me. "I'm such a bird-brained idiot."

"Not sure I'd go that far."

"Hey." I fake punched Aisha in the arm. "I picked up on the poison used on the dagger, so tomorrow morning before the hunt, I just have to be on guard for that same smell on the entrants. Might work."

"If they have it on them. What if they've hidden the weapon in the woods?"

I stared at Aisha. "The woods are too vast to search now, and considering we don't even know what we're hunting tomorrow, how would the assassin know which direction we'd be running?"

Aisha shrugged and glanced out the window. "We don't know."

How could she remain so calm? "I'll still sniff the area for the scent. Got to cover all bases."

"Nothing to lose."

Sick of rehashing this, the urge to kick something real hard struck. "How 'bout we head outside so I can practice."

"Yes!" She spun and bolted toward our bedrooms. "I'm bringing Klaus and Grit with us."

My mouth opened to stop her, but maybe having them along would stop anyone from trying to assassinate me ... in case we had this all wrong, and I was the target.

—

ithout knowing the venery rules, I assumed the worst: no weapons. Fine by me, as I'd hunted animals without them, though it could involve tracking down a hidden object.

Surely not.

We moved away from the dim castle corridors that always made me tense. At the age of nine, I had been accidentally locked inside a dungeon cell while playing down there. For two days, I was trapped in pitch blackness, screaming for help, crying, terrified.

Finally, a guard retrieving a set of keys discovered me. But I'd never forget the foreboding feeling of darkness pressing down on me, the sensation that I'd die in those cells and never see my family or friends or the sun again. Just death and me in one room. I never planned to go there again.

Huffing, I traipsed amid a cluster of trees on the west side of the castle to avoid the open land where anyone could spot us. My feet sunk in snow to my knees, and damn, this hunt was going to be more difficult than I anticipated. It never snowed like this in Turkey. What we were experiencing here was the aftermath of an avalanche.

Grit pounced past me, tongue sticking out. Klaus raced after him.

"Hey," Aisha called out, rushing after them. "I tagged you, Grit. You're supposed to chase us, not the other way around." She stumbled to her knees but got up and kept going.

If I was ever going to keep up with Marcin tomorrow, I had to get used to the environment. I leapt after the trio. My attempt at running turned into a half fast walk, half knee lift. Damn. Maybe the answer was to transform. At least that way, I'd be as fast as the dracwulves. Except, I ought to raise my stamina in human form just in case.

I passed Aisha and turned right after Klaus, who kept glancing back to make sure he didn't lose sight of us. "Hurry up, lazy bum," I said over my shoulder.

Aisha had slowed the pace, her cheeks glowing bright red.

When I refocused on the path ahead, I spotted Grit darting left, faster than a bullet, chasing a bouncing animal—a rabbit.

Challenge accepted.

"Aisha, chase the bunny." I swerved and sprinted after Grit, unable to stop the giggles building up in my chest. Back home, Aisha and I spent hours trying to catch the loose chickens that escaped from a nearby farm. Besides, my scent always calmed animals and put them into a kind of sleepy trance, so if I could get close enough, I'd try to save the rabbit. It had been that way ever since I was born. But more than a month ago during the red moon, also called the Lunar Eutine, my ability strengthened when I transformed from a moonwulf, when the full moon would control my shifts, to wulfkin status, where I mastered my wolf.

The distance between Grit and me widened, and the rabbit he chased headed for the cluster of trees. I'd never catch him while clumsily plodding through the snow; my hip ached to high hell from the long strides. Aisha wasn't anywhere near us, having collapsed into the snow behind me.

Time to play dirty.

I stopped and yanked my jacket off, then my top and bra. In two seconds, I shed my other clothes and boots. And right there, in the center of my chest was a presence—my wolf— pushing against my human side. My flesh rippled, and the wolf exploded free as brown and white striated fur spread across my body. My limbs elongated and reshaped, bones cracked, and skin split into a four-legged form. *Catch rabbit.* A howl that could carry for miles slipped past my lips as I shook off the last remnants of my human form and threw myself into a huge drift of snow.

Fast strides were a breeze, and my hip didn't hurt while in

wolf form. I closed in on my target, inhaling Grit's muddy scent along with the furry smell of the sweet morsel. *Delicious.*

A white tail bounced into the woods. Not far, Grit skidded to a halt and bolted after his meal.

I pushed ahead. Catch the bunny. I careened around a large tree and merged into the shadowy woodland. My paws dug into snow and soil, the wind swooshing through my fur. *Where are you?*

Then a guttural growl bellowed. Not the kind I'd expect from hunting down a tiny mammal.

Grit!

A scream followed.

My chest tightened. Goddess, no. My insides deadened and only one vision dominated—Grit attacking a wulfkin.

I pounced toward the sounds, but my back foot skidded and sent me flat on my side like a drunken fool. Back on my feet, I moved fast, weaving around trees and leaping over dead branches, the heavy stench of earth and wolf filling my nostrils.

Then I came to a jarring halt near an old pine, stripped bare of needles.

A male wulfkin with a large hooked nose was gripping a knife with both hands. The first ripples of his transformation caused his body to shiver. Across from him stood Grit, all one hundred pounds, seemingly confused as his head danced between the wulfkin and me. He kept sniffing the ground in a circle, searching for his bunny.

Father had warned us. If the dracwulves caused trouble again, he'd send them away forever. It would break Aisha's heart. I couldn't bear to lose them. Klaus and Grit had been our pets since they were pups.

"I'll kill it." Hook Nose guy lunged forward, his blade swiping the air, inches from Grit's face.

I threw myself between them and forced a shift back into my human body with as much ease as slipping off a coat. The snap of coldness swathed around me tightly.

"Stop," I said. "He won't hurt you."

Hook Nose's head jerked in my direction, his wide eyes

tracing the length of my naked body, and a grin pulled at the corners of his mouth. But it vanished the moment he looked down at Grit while readying his knife for another attack.

Grit was by my side, snarling at the wulfkin. I reached behind me with a hand, patting him. "It's okay, boy. You can calm down now."

"Dracwulves are banned and should be killed on sight."

Grit's snarls eased, replaced by heavy grunts, his hot breath on my hand as he licked my fingers.

"Get out of the way." The wulfkin stepped closer. "I have to finish it." "He's my pet."

His shoulders shot back. A genuine surprised look, complete with a furrowed brow and parted mouth, greeted me. "Then you deserve to be hunted down and killed too."

"My family doesn't follow your prehistoric Varlac rules." I hadn't intended to sound so angry, but this wulfkin irked me.

Snow crunched behind me. My spine stiffened, but with a quick inhale, I released the breath I'd been holding.

Hook Nose guy spat on the ground between us. "Turks. Not good for anything but bait."

"Fuck you."

"I'd fuck you since you already undressed for me. On second thought, Marcin can have you for now."

His comment caught me off guard, and I stared at the guy, the question of what he meant at the front of my thoughts, except I refused to spend another second in his presence.

"Sanyi, where are you?" a male's voice called out from deeper in the woods. Another burly guy emerged, his gaze locked onto me.

Too much company for my liking.

"Selena?" Aisha appeared, my clothes bunched up in her arms.

Despite my nakedness, the fire burning through my veins wiped clear the frostiness, and my hand curled into a fist as I stared at the arrogant son of a bitch with a huge nose.

Aisha grabbed my elbow.

"Don't waste your time with these losers."

Of course, she was right, but hell, I considered breaking that ridiculous nose of his in three places. Sidestepping Grit, I nudged him toward the castle. "Let's go, boy."

I clenched my teeth and rushed after Aisha and Grit, well aware that Hook Nose guy probably voiced the opinion of most Hungarians. Maybe fearing Levin wasn't my only problem—it seemed the Hungarian clan had enemies on the inside too. Could Hook Nose guy's hatred of Marcin be in any way related to the missing dagger?

CHAPTER 9

MARCIN

*E*nre's expression twisted, and he jerked to his feet, the chair behind him falling over. "I'm sick of waiting in this hellhole. And why the fuck hasn't Father come to see me yet? I want out. Let me represent myself at the venery. I'd run circles around all of those other fools."

Never been called a fool before, but I bit my tongue. "With the Turkish clan here, Father's trying to run things by the rules for once. Don't give him any reasons to dispute your freedom."

Daciana stepped closer to my brother, her deep, gray eyes striking against her pale complexion. "Enre's right. Let us represent ourselves. We're not helpless."

"If it were up to me, you'd be back home already. Stay put awhile longer, that's all I ask."

Enre's gaze never left me. His stubble was in need of a trim, and his black hair was a mess as if he hadn't combed it for weeks. Probably hadn't.

I understood he was pissed and frustrated, but welcome to my world, twenty-four seven. For my brother, I'd risk my life because he didn't deserve the upbringing he'd gotten.

Enre leaned against the window frame, arms folded across his chest. Daciana lifted the overturned chair and sat on it, releasing a low sigh. The fire behind me hissed and sputtered, and despite its warmth, iciness clung to my skin. With Enre's hunting skills, developed at a young age, he would have made a powerful alpha from the get-go. But without support, he'd spent his days finding ways to avoid Father. I helped where I could, but the worse Father got, the more distant Enre grew. And then one day, he had left without saying good-bye.

"What are we supposed to do?" He spoke with his back to me. "Sit here and wait like trapped foxes? It's fucking bullshit. Father hasn't changed one bit."

"He's gotten worse since you left."

Enre turned around, the bridge of his nose creased. "Find that hard to believe."

"Trust me. Everyone's an enemy to him. He doesn't hesitate before striking." Like the small Moldavian pack in Romania he'd ordered attacked. By the time I found out, half the wulfkin were dead, and Father had claimed the territory as his own. He had set himself up to take over Transylvania because of its easy access into Turkey and Russia. No use dredging up horror stories with Enre when I intended to put my brother at ease.

"Except you, his favorite."

His words left a sour taste in my mouth. "I'm in the challenge to gain your freedom." "You don't owe me anything."

I shouldn't have responded because I doubted anything I said would make up for the years of separation or the fact that Enre blamed me for never sticking up for him. He couldn't be more wrong. I wasn't here to convince him otherwise. My purpose was to save their lives. Then maybe we could relook at mending our relationship.

"Blame me all you want, but nothing is as clear-cut as you think. I've done things like this my whole life to help you out, and maybe one day, you'll listen to my side of the story."

Enre's narrowed gaze gave nothing away. "You're not getting any sympathy from me.

For all I know, this whole incident is some kind of trick you and Father concocted." Daciana cleared her throat, drawing my attention. She tucked dark chocolate hair behind her ears and leaned forward in her seat.

"Tomorrow's the day of the venery, then?"

"Yep. A number of wulfkin were selected this morning." I returned my attention to Enre.

"I'll win the challenge and prove your innocence." I'd hoped for Vincent, my second-in-command, to participate alongside me. Unfortunately, his name wasn't drawn out of the bucket. Most of the ones called were wulfkin from Father's side and were the kind who'd kill anyone who stood in the way of their boon. They wouldn't care what Father threatened them with if it meant getting a free ticket to anything they wanted. That came from building a pack of followers through fear.

"Not going anywhere without Daciana."

I shifted in my seat. "I give you my word, you'll both live."

"Will you keep us posted about what's going on?" Daciana asked.

"Of course." My cell beeped in my pocket. I grabbed it. A reminder for dinner with Selena in five minutes. She'd invited me, which had me all kinds of curious, especially since I suspected it might have something to do with the missing blade from the weapons room.

I stood and brushed down my shirt.

"Good luck," Daciana said, her voice softening as did the look in her eyes. Enre didn't say a word.

The invisible wall between us wasn't coming down anytime soon. Once this song and dance tournament was over, we'd address that.

I gulped back a mouthful of blood wine. Tonight, my expectations weren't on food but on Selena arriving. I set the silver goblet down a bit too hard, crimson splashing over the edge and dribbling onto the wooden floor. I shifted on the bright green cushion, crossing my legs, unable to get comfortable. How does anyone sit on these things and not lose sensation in their legs? Father would have a fit if he saw us eating a meal sitting on the floor.

The room had been decorated in a strange fusion of Eastern

Europe meets *The Arabian Nights*. Tapestries covered three walls, each showcasing wolves running through a field. Silvery moonlight bounced off their gray pelts, and the grassy meadow seemed to almost move if you looked at it long enough. All the furniture had been removed and replaced with a rainbow of cushions in a circle in the center. The thick layer of incense burning in the far corner burned my nostrils, a cross between frankincense and sandalwood.

I checked my phone. Fifteen minutes late to her own dinner invitation. Should I be disappointed or surprised? The only reason I remained was curiosity. Tonight was about discovering what Selena concealed and, most importantly, why.

Footsteps echoed from behind the door before it opened. I untangled my legs and stood.

Selena strolled in, her hips swinging in a rhythm that called to my wolf and pelvis. She wore the bluest dress with a corset emphasizing her cleavage, the sheen fabric billowing around her feet with each step she took closer.

Regardless, in my mind, I already had her up against the wall, skirt pulled up to her waist and me buried deep inside her. Her soft murmurs in my ear, begging me for more. Hell, I'd imagined myself with her nonstop since her arrival.

Then my sights slid to the dracwulf on her leash, and the fantasy disappeared. My inner wolf snarled in my chest.

The dracwulf's head shot up, his eyes locked on me. Did he see me as a snack? These animals were stronger than regular wolves, and ten times more territorial.

Selena held her chin high. Her smile radiated with glossy lips that glistened against the candelabra's flames. Maybe I'd misread her invitation as something more than discussing the assassination attempt.

"You look spectacular." I swallowed hard. "Should have told me we were going full out. I might have worn my good jeans."

She broke into laughter, the sound soft and soothing, except it wasn't real in the slightest—from the twitch at the corner of her mouth to the tightness with which she gripped the leash. Even the tone of her laughter was gone.

"I'd pull your seat out, but ..." My gaze fell to the custard-colored square cushion a few paces across from mine, curious if this was how Turkish females normally dressed when seated on the floor.

"Klaus, sit."

The dracwulf lay down on his belly alongside Selena's pillow with his front paws stretched out toward my side. I couldn't help but feel intimidated by his size. Klaus's head was easily larger than mine, and yet he sat there, tongue hanging out the side of his mouth like an obedient dog. I inhaled a tidal wave of wet fur and dirt scent. Wulfkin had hunted dracwulves to extinction in ancient times for a reason. They killed anything in their paths. Yet the Turkish kept them as pets—a spiritual connection with their ancestors. I had no problem with the spiritual part, just the dracwulf one.

"He won't bite." Selena's voice carried a hint of amusement. She stepped in front of her cushion and sat, her bent knees dropping to one side, revealing blue heeled boots.

The only bite I'd ever accept was from Selena. And that single thought had my wolf wide awake, ready to party.

"I'm surprised you've got Klaus under such control." The animal was so close to me that one wrong move and he'd take my head off.

After a quick sip from her goblet, she licked the red from her upper lip in a way that made me suddenly relax in all the right ways. "He's been trained from a young pup," she said. "Thanks for having dinner with me. Figured we didn't really get a chance to catch up. Well, we tried, but ..." She paused. "It didn't go according to plan."

My idea of a relaxed night involved a simple plate of raw steak, lots of blood wine, and chatting with my pack in the main hall, but maybe in Turkey it meant dressing up, being watched by a dracwulf, and having your legs cramp up as if they were an elastic band. But for the chance of sharing alone time with Selena, I'd run naked through the .

I drew my foot in closer, but it only sent a twinge up my thigh. Terrible idea.

"If you're not comfortable, we can go elsewhere." She shrugged. "Thought we could lounge a bit."

"You get all dolled up when lounging at home?" Back in Turkey, she'd spent her days in jeans and T-shirts.

She stared at her dress and ran a hand down the gorgeous curve from her bust to her tummy. "Kind of wanted to impress you."

The escalating pounding in my chest demanded I reach over and kiss her at once.

Selena had openly admitted to trying to make an impact on me. And while I was excited about the possibilities this brought, a niggling sensation still churned in the pit of my gut. "Even if you wore sweatpants, I'd be impressed."

She smiled, and her lips could have melted the snow-caps off a mountain range. Selena was no stranger to getting her way with those looks, and I guessed she'd used them plenty of times.

The door jerked open, and my muscles tensed.

Klaus jumped to his feet, towering over us, his bad breath flooding across me. Selena patted his back. "It's okay, boy. Sit down."

A kitchen girl froze in the doorway, her gaze locked on us.

Just the food. I waved her forward. Goddess, I had to calm down.

The servant, who I didn't recognize and assumed belonged to the Turkish clan, skirted around to the other side of us, away from Klaus, and set a large plate on the floor between us. She then hurried from the room. Strips of raw meat coated in an earthy marinade filled half the plate; the second half was covered in strips of flatbread.

Selena leaned forward, grabbed a slice of bread, and used it to scoop up meat. She popped it into her mouth. I followed suit, inhaling the spicy fragrance that tingled across my tongue. I swallowed the food and was going in for another.

"Do you like it?" Selena asked.

I swallowed the food. "I might just marry this sauce."

She wiped her lips with a napkin and smirked. Black makeup swept across her eyelid, curving upward at the corners and giving her sexy cat eyes. When we first met in Turkey, she'd never worn makeup and her beauty still radiated, though the theatrics of her new look definitely held my attention.

"So, do you know what we're hunting tomorrow?" Her question was quick and precise as if she'd practiced it many times.

"We? Didn't your father prohibit your entry?" I took another bite of food.

She cut me a hard stare as if ready to challenge me. "I'm in. Father was worried at first, that's all. But he's fine with it now."

"Even with a potential assassin out there? Maybe it's best you sat this one out."

Her fierce glare told me to back off. "Wouldn't the same apply to you then? What makes you think you'll be safe? Maybe you should focus on who your enemies are?" Her spectacular green irises sparkled under the glow of the candles, though the emphasis she put on the word *safe* left me wondering what exactly she meant.

"I've spent the day speaking to every entrant, and I didn't detect a single lie. I doubt the attackers are in the race. Though, I haven't questioned anyone from the Turkish clan."

Her lips thinned, and when she responded, her voice was dark. "I'm here, grill me if you really think I'm the enemy."

"Doesn't everyone have enemies of sorts?" Something wasn't sounding true here.

Her cheeks flushed. "I'm more than capable of looking after myself. Nothing you say will change my mind. But I'm curious. What sort of enemies would the son of the great emperor have?"

I studied her, the stiffness of her posture. Despite her innocent tone calling me like a goddamn moth to bright light, she was beyond stubborn. And she was fishing for information. Subtlety wasn't her forte.

"Someone different takes reason to dislike me on a daily basis for my father's actions.

But since we're being so honest with each other, let's talk about what happened in the weapons room last night."

"Sure." Shifting on her cushion, she bounced around slightly, causing my eyes to focus on her breasts. As much as I tried not to, they locked onto her cleavage.

"When I searched the room, I didn't find the weapon thrown at us. Isn't that strange?

Especially since you were alone in there after the attack."

"Yeah, so? We didn't find a weapon." She patted Klaus, her fingers zigzagging down his back, evoking a guttural whimper from the animal.

"You're going to make me come out and say it, aren't you?"

Her hand stopped halfway down Klaus's back, and her cheeks morphed into a darker rosy hue. "Are you accusing me of something?" Her voice had steel behind it.

"Help me understand what happened after I went to look for the attacker." She shrugged nonchalantly. "I searched the room and found nothing."

Picking out deceptions was my specialty, and Selena's shaky voice and averted gaze screamed liar. "I don't plan on getting you or anyone in trouble. Whatever you tell me stays between us. Please, Selena. Do you know anything?"

Her face softened, and her posture slackened. She gave a nod so tiny she probably didn't even notice doing it. Dead giveaway she hid something. "I ... I don't know anything."

I reached across the platter of food and took her soft hand in mine. "I found the puncture in the fireplace mantel. It had to be made by a small blade."

She spread her fingers out in a fan against her breastbone with her free hand. "And?

That was probably there from long ago." Her lips pinched to the side.

"Selena, there's been a lot of crap between our families over the years, but I would never harm you. I'd rather throw myself over a cliff before letting you get hurt. You can trust me."

She licked her lips, and her vivid eyes blinked. "But do you trust me?"

"Absolutely." No hesitation. I may not completely trust the sultan or his intentions, but I did when it came to her. Foolish as it sounded, I would wholeheartedly put my life in her hands.

"Then believe me when I say I did not find anything in the room." Her words were fluid without a hint of a tremor.

Were my feelings for her clouding my judgment?

I squeezed her hand in mine before she pulled it away and continued eating.

Obviously, my direct approach wasn't working, and I had no idea why I'd suspected it would. This was Selena I was dealing with, stubbornness extraordinaire. If she had a secret, she'd face a lashing before spilling. She had once refused to tell the sultan where Aisha was because she'd promised her sister to keep the secret. Never mind that the full moon was out that night, or that Aisha had last been seen heading into the city. With only a few hours to sundown, I'd snuck away from the families and tracked her down at a friend's place. A human's home where other young girls and boys were spending the night. In her excitement to be invited to a party, she had insisted the full moon was the following night. We'd made a hasty escape before she turned her newfound friends into snacks.

Yep, Selena hadn't changed one bit.

We finished the rest of the meal in complete silence. I wiped my mouth and stood.

"Come, there's something I want you to see." I offered her an outstretched hand, and she stared at it for a few long moments before accepting my offer.

"What is it?"

"You'll see." Retrieving my long coat from the stand in the far corner, I wrapped it around her shoulders and opened the door.

She grabbed the dracwulf's leash and brought Klaus along. Of course, she would. Guards from both packs followed us, but remained a fair distance away. In all honesty,

since she was packing a dracwulf, it wasn't Selena who required extra protection, but me. I'd take my chances, not believing for one second Selena would ever harm a soul. But that didn't mean she wouldn't hold out on relevant information if she'd made a promise to someone.

At the end of the hallway, I guided her down a dark passage and away from the main courtyard, toward the rear of the building. Klaus's nails click-clacked against the stone floor as he trotted between us. Quite the chaperone.

"You know that lookout place you once showed me in Turkey?" She glanced at me, her eyes wide. "You still remember?"

"Yep, why wouldn't I?"

She shrugged. "Just thought ..." Her words drifted on the breeze whistling through the corridors. "Now you've got me curious." Her mischievous smirk tightened my insides.

Klaus pulled on his leash. Selena rushed after him, her long hair waving against her back, the blue fabric from her dress set in a motion of waves around her legs. Candlelight colored her silhouette across the walls. She broke into a laugh as she ran.

I chased after her and passed them, curving up three flights of worn steps that were rarely used these days. For those few seconds of us running, our breaths labored, and it was as if we were back in Turkey without a care in the world. As far as we had been concerned, we'd be together forever. Our future was set. That was a lifetime away, but I'd take a few seconds of pretending.

I swung left and entered another hallway, darker than the last, but the whispering wind guided me to the back door. I shoved it open, and Selena was right there alongside me.

Klaus pushed between us, leaping outside into the freezing cold night on the upper balcony surrounding the far west wing of the castle.

The dracwulf dragged Selena by the leash, dashing toward the passage that branched out from the veranda in a long passage built on stilts. I kicked the door shut behind me, hoping the guards got the message, and strolled after her.

Wooden beams creaked beneath my footsteps. The outside corridor was overdue for maintenance, but considering no one but me visited the place, it wasn't a priority.

Ferocious winds battered us.

"This post was once used by guards who spend nights here, watching for approaching enemies from the forest. Kind of suits the name of the land: Őrség, meaning defense area."

Up ahead, Selena stopped at the end of the lookout point, a small circular area, and turned toward me. "I love it up here. So free." The wind swept through her hair, blowing strands across her face, which she pushed away.

If I were to ever grill Selena for information, now was the time to do it.

Her eyes crinkled in the corners when she smiled, and my pulse skipped into a race.

How could I have let someone like Selena slip through my fingers?

I stepped alongside her and inhaled her crisp scent of clementine spiked with a hint of honeysuckle. Was it wrong of me to imagine her naked and me kissing every inch of her?

Behind her, the great expanse of the forest was draped in night's cloak. I resisted the urge to take Selena into my arms and taste those lips. "If you look straight ahead, you can just make out tiny lights. That's the closest city in Slovenia, on the border of Hungary."

She inched forward, and my hands tingled to lift her against me. "Yes, I see them. Wow." Then she glanced upward at the clear sky, stars sparkling the heavens overhead like they had back in Turkey.

A howl broke from somewhere in the forest, filled with forlorn pining, stirring Klaus into his own tune. His paws were soon up on the railing, and he too was peering out.

The beautiful smile gracing Selena's lips had my insides flipping. I stared at my girl from years ago, the wulfkin who risked her life to run away with me, who had the confidence in me to keep her safe. Despite every piece of crap that had gone down between our clans, the short stint in Turkey had held some of my fondest memories. It all centered around her. Even following the fucked up turn of events after our attempted escape, maybe the life we'd wanted was still possible. And maybe Selena could be mine again. Hope swirled in my chest.

And for that small space of undivided time, where reality was a world away and a sparkle glimmered in her eyes, I let myself pretend it was the case.

CHAPTER 10

SELENA

White blanketed the terrain farther behind the castle, free of tracks, and sloped downward to empty, flat land. The morning breeze washed through my hair, awakening my senses, my wolf, my anxiety for the venery about to commence. In the far distance, pines stood side by side, partially concealed by low-hanging fog. The trees fanned out like an army ready for battle.

Near the castle, spectators huddled closer, chatting, while in front of them was a small pocket of wulfkin stretching and mock-punching each other in a kind of macho show.

These pack members stood no chance at fighting an army the size of the forest.

When I was a child, my grandmother often recited a grand tale about an enormous army attacking a Turkish village at a time before wulfkin. A gruesome battle ensued, and everyone was murdered, except for a young boy. Alone, he was found by a female wolf who took him under her care until he grew into a man. The legend said the man and she- wolf mated, and she gave birth to ten sons. Eight became the first race of wulfkin and spread across the world as great leaders, while the last two were neither wulfkin nor wolf, but a blend of both. Dracwulf.

Aisha brushed past me and grabbed my elbow, dragging me

toward the group of wulfkin. "You're not going to win if you start all the way back here."

I stumbled after her. "Hey, I was warming up." "How? By staring into the distance?"

Fine, she had a point. Not that I had an issue with being the only female or Turkish entrant, but each time they glanced my way, they sneered. Don't get me wrong, their glares only pumped my adrenaline into a challenge to beat their asses, but I had zero intention of feigning camaraderie.

"Okay, you can let me go now." I pulled free from Aisha's death grip. Damn, she had iron fingers like Father's. At the moment, my mind was drifting with ideas of how to keep Marcin safe, to stay alive, and to protect my family. Last night, I had contemplated telling Marcin about the daggers, but what if it backfired and he told Levin? My family would be in so much shit. No, I'd stick to Father's suggestion to keep it to ourselves for now.

Zeki, the Turkish captain of the guards, approached, standing so close to Aisha that for a split second, I swore they were holding hands, but it couldn't be. He wasn't wellborn enough to be able to mate into a Varlac family.

"Use those back kicks I taught you," Zeki said. "Don't be afraid to cause damage to slow down your opponent. Do what it takes." He smirked, revealing dimples in his chin. With his deep midnight eyes, any wulfkin could easily fall in and get lost, but I often wondered why he didn't have a girlfriend.

Aisha leaned close, lowering her voice. "Use your animal ability, and show them that girl power rocks."

"If we're hunting an animal," I said.

Aisha's eyebrows cocked. "True. But hey, while you're doing all that heroic stuff, why not win as well?" She slipped back to the line of spectators, which included Father and several of his guards and servants. Zeki joined them.

Father approached and touched my arm, squeezing lightly. He didn't need to speak because the worry behind his eyes said it all. Stay safe. The corners of his mouth twitched, probably with a last-ditch attempt to pull me out, but he and I both knew that protecting Marcin meant keeping our heads intact.

Of course, I intended to give it my all. Just the notion of outmatching the sneering Hungarians made me cocky enough to kick their butts. Why the hell not?

The crowd hushed, and I glanced farther behind us. Levin, his guards, and Marcin strolled toward us in a silent march, reminding me of gangsters. It probably wasn't far from the truth.

Marcin wore a plain T-shirt and sweatpants—for easy transformation no doubt. Even in his scruffy gear, my gaze fastened to his broad chest and how tight the shirt stretched across it. I had to admit his strong arms were a fetish for me. If there were ever such as thing as arm porn, Marcin would be the hottest superstar. And with that, warmth dove south. Goddess, this was the worst possible time to get all hot and bothered for Marcin.

Last night's conversation rolled through my mind, along with his constant questions about the dagger. He had no idea I took the weapon, and it would remain that way.

He might suspect me, but I had to remind myself he was a lot more dangerous than I'd initially given him credit for being. Then again, if that was the case, why hadn't the Hungarian guards imprisoned us last night? Meant he hadn't told anyone ... yet. Either that or Levin was playing a mouse and cat game. Wouldn't put it past him.

Marcin's word against mine. He had no proof, unless whoever stole the second dagger made a reappearance today. The urgency to keep Marcin safe during the challenge bulleted through my veins like an unstoppable train—ferociously fast and promising a spectacular crash.

My father approached Levin, both chatting casually, but the storm clouds overhead weren't dissipating anytime soon, in reality or with their underlying distrust.

Adrenaline had me bouncing on my toes. Father cut a glance my way, the expression on his face taut, his smile shaky. A quick nod confirmed I continued as planned, though his trepidation now crawled up the back of my legs. So much rested on keeping Marcin safe, though in all honestly, there was no guarantee the assassin would even show. If it were me, I'd pick this time and place. Fewer wulfkin around and plenty of space to make a break for it.

Forcing every emotion from my head, I wove through the twenty or so wulfkin huddled in front of a makeshift podium—a tree stump big enough for six people to stand on. I inhaled the breeze for the poisonous scent. Perspiration, dog fur, and musk strangled me. Nothing else.

While Levin climbed up on his pedestal and called over to someone to stand near him, I continued wandering through the crowd with no success. Either the assassin wasn't here or they'd hidden the weapon in the woods. Or a more likely scenario, they waited in the woods. Wouldn't that mean they were well aware of what we were hunting? If so, that was interesting how Marcin deflected my question when I grilled him about it last night.

A sexy, masculine smell of musk teased my nostrils, the kind that roused my wolf awake for all the wrong reasons. I turned to find Marcin standing next to me. He might be deadly silent in his movement, but his scent always gave him away. It also made me want to jump his bones, but we weren't going there.

"You ready?" He smirked as if he concealed something behind the grin. I straightened my posture and lifted my chin. "Sure am. You?"

"Got this in the bag." The cockiness in his voice grated on my nerves. As the alpha's son, he had the world's best advantage. He had to know what we were hunting and where.

"I'm sure you do."

He narrowed his gaze, and his lips pinched to the side. Goddess please help me, but every inch of me implored that I lean in and steal a kiss. Just like we used to do.

"What's that supposed to mean?" His words snapped me to reality. "I'm sure you can figure it out."

"Welcome," Levin's voice cut through our conversation. "This is the first venery challenge we've held on these grounds in centuries. These are exciting times, and I'm grateful to our visitor, Sultan Boran, for suggesting the battle of innocence."

Sure you are. Even as he spoke, the undertone of his words was spitting malice at Father's proposal. Damn, I never should have told Father to interrupt the council meeting, then we wouldn't be in this position. Yet, I could never have lived with myself if I'd sat there and did nothing as Levin sentenced Enre and Daciana to death. For all I knew, the daggers could have been stolen before Father's interference at the council meeting. My stomach churned, but there was no time to let doubts into my mind. Focus on the mission at hand.

"Two stags were released into our forest last night. Each wears a red collar to ensure you bring back the correct animal. The two wulfkin who return the stags, dead or alive, achieve the title of champion and will automatically enter the final battle of innocence. One winner will represent Enre and the second will represent Daciana. If each champion wins the final challenge in the battle of innocence, then Enre and Daciana will be proven innocent, but if the winners fail, Enre and Daciana will be found guilty. It's possible that a winner will find Enre innocent while the second challenger fails, making Daciana guilty. And to make it clear, as I've received many questions about this, the final champions will not be fighting one-on-one to the death. They will be given a challenge to complete." His voice deepened, while several spectators booed.

Hunting stags I could do, but with all these pumped up wulfkin, this could easily turn into a bloody mess.

"And as was promised," Levin continued. "One boon will be on offer to the first champion to complete the final round. Nothing like this has been done before, and I doubt it ever will again. But don't forget there are restrictions on what you can request for your boon, such as asking to replace an alpha's posi-tion." Levin broke into a nervous chuckle. His gaze swept across the group, stopping on me momentarily, his lips spreading into a grin.

Fuck him, his grimace, and everything he stood for.

"Rules," he bellowed. "You can't transform until you've crossed the open land and reached the woods. Bring back the stags, and do whatever it takes to do it. If anyone gets hurt or accidentally killed, there will be no blame issued. So if you want to pull out, now's the time."

Silence fell over the assembly like a heavy curtain, and Levin's gaze landed on me again. No way would I give him the satisfaction.

"Let's get started," I called out and broke into a woot. Other wulfkin joined in, the atmosphere bubbling into a rupturing volcano.

"Wulfkin, take your places." Levin raised a hand and pointed to the line in the snow to his left.

We all converged along the line, overlooking the landscape. Marcin stood a few paces away.

I drew my hair into a ponytail and spotted Marcin taking his shirt off, then tossing it behind him.

Despite every strand of rigid concentration weaving through my body, my gaze lingered on Marcin's muscles, the goose pimples on his flesh, the way his pants hung low on his hips, accentuating his tapering V.

When had he buffed up so much?

For a few seconds, I'd forgotten about the tournament, the thumping of my pulse echoed and sunk deeper through my belly. I chewed on my lower lip as I glanced up at the god of a wulfkin, then noticed him staring my way. *Crap.*

He offered me a cheeky grin and winked just as the horn sounded. Wulfkin burst forward, legs pumping, arms swinging.

I lunged after them.

"Go Selena. Woohoo!" Aisha's shouts faded in the background.

The turf and snow flew beneath me; wind whipped my face and tugged on my clothes.

Wulfkin branched out in every direction, targeting the circular band of trees ahead.

Marcin plowed onward, his strides long and powerful, and the distance between us widened by the second.

I pushed myself faster. The pinching ache in my hip lanced down my leg each time that foot hit the ground and sunk in snow to my ankles.

Half a field to go. Keep going. Don't think about it.

My inner wolf was there, curled tight in my chest, waiting for her chance, snarling for release.

Soon.

Ahead, two wulfkin tracked behind Marcin, who'd already vanished into the woods.

Were they the assassins? Or somehow involved? Two against one was never a good move.

Other pack members disappeared into the folds of the forest around me, and several howls broke out.

My heart hammered against my chest. Pushing past the wrenching waves of pain, I ran with a limp.

Almost there.

The wulfkin tracking Marcin bled into the tree line.

I refused to look behind me. Who cared if I was the last one to leave the field, though I pictured Levin smirking and belittling my attempt. *Son of a bitch.* I gritted my teeth and pushed on. When I burst through the threshold of dense trees, I unleashed my inner wolf.

She gushed free like an exploding dam—skin tearing, limbs stretching, jaw realigning.

Shreds of clothing fell away. I threw myself forward, and in midair, chestnut and white fur bristled across my body. Gone was the cruel agony in my hip and the heaviness of my human form, now replaced by a light and refreshing surge of energy.

I landed on four paws and launched ahead, swerving massive trunks. Marcin's fresh kindling and musky scent led straight.

Footfalls pounding the earth and heavy breathing echoed in the distance.

With the stags released last night, they could be anywhere. The animals would head deep into the woods to a safe location. Their keen sense of hearing meant they'd detect anyone sneaking up on them and bolt, so the idiot wulfkin howling weren't getting their prize today.

Leaping over a log, I caught the faint whiff of something metallic. I smelled it again; the coppery tang of fresh blood coated my throat.

Was it Marcin? Had those two wulfkin caught him? Images of Marcin bleeding to death and his stomach sliced open seared my thoughts.

I bolted over the snowy ground, ignoring the branches and twigs snagging on my fur, poking my legs.

Several paces away, I spotted it.

Discoloration marred the powdery snow, traveling in a speckling path ahead of me. I inhaled the blood, its metallic fusion carrying the faint undertones of fresh kindling.

Marcin's blood. I'd recognize him anywhere.

Several sets of paw prints, definitely wulfkin from the sizes. I burst after the trail, my body numb, my veins on fire.

The weight of the world crashed onto my shoulders. I should have run faster and should have told him last night about the potential assassination attempt.

I should have kissed him.

Please don't let it be too late.

CHAPTER 11

MARCIN

I sprinted through the woods, my back leg burning. Sanyi—Father's dungeon guard—had just attacked me, ripped at my leg with teeth, though I shouldn't have been surprised the weasel played dirty. A quick glance behind me revealed Sanyi and his pal, Alex, chasing after me. I wanted to rip Sanyi apart. I wanted to make him pay for touching that kitchen girl. I wanted his blood. The desperation scorched through my veins.

But two against one meant a lengthy battle, and I had a venery to win. That was paramount. No time to waste. When my quest was won, I'd claim the Transylvanian land for my brother and Daciana, making them untouchable by Father. It went against everything the great Varlac leader demanded, but fuck him. I just had to do a better job of convincing Father I was on his side. With recent actions involving the Turkish clan and Enre, Father had set in motion repercussions that could never be retracted.

My paws sunk into snow with each hasty leap. The bleeding in my leg had ceased, but the stabbing ache traveling up my thigh hadn't. The scent would give my position away to anyone determined to follow me.

Behind me, the duo fell farther behind.

I inhaled wulfkin scents to my right—not too far away.

Better it stayed that way. Pine smells and timber prickled my senses, along with the musky, mothball stink of several red deer. But they weren't my target.

Sure, Father had confided in me where he'd released the stags. He'd sent several wulfkin into the woods last night to ensure the animals ran straight ahead, but they could have changed course by morning.

The land sloped upward, and I dug my claws into the ground for leverage.

Grunts and thunderous footfalls echoed behind me. A quick look over my shoulder— two wulfkin swerved through the forest, far enough back they wouldn't catch me anytime soon.

Closing in behind them was another wolf—white streaked with mocha. A smudge against the ashen backdrop.

A part of me expected more than three suckers realizing I was privy to the stags' direction. But with the heavy snowfall overnight, the tracks had been covered, and I still hadn't caught one of the buck's scents.

Forget that. Go faster.

The winds were relentless, shaking the branches overhead. Snow fell across my back. No stopping.

The crisp air pinched my nostrils, but still no stag. Had I taken a wrong path?

I fell back to a trot, catching my breath before breaking into short bursts up the gradually ascending terrain. Over the hill lay open land, free of trees in the near distance.

My chest heaved for air.

Behind me, no visible sign of my pursuers. Didn't mean they weren't near. The wild gusts of wind attested to their presence, faint, but there. Had they discovered the stag?

I would have smelled them. But with the animals' 310 degree view, sneaking up on them wasn't an easy feat. I doubted they were out in the open. Deer remained in the woods to escape chilly winds and predators.

A wolf's piercing whine reverberated behind me. It had made the kind of sound belonging to an injured creature. My skin crawled. I turned around to a forest coated in snow.

Snarls followed. Multiple. A fight.

The air current brought with it several scents—definitely wulfkin, and one I recognized. Wolf swirled with honeysuckle.

Selena!

Terror sunk into my flesh, and my primitive instincts kicked in. I bolted toward the escalating commotion, half skidding down the slope. I swooped though the woodland.

Where was she?

My nose led me straight ahead. Fast and furious, I sprinted, kicking snow and ignoring the ache in my wounded leg.

Fifteen paces away, I spotted three figures skulked in a circular dance. Selena was the brown and white wolf. The two others I recognized from Father's pack. They'd attack anything in their way.

Selena lunged at the black one, biting his front leg. She leapt back, licking her nose.

A whimper came from the injured wulfkin. Not the one I'd heard wincing before. That was definitely Selena.

The other wolf lunged and crashed into Selena's side, bringing them both down. He pinned her beneath him, fangs inches from her jugular.

Urgency pulsed within me as I lunged.

Selena's back legs kicked for purchase, but the beast on top of her wasn't budging.

The second wolf lay several feet away, whining from his injury.

My sights targeted the wolf squashing Selena. I head-butted him in the ribs, sending him reeling sideways.

He faced me ... teeth exposed, with drool dripping from them. A deep, menacing growl shook his chest. All show.

No one touches my Selena.

Fire bled into my veins, and I charged.

At once, the culprit retreated, crouching low near a tree, a cry curling in his chest.

I snatched the scruff of his neck in my jaws, bit down hard enough to hurt, but not to rip away flesh. A warning, loud and clear. *Mess with me, and you'll pay.*

The wolf dropped to his belly with his chin buried in snow, motionless. I released him.

Only cowards ganged up in an unfair fight.

He didn't move at first, then scampered in a mad rush as he bolted away from me with his tail between his legs. Without a thought, I swooped in on the other wulfkin who was back on shaky legs and recoiling into the woods. A deep howl came from within, the sound vibrating across my chest.

My head jerked around in Selena's direction as she dragged herself to her feet, back in human form. Blood rolled across her back from a gash streaking her shoulder blade, a stark contrast against the paleness of her skin. Scratches and bite marks dotted her legs.

My gaze curved over her full breasts, budded pink nipples, and a flat stomach, dipping lower to the dark curls between her legs. I shoved my wolf aside and called to my human form, fur vanishing, bones cracking, spine straightening. My warmth ripped away.

When Selena faced me, she wiped the blood dribbling from her scratched chin, her gaze wide, then her hands covered her mouth. "I thought you were ... dead," she stammered. "Blood in your tracks. The wolves chasing you." Her words sped up. "And I thought ..." Her gaze fell to my injured leg where the branch had sliced me open.

She actually worried about me? Flutters of excitement raced through the pit of my stomach at the idea of her caring for me so much. "Thanks for looking out for me, but I'm fine. Are you all right?"

"I had it under control." She shrugged and continued wiping the blood with a palm. "If you're hurt, I'll escort you as far as the open terrain."

"Ha ha. You're funny." Selena stretched, hands pressed to her lower back, bones cracking. "I'm not tapping out because of a few cuts." A faint breeze weaved past, throwing hair off her shoulders, displaying her in her full, gorgeous glory.

This was the Selena I'd fallen for all those years ago—confident and brazen. But she'd never carried such sexiness.

Goddess, I'd had so many fantasies about burying myself in her. And yet, here she stood naked. Blood raced to my cock, but one touch and she'd probably rip my arm off.

"Enjoying the show?" she asked.

My head shot up just in time to notice her gaze also lifting. "Are you?" She shrugged. "Maybe." A wicked smirk split her mouth.

Now, this flirty side of Selena was new, at least since arriving in Hungary. Was it the adrenaline of the fight driving her actions or her true nature surfacing?

I moved toward her, our bodies so close that the fire on her skin leapt across to me.

She lifted her chin, her inhales racing, her lips parting. The sweet honeysuckle scent fogged my mind, and I didn't give a fuckin' shit about anything right then, except Selena against me, us alone in the woods, the world as far away as possible, our problems a distant memory. My wolf was in my head, reminding me of our attraction, our connection, our future.

My arms swept across her waist and drew her closer, the softness of her breasts grazing my chest. I leaned in, my lips grazing hers, an inferno scorching between us. My wolf prodded me to go further, to reaffirm her as our claim.

Her wolf was there too, heating me, embracing me.

Selena's body softened into me, her hand gliding behind my neck, pulling herself closer, her lips kissing me with a savagery I'd craved from her for too long.

My tongue surged into her mouth, and she sucked it, a mewl vibrating in her chest. My cock nestled between us, and my hands skipped down her back to her butt, hauling her closer.

I broke our kiss, our foreheads and noses touching. The thought of taking her here and now, tasting every inch of her, teased me. *Do it already.*

The wind carried the scent of wulfkin nearby and, with it, the reality of the venery, saving Enre, and what was at risk if I lost this challenge. It crashed through me like a tsunami, ripping away everything else.

"Hell, Selena. Any other time, I'd be buried so deep in you

that the next country would hear you scream my name. Fuck. I want you so bad. But ..."

"A little diversion won't hurt anyone." She batted her eyes.

My cock pulsed at the temptress asking me to take her, but the truth was, a little diversion was me gambling with my brother's life. Despite the overwhelming hunger surging through my body, I untangled myself from Selena, our fiery warmth replaced by an arctic snap.

"I can't tell you how long I've waited for this moment," I said. "Then stop talking."

My mind spun from Selena's sudden show of physical attraction, to the question of *why now* and not the previous night when we weren't in a venery. Besides, she hadn't once admitted to also wanting me or dreaming of me. Hell, I sounded like the fuckin' girl here. This had to stop.

"Why did you really enter this challenge?" I rubbed the cold from my arms.

Her loving expression wavered ever so slightly—a small twitch at the corner of her mouth, the straightening of her back. Damn. She had some ulterior motive for her sudden passion all right, and I fell for it like the biggest sucker in the world. Hook, line, and sinker.

"Why did you?" she asked.

Lava burned through my chest. Was this challenge a joke to Selena? If she remembered anything about us, she would've forced me back into the race immediately. But it was my fault for staying around, for kissing her, for believing it meant more.

"You've wasted enough of my time." My voice deepened. "This challenge means more to me than you could ever imagine, but thanks."

"I wasn't trying—"

I spun and couldn't shake the guilt of my words, but I'd lost enough time. Calling my wolf, I ran, transforming during the sprint and refusing to look back.

What the fuck had just happened?

If Selena wasn't interested in the race, why follow me? No matter how much I denied it, the weapons room and the missing blade came to mind. Selena clearly hid something, and here I was the idiot falling into her web.

I'd track down this goddamn stag and win a spot in the battle of innocence, just as I'd promised Enre and Daciana. And nothing else would put me off my game. Not a wulfkin trying to assassinate me ... not the stags who could have already been tracked ... and definitely not one sexy Turkish wulfkin who might have just outed herself as being as dangerous as Father.

CHAPTER 12

SELENA

W ell, that situation deflated quicker than a busted-up air balloon. The two fuckwits following Marcin had turned on me, their hatred for the Turkish far outweighing their reason to pursue him. And my so-called *quick thinking to kiss Marcin in hope that he'd stay close in case the assassin struck* idea had gone to hell.

How could I have been so thoughtless? *Excellent job of building a bridge between us,* and it couldn't have come at a worse time.

Didn't matter. I'd live with the embarrassment and my mistakes if it meant keeping Marcin safe. I squared my shoulders and called my wolf. Time to get moving.

I fell on all fours, fur sprouting across my body. The cold eradicated, shadows around me sharpened, and scratchy noises of birds in the trees rang in my ears. I sprinted after Marcin, wind tugging against my pelt. Too many trees in my way, but Marcin's prints in the fresh snow were breadcrumbs I could follow. His musky scent kept wavering on the breeze, so I hurried, careening around humungous trees, several bunnies bouncing out of my path. Any other time, they would have made a delicious snack. Not today. Too much other shit going down.

Amid the jungle of pines, Marcin's wolf pounced.

Come on, girl, let's catch him.

Pulse thudding in my ears. Only one target in mind. Catching Marcin and keeping him safe.

The distance between us closed, each rapid leap quicker, unstoppable. Thirty feet away, Marcin took a sharp left and his pace intensified.

He'd picked up a scent.

I skidded left, cutting through the woods.

Faster.

No time to catch my breath.

He was close now, only fifteen feet away, and he hadn't once glanced over his shoulder. Marcin was on a mission, gunning forward.

And then the scent smacked into me: the peppery smell of a deer and the wet dog fur of wulfkin.

Marcin swerved right before coming to an abrupt stop.

I hit the brakes, swinging in alongside him, and kicking up snow against his back legs.

Mist billowed from our rapid breaths, curling into wisps.

Before us, two wulfkin in wolf forms skulked toward a stag wearing a red collar.

The spectacular buck was melanistic with its dark, almost black skin. It recoiled from its attackers, head low, and its twelve-point antlers aimed at the wolves. The stag was larger than a stallion. Shards of sunlight pierced the canopy and glinted against its pelt.

It made a deep, heavy bawl sound, steam threading out from the sides of its mouth.

My heart trembled at the idea of the buck being torn to pieces. Running was useless for the animal, so it faced its enemies for a final showdown. But it stood no chance. Not against savage wolves.

The white wulfkin inched closer. The fur behind its neck bristled while the brown one swept outward. They'd work together, but once the stag was dead, they'd turn on each other to claim the prize.

A faint whimper fell from my mouth, and I stepped closer.

The stag's head jarred upward, our gazes locking for a split second. The terrified look behind its eyes shattered my insides. Death was imminent, and like a deer might call its mother, it made the bawling distress sound.

I had no problem with hunting down my meals, but senseless animal killings never sat right with me.

A snarl rolled from Marcin's chest.

I threw myself against the white wolf, my teeth latching onto his hind leg, biting down hard, blood smearing my tongue.

He bucked, tossing himself about, snarling.

Submit.

He swung his head around, his jaws snapping at my side, ripping fur from my rump and tearing skin.

Ignore the lacerating ache. Save the stag.

Next to me was movement.

Marcin and the brown wolf leapt into a brawl, legs and fur knitted together, their gravelly snarls a war song against the tranquil backdrop.

Another bite to my side, stinging. I whined. My grip eased.

The white wulfkin, Snowy, slipped free, his back leg buckling, and he jarred around to face me.

A snarl reverberated through my chest. My wolf insisted we fight, and I was ready, despite the blood tainting the snow around my paws.

Marcin and his sparring opponent were a few trees away now, both matted with blood and neither giving up. I lowered myself, muscles tense, and faced my foe.

Snowy charged, and I hurled myself head first, teeth exposed. He ducked low and seized my neck with his jaws.

No way. That's not how I'll die. My eyes blurred from the frightful piercing. A large figure dashed to my right and drove into Snowy, pitching him off me.

I shook my head, my neck cramping up from the bite. I'd expected the savior to be Marcin, but instead, in front of me stood the gorgeous stag, the pointy tips of its antlers dipped in blood. Behind him was Snowy in a crumpled mess at the base of the tree, eyes wide and huge. Dead.

Goddess, he wouldn't have had to die if he'd just backed away.

Another figure encroached from behind Snowy. Marcin staggered closer in wolf form, as blood and snow congealed his fur along one side. He wasn't limping enough to warrant that much blood loss.

Farther behind him, the brown wolf lurched away. He broke into an otherworldly howl, mournful and despairing, the kind that called to other wulfkin. And with the waft of blood in the air, we'd be swarmed with fighting rivalry in no time. We had to leave.

I pushed myself to my feet but stumbled a few steps.

Marcin glanced at Snowy, then lifted his head toward the stag who stood alongside me like a guardian. The buck's nostrils flared, and it scraped a front hoof into the ground, telling Marcin to back off.

I didn't give a shit if Marcin judged me because of my connection with animals. And under no circumstances would I allow Marcin to hurt the stags.

He wasn't making a move, but stood there, lowering his head to appear as nonthreatening as possible.

A guttural growl spluttered behind me.

I spun around. Several trees back, a dark wolf appeared from within the shadowy folds of the forest, fangs exposed. Howls broke out in the distance. More wulfkin approaching.

Flames zipped through my veins. Movement to my side.

The second stag padded toward us as if it had watched us this whole time, and now both of them stood on either side of me, facing the encroaching enemy.

Okay. New set of plans. Save Marcin and these animals. At any cost.

Marcin sprinted past us, toward the enemy, but a loud metallic snap sounded. He tripped, tumbling face first into the snow, and his high pitched whines shattered my heart. A hunter's bear trap.

I raced to his side. Blood pooled around a hind foot, his whimpers shredding my insides. He pushed himself up by his arms but collapsed back with a whine. I sniffed him, nudging him to stay still.

The dark wolf encroached.

Fuck, fuck, fuck.

Marcin's body quivered and morphed into his human form. His limbs stretching, skin replacing fur. He lay there, body curled, face scrunched. The bone in his leg had snapped judging by the deformed angle of his ankle.

If I left him here, he'd die, but if I didn't save the stags, they'd be butchered. The black wolf lunged, sidestepping Marcin and me, going for the stags.

I trembled with rage. In a swift move, I darted for the predator, teeth piercing his neck, pinning him down with the mere force of my attack. I stood on top of him, demanding he submit. Instead, he snapped at my front paws.

A wave of dizziness washed through me. Too much blood loss. I roared more like a lion than a wolf into his face, spittle flinging across his muzzle.

He jerked upward, nudging me off, but I charged after him. Lava burned my chest.

Teeth bit hard into his shoulder. Claws raked his body. Snarls rolled from deep within my gut. I drove him backward.

The sucker shook in my grip and slipped free, but not before his mouth latched on to my side. Inside my head, I was screaming, the excruciating ache was a blade through my ribs. My legs wobbled beneath me.

But he flew backward in an instant, and alongside me stood the stag, watching over us.

I sprinted back to Marcin and transformed into my human form in haste, my wounds stinging as if someone poured acid on them. "Stop struggling. I'll free you."

My hands shook violently as I reached for the rusted, metal jaws that swallowed his ankle. If I didn't remove it, he'd lose a foot. And what if the assassin was on his way here with the other wulfkin?

"Listen to me."

He didn't respond, and his eyes glazed over. "Marcin! I need your help."

A howl, much closer this time. Another in the distance.

The hairs on the back of my neck spiked.

I grabbed Marcin's arm. "Push past the pain one more time. Please."

He lifted his head, face paler than snow, his eyes engorged with torment. In all honestly, most people would have passed out by now.

"I'm going to pry the trap open. But you have to get your leg out as best you can. Can you do this?"

At first, he didn't respond, then nodded. He was miserable.

My world faded away for those seconds because the affection I had for Marcin embraced me so hard it twisted my insides to knots. It had always been there, no matter how much I fooled myself. He was my true mate; I felt it deep in my soul, in my heart. Every part of me shook, and tears pooled in my eyes at the way it blossomed in my chest. Now I was so close to losing him. If I didn't free him, the assassin might kill him or other wulfkin who hated him would. Just like the jerk, Hooked Nose Guy, whom I had bumped into in the woods.

Not the time to fall apart. I gripped the metal jaws and pulled them apart. My arms quivered as the springs fought me.

Distant growls reached my ears. The stags were stomping the ground behind me.

I called to my wolf. Biting my bottom lip, I squeezed the jaws in my hands, slowly folding them down, the sucking sound of flesh making me cringe. The hinges groaned, and Marcin whimpered.

"Now, pull your leg out." I grasped the trap, my hold convulsing. Growling closed in around us. Paws hitting snow. *Shit.*

Marcin reached over, gripped his leg with his hands, then pried it out from metal teeth biting his flesh. His body shuddered. He never made a sound.

After jerking his leg back, he collapsed onto the ground, his hands into fists, his body twitching.

I released the trap, and the jaws snapped shut. Threading an arm around Marcin's waist, I dragged him to his knees. "Time to go."

A stag approached and knelt down next to us.

"Oh, you read my mind," I said. "You're an angel."

Marcin's flesh was cold and sweaty against me. He used me for balance, and we wobbled toward the animal. I pushed him into a straddle across the stag's back. He slumped across the animal, hands wrapped around its neck. The stag was on its legs, and Marcin held on.

"Let's go home." I caressed the stag's neck. "I owe you my life. Now, follow me. We have to be fast."

He grunted and the second stag was alongside him.

We broke into a run while I transformed, and every hair stood on end. If we got out of this alive, it would be a miracle.

The repetitive thump of paws trailed us.

We plodded our way through the woods. I picked the widest path where possible. The low-hanging branches swiped at me; bushes snagged my fur.

A quick look behind and I noted that Marcin hadn't fallen. Thank the moon.

But farther behind them, weaving through the shadowy woods, were dark silhouettes amid the unfurling mist. At least ten wolves, and they were closing in damn fast.

I ran faster, lungs pumping furiously.

Growls rang out behind us.

I swung around a large pine to a section of woodland where the trees were sparser, but the snow was fresher. With each long pounce through the deep powder, my body strained for air, each muscle quivered, but the stags were keeping up. The terrain sloped downward beneath my feet.

Over my shoulder, Marcin sashayed across the stag's back, but his grip around the animal's neck never faltered.

The clearing came into sight, and my chest exploded with joy. My second wind kicked in, and I broke free of the woods. The wind seemed gale force, sending me sideways with its unrelenting surge.

Nothing will stop us. Not the weather, not the wulfkin, at least not until I inhale my last breath.

One stag was alongside me, the one with Marcin, the three of us running in a mad rush toward the castle ahead. The sight was a beacon of salvation. Tiny dots in the distance revealed wulfkin waiting.

My heart crashed against my rib cage, my body sprinting on pure adrenaline. Focus.

Faster.

Don't stop.

A glance behind.

Wolves broke cover. Massive leaps. They funneled in from all sides. One in particular, a huge one, sped up quicker than the rest. He'd be on us in no time.

I fell back on purpose.

The stags continued onward. The large wolf swung right, obviously going for the slower buck, the one carrying Marcin.

I placed myself between the buck and our enemy, all of us running in a line. No time to be scared. *Focus.* Too many lives at stake.

Several feet away, movement. The black wolf now ran alongside me. He snarled my way with teeth bared, warning me away. Fuck that and fuck him.

I swerved and crashed head first into his side, throwing him off his feet. Catching myself, I leapt onward again, chasing after the stags, noting the other wolves were closer.

Only fifty feet away from the castle.

Wulfkin stood near the finish line, staring our way. So close.

Then a heavy weight slammed into my back, a crunch to my back leg. I whined as the sting threaded through my thigh. My knees buckled, and I crashed to the ground, my face buried in snow.

No time for this. No fucking time.

I jerked to my feet, ignoring the torturing blaze burning my back leg, the blood, everything, and threw myself forward.

Too many wolves were close now, fanned out around me, their breath practically on my neck. But the problem was in front. The large, black wolf had closed the distance between him and the stag with Marcin.

I lagged behind. I drew on my last strands of strength, thanking Zeki for his relentless training, for forcing me to run nonstop all day, for never letting me give up. I closed in on the wolf's backside. He slowed and snapped his jaws at my face, snatching my ear. I lost my footing, and we both rolled to the ground from the momentum.

No waiting.

I bound back to my feet and was off again, shaking the sting in my ear.

Other wolves were close enough now to pounce on the stags. But the castle ... *Oh, please* ... We were so close. I could nearly reach out and touch it.

Aisha was there too, jumping up and down, her hands in the air. Zeki and his guards were in wolf form, near the line, ready to intercept.

Almost there.

A wolf approached the stag farthest from me. My lungs squeezed. *Push past it.*

I careened around the bucks and inserted myself between the stags and the encroaching foe, forcing my side against his, driving him away.

He snapped at my face, ripping at fur below my ear.

I bit back, but he recoiled and tripped, tumbling into a roll.

Fuck, yeah!

Father's guards parted for our passage. The stags passed the finish line, and I crashed in after them. But they weren't stopping. I sped up and curved out in front of them before slowing my pace.

Gradually, we came to a halt, and my legs collapsed from under me. My wolf glided away, fading deep inside me, and I now lay there in my human form. The stags both collapsed on bent legs, and Marcin rolled off the animal, landing flat on his back in the snow, a trail of blood smeared across the stag's back.

Aisha and Father ran to us. Her eyes were panicked.

"Help Marcin." I lifted my head, glancing toward the field

where Zeki and his pack were in a standoff match against the wulfkin from the venery. Slumping back down, I stared at the dark clouds overhead, gasping for air, my lungs straining with each inhale. I was convinced I'd never be able to stand again.

Levin trudged toward us, his arms tight by his side, his mouth a grimace. He glanced down at Marcin near a stag, then toward me. "It seems we have our two champions." He lifted his chin, and called out, "Someone call Barka to tend to their wounds." He spun on his heels and walked away.

I didn't give a shit about the challenge, only about making sure Marcin and the stags weren't hurt. Levin could go and fuck himself. I rolled over and crawled on all fours toward Marcin.

His eyes were shut. Blood pooled around his leg. I ran a hand down his cheek, and his eyes flipped open, agonizing torture behind them.

"Selena." His voice flatlined, and his eyes slid shut. "Please, be okay, please."

My father kneeled at Marcin's feet, examining his wound. "We have to stop the bleeding immediately." He called several guards, instructing them to take Marcin to the castle. "Aisha, bring Selena."

CHAPTER 13

MARCIN

My eyes fluttered open, and I jarred upright, my heart banging so hard against my chest, I swore the bed shook beneath me.

An excruciating stabbing pulsed across my ankle, traveling up my calf muscle. I fisted the bedsheets as the pain washed through me.

Venery. The word steamrolled through my mind, along with the bear trap I'd stepped into. Riding a stag and Selena racing us over the finish line. I owed her my life, though being carried over the final line wasn't the way I'd pictured myself winning.

I threw the fur blanket aside, noting I wore only boxers. My leg had a splint against it and was wrapped in bandages all the way to my knee. Even with my wolf healing, such damage would take a few days to repair, maybe more. But I sure as hell wasn't going to sit around in bed like an invalid, especially with Enre and Daciana in custody.

The door to my room flung open, and the bronze handle left a dent in the white wall behind it. Father stomped inside, hands deep in the pockets of his coat and shadows gathering beneath his narrowing gaze.

"You're a disgrace." He passed my bed and stopped near the window that overlooked the nearest snow-capped mountain.

"I could have lost a foot or my life, but hey, let's not worry about that." Grunting as I forced my legs over the edge of the bed, I tensed as the shooting pain sparked up my thigh. I scanned the room for something to lean against. The chairs near the table were halfway across the room; the closet offered me nothing but clothes. Then my sights landed on the poker near the fireplace. Too short. Damn it.

"You were carried over the line on a fucking stag." Father shook his head, all the while staring outside as if looking at me pained him. "And to make it worse, you let a Turk bring you back." He spun to face me; his posture curled in on himself. "Fucking hell, Marcin. You've just won the golden medal for weak-shit-alpha."

I pushed off the bed and hopped over to the chairs. "I don't care what you or anyone else thinks. I won, isn't that what you wanted? So what the fuck are you harping on about?"

He stalked closer, his stomps striking the floor with haste, and he gripped my arm before kicking aside the chair I balanced against. My bandaged toes hit the ground, and I cringed. They stung as if a vice clamped down on my foot.

Venom oozed from Father's grim expression. "I raised you to show no weakness, to be the best and most feared."

Hell, you'd think I murdered someone. I ripped my arm from his and balanced precariously on one leg. "I'm one of the champions now, so get over your embarrassment." Hopping back a step, I pressed my back against the wall.

For those few seconds, Father almost looked thoughtful with a hint of a smile, as if he was secretly pleased I'd won but wasn't going to show it.

On his next breath, he morphed back into the brute I knew. "You don't get it, do you?" He drove his boot into the chair, sending it skidding across the room. "That bastard sultan set this up. He insisted on the challenge then put his daughter in there, whom no one suspected, including you, and now she's in the battle of innocence. She's going to try to win that boon to claim our land as their own."

"Bullshit. Why would she save me then?"

He tapped his temple. "He's trying to pull the wool over our eyes."

Father was delusional, simple. Though, I couldn't ignore Selena's secretive behavior over dinner or her insistence to get it on during the venery. I shifted my gaze to Father, who studied me as if I were a target board.

"Are you pissed because a girl saved me or because you believe they want your land?" He snorted. "Is this a joke to you? Maybe you ought to be locked up with your brother.

Although, I'm not sure anyone would call it imprisonment. I've been to hotels that treated me worse than the way Enre and Daciana are living in the guest wing."

I shrugged. "He's my brother. Besides, you're the one who invited the Turks here, not me."

"Yes, but not for this."

I hopped toward my closet for clothes and to shake away the chill clinging to my skin. "That's right. You planned to mate me to Selena so you could get their land. Maybe the Turkish leader isn't like you. Have you ever considered that?"

Back in the woods, Selena had risked her life to save me. She showed no sign of trying to win. Otherwise, she'd find herself a weak rival to go into the battle of innocence with. Not me. Besides, how could she have known I'd step in a bear trap? What happened in the woods wasn't orchestrated one bit.

I reached the closet and held on to the door with a death grip.

"Sorry to burst your bubble," Father said. "A day ago, you were almost killed by an invisible assailant, which happened after the Turkish clan arrived here. Then Selena's name gets mysteriously entered into the venery. And now she wins. The truth's smacking you in the face, but you're ignoring it."

I seized a pair of jeans from the closet and glanced over to the chair behind Father.

Might be easier if I sat down to put these on. "I can see what's going on perfectly. You've got a bit of competition, and you're paranoid. I wouldn't worry. Anyway, what have you got planned for us in the final challenge? Let's talk about that."

"You've gone soft-cocked for Selena, haven't you? The sultan mating his daughter to you isn't enough for him anymore, not with a boon on offer. He will claim Hungary as his own and move his pack here, overthrowing us."

This was new. "Where are you getting this from?"

"Does it matter?" He marched toward the door. "Get your shit together, decide whose side you're on, and heal because you have a boon to win if you intend on living this cozy lifestyle. And remember our little deal. Claim the boon for me, and I'll leave Enre and Daciana alone forever." His voice deepened, underlining his real threat—cross me on this, and I'll destroy everything you hold dear.

I had to play the game.

"I'm postponing the battle of innocence until you're better, but don't drag this out." He vanished and thumped the door shut behind him.

I slumped against the closet behind me, jeans in hand, staring at the fire spitting embers into the metal guard across the room. Dealing with Father was like playing Russian roulette. Winning the boon would save my brother, but what exactly did Father have in mind to claim? Did he still want Transylvania, or were his sights on something much bigger now?

First, I had to get my facts straight because if the Turks intended to take over our territory, then I was no longer dealing with the Selena from years ago, but a deadly adversary. And if that was the case, then I'd gladly help Father destroy them.

Wobbling my way to the chair, I crashed down and wrestled to get into my jeans, unsure what pissed me off worse: Father's constant paranoia, Selena's strange behavior, or my foot, scalding with sharpness each time anything touched it.

A knock came from the door, and I still hadn't put my pants on. I tossed them aside. "Give me a sec."

"It's me." Selena's soft voice filtered from behind the metal-studded door. "May I come in?"

"Sure." I stood in my black boxers and gripped the back of the chair for balance. Selena entered, dressed in tight black pants, knee-length boots, and a turtleneck top.

She was the epitome of a ninja, and this was the complete opposite of her attire on the day she'd arrived. Her chocolate locks draped over her shoulders, and her cheeks glowed bright red. But I couldn't quite pinpoint the purpose of the bath towels tucked under her arm.

"You either just returned from breaking into a high-security location or ..." I scratched my head. "You're about to go swimming? The lake's frozen over by now, so you might struggle with that."

Her response came in the form of an arched eyebrow, while her dipping gaze didn't go astray, and she obviously made no secret about checking me out. Absolutely fine by me. If she asked, I'd remove my boxers too.

"Actually, I was sword practicing."

Images of her dancing with her blade during the dinner swarmed through my mind, along with how precisely she sliced that silk above Father's head. Not to mention her bouncing breasts and the length of her tanned legs. I pictured our kiss in the forest and the passion in her embrace, except I had no idea if she had played me or not. In truth, I hadn't fully deciphered Selena's intentions, and with Father whispering so much crap in my ear, it all congealed into a confusing knot.

"How's your injury?" She strode closer, her gaze locked on my leg. "Can I take a look?"

Before I could respond, she pulled another chair close, positioning it in front of mine, set her towels on the floor by her side, and kneeled down near the seats. "Sit and prop your foot up."

"Give me a few days, and I'll be stronger than before."

She glanced at me, wearing a *whatever* expression with her tilted smile. "Maybe I can help."

I collapsed in my chair, grateful to be off my feet, lifting the leg with my hands. "And how will you do that?"

She unclipped the butterfly hook and unraveled the white bandages. "I have my ways."

If Father had spoken the truth, then why would Selena even bother caring for me? It made zero sense.

"How did your father take your win in the venery?" I asked.

"Pretty pleased with himself."

Father's words came back, the ones about the sultan wanting the boon. But was it to claim Hungary?

"So, we're both in the final. You must be excited."

Her gaze lifted, and her green eyes, the color of a fresh meadow after a rainstorm, were crammed with curiosity. "Not really, but I bet you're excited. Regardless, do you know what the final challenge will entail? Animal hunting? A race?"

"No idea. But I'm sure your father would reward you well if you won the boon?" The bridge of her nose creased. "Is that all this is for you? Winning the stupid boon?"

She pulled a bit too tight on my bandages as she removed the splint, and a shooting ache stabbed my ankle.

"Careful." My body tensed harder than a block of cement.

"This boon thing is bullshit." Her unwrapping quickened, the softness replaced by bumps against my wound, and I grimaced each time she nudged me. "It's got your father all riled up, and obviously you too. If I win, I'd use it to help someone in need, not feather my own nest or bluster my power or kill other wulfkin. That's where we obviously differ."

"Whoa, you're jumping to major conclusions here. Since when did I become a power- hungry lord who wants to kill pack members?"

She shrugged nonchalantly as she peeled away the last bandage and studied the trap's teeth marks dotting my ankle. Dried blood marred the flesh near the healing lesion.

Purple bruises covered my shin, and my foot was swollen to twice its size. The bone seemed to be healing since the sultan had straightened it yesterday. I passed out after that. The sultan didn't have to help me ... yet he had.

"You ready?" She headed to the door, opened it, and waved to someone outside. I stiffened. "Ready for what?"

Several servants careened into the room, each carrying two buckets of water with steam curling from them.

"You really should invest in proper plumbing in this place." She retrieved the towels from the floor and headed to my en suite bathroom at the back of the room. "I'm running you a bath and have a healing concoction that should help your wound heal faster. It'll deaden the pain for a while and reduce the swelling."

My head hurt trying to make sense of Selena. She accused me of being barbaric, yet still cared enough to help with my injury.

"Thank you," I called out as she vanished into the room.

Despite Selena giving off mixed vibes, it was clear she had me all wrong and had pigeonholed me into the same category as Father. I couldn't blame her. After years of war between our clans, we were just now striving for peace. But her words came back to me, the ones about using the boon to help a person in need. Whether it was a general comment or referring to a specific person, it probably didn't matter. What counted were her intentions.

So, if she had no desire to win the final boon, then the rest was straightforward. I'd claim the prize, defeat Father, and set my brother free. But first I'd have to convince the council to back me.

The maids fluttered out of my chamber and shut the door behind them. Selena appeared in the bathroom doorway, the sleeves of her shirt pushed up to her elbows. "You'll have to take your boxers off."

"How can I resist when you put it like that?" I pushed myself to my feet and hobbled toward her. My attention fell on the porcelain bathtub on silver feet that Father insisted on fitting in all the bathrooms, despite having no plumbing in half the castle. Leaning against the open door, I dropped my boxers and kicked them aside as Selena sprinkled what looked like dried herbs into the half-filled tub and mixed them into the water with one hand.

"Soak your leg and keep your foot submerged for at least an hour. I'll get the girls to keep topping up the warm water." When she turned around, her gaze dipped and her cheeks glowed.

"You're blushing?" I asked.

"No, I'm not." She spun around to the bathtub.

Warmth spread through my gut, and I couldn't help but smile. "Can I get some help with this?"

She offered me a hand.

I limped closer and leaned on her outstretched arm as I climbed into the tub; the water was scorching hot. In slow motion, I lowered myself into its burning cocoon, my injured leg submerging last. The heat swathed my foot, the wound stinging as if a fresh blade sliced it back open. I clasped the edge of the tub, waiting for the pain to ease.

Selena's fingers caressed my shin, softly kneading away the pain. Then she broke into a hum, the sound sweet and calming.

Leaning back against the tub, I closed my eyes and focused on the softness of her voice. "You have magical fingers."

She continued her tune and gently massaged my leg. The strange cocktail of my foot throbbing, Selena's tranquil song, and the ease with which her fingers glided over my skin left me strangely relaxed and maybe a bit turned on. Okay, a lot. With each stroke, my muscles flexed, and my inner wolf stirred inside. *Take her, claim her. She's ours.*

Well, not sure Selena would agree.

"The healing brew is from your medic, Barka, so I can ask her for more," she said.

I slid my eyes open, studying the way she knelt next to the bathtub, one bent arm leaning against the edge, the other in the water, and her gaze locked on my leg. "They smell girly."

Her gaze swept across my body. "Maybe you should be careful, stay indoors. At least until you've healed."

I wasn't used to the protective nature, her worries about my well-being. Father rarely asked me if I was okay, and his encouragements came in the form of insults or backhands. As an alpha of my pack, showing weakness wasn't a smart option, especially surrounded by Father's minions who'd rip my heart out the moment I showed a hint of frailty. Back at the venery, I'd expected one of Father's wulfkin to kill me. Getting rid of me meant everyone else could clamber for my position to inherit the title.

"Thanks for helping me again." I slid deeper into the water. "But I'm curious. Why didn't you leave me behind in the woods?"

A strange expression crossed her face, a blend of shock and

pity. "That wasn't ever an option. Maybe that's how things work in Hungary, but I'd never leave behind an injured wulfkin."

Okay, we were derailing fast, so I changed directions. "How did you control those stags in the forest?"

She pushed a loose strand of dark hair behind her ear. "A small gift from the moon goddess during my transformation from moonwulf to wulfkin. My scent and voice calms animals, makes them feel safe around me. Sometimes I think they can understand me, but I'm not sure. These blessings don't really come with a rule book, you know." She removed her hand from the water and wiped it on a towel as she climbed to her feet.

I grasped her wrist and pushed myself into more of a sitting position, water sloshing out of the tub. Fire from the main room reflected off her hair, her plump lips teased me, torturing. I ached to touch her just as I'd done in the forest, to hear her moans, and to see her cheeks flush with desire.

"I owe you my life. I want to show you I'm not the wulfkin you think I am."

At first, she said nothing, but stared at me, then slipped her hand free from mine. "I can figure out what kind of wulfkin you are."

"Maybe you've got me wrong."

She strolled around the end of the tub and headed to the window overlooking the yard below. "I'm—" Her words died as she leaned closer to the window, her hand pressed to the glass pane. In the next instant, she spun around and bolted across the room. "I've got to go."

"Wait. Selena." I started to climb out of the tub, but my leg stung to high hell, and I slipped back in, water splashing out of the tub. "What's going on?"

Her footsteps faded away, and the door clicked shut. What the fuck was happening now?

CHAPTER 14

SELENA

From Marcin's window, I had spotted Zeki, captain of the Turkish guards, handing over a package to a Hungarian wulfkin. Their heads were low; Zeki continuously glanced over his shoulder.

Had he really betrayed us? Surely not. Still, my insides quivered with the dread of such a possibility.

I sprinted down an empty corridor, my chest tight.

Zeki had been with my family for the past five years. Father even showed him support and trust by encouraging him to start his own pack. Maybe I jumped to conclusions, but considering one of Father's daggers was still missing, I couldn't ignore the possibility.

I burst out into the courtyard, my hasty steps crunching snow. When I careened around the well to an empty yard, I bolted to the nearest open door and entered a barren hallway.

No sounds.

Where did they go? I sprinted to our guest room, which was empty. In Father's room, I pulled out the duffle bag from under the bed and unzipped it. The dagger box was in hand. *Please don't let another one be missing.*

In slow motion, I unclipped the latch, then lifted the lid. Still only one dagger missing. "Thank the moon goddess."

I closed the box and slid it back into the bag, stuffing the whole thing under the bed.

My head was in a vice of confusion. The room seemed to be closing in on me as I struggled to make sense of Zeki's behavior, so I headed back outside in case he returned. Maybe fresh air would help my paranoia.

I tucked my hands into the pockets of my coat. The morning sun wasn't doing much against the freezing temperature.

Footfalls echoed behind me. Irmak, the Turkish ward living in Hungary, approached. His hands were curled up in the pockets of his jeans, his expression marred by a furrowed brow. We'd grown up together, played on the same field back home, and used to joke about what we wanted to be when we were adults. I'd said ninja, while Irmak was adamant he'd become a firefighter after his parents had died in a tragic blaze. Foolish dreams on both our parts, but neither of us could have guessed he'd end up being sold to the enemy as a ward of the state to keep a treaty that said neither clan was to cross the border of our territories. It had worked, until several Hungarian wulfkin were spotted skulking on our land.

A light breeze fluttered through Irmak's dark blond hair, and his gaze lifted, meeting mine. A half-crooked smile tugged at the corners of his mouth. He'd grown since I last saw him, his shoulders wider, his eyes a deeper shade of mocha.

"Selena, you've become more beautiful than I could have imagined." His voice was deep and manly. Not the young boy I used to play hide-and-seek with back home.

I broke into a laugh. "It's only us, drop the act."

His shoulders softened, and I took him into an embrace that he returned, squeezing me into him as if it had been too long since he'd had anyone to hug.

"Come, sit." I drew him by the hand to a bench beneath an awning. The sunlight warmed the spot, and I crossed my legs, half turning to face him. "Tell me everything. How have you been?"

He shrugged and leaned against the wall, his hands resting on his thighs. The angle of the sun cast shadows across his face, accentuating his chin and square jaw. He'd grown into a man and a handsome one. Surely, he had a number of wulfkin females chasing him.

"Things are never as they seem, but you know that better than anyone," he said. "Are you being treated okay?"

He nodded. "Doesn't mean I'm not an outsider."

I took his hand in mine. "You're Turkish, and your home will always be with us."

The way he glanced at me, rawness behind his eyes and his posture stiffening, told me he didn't agree. "Turkey is not your home anymore either."

"It will always be in my heart. No one can take that from me … from us."

He pulled his hand away. "It's okay. I'm no longer a child. I accept my place. And you will too, once reality sinks in."

Tightness coiled in the pit of my stomach. Was this going to be me in a few years— bitter, resentful, and defeated? "We'll have each other. And I'll speak to Father about you returning home after my mating." The words poured out so easily that for those few seconds even I believed my future was set with Marcin. Until the challenge, the dagger issue, and me learning to trust him again, I had no idea what my future held. Of course, I hoped for the best and that it involved Marcin.

Irmak didn't look at me but studied the slush of snow by his feet. "Selena, you've always been kind to me. After my parents died, after your father adopted me, and even now, you're the only one who talks to me as if I'm part of the family rather than an outsider. But things aren't the same anymore. Your father sent me away without hesitation. I've lived here seven years without a single message from him." He paused for a moment, his hands curling into fists. "I'm a drifter now, but karma will make her presence known soon enough."

His words echoed in my mind. "Karma for what?"

"Please don't tell your father I said that." Without a glance my way, he stood. "I'd better go, or they'll be searching for me in the kitchen. Take care, Selena." With hasty steps, he crossed the yard and vanished through a side doorway.

The ache behind my rib cage deepened for Irmak, not for being abandoned by Father, but because he'd lost his spirit. Father had to make this right again. But what exactly did Irmak mean by karma? I couldn't help but connect it to the assassination attempt. Surely, Irmak wouldn't have taken the dagger or targeted Marcin to get back at Father.

I stood and wrapped my arms around myself, rubbing the cold from my body, convinced the only wulfkin I could trust were Aisha and Father.

With the first icy flakes of the day cascading, I retreated indoors.

The moment I shut the door to our guest chambers, Father emerged from his room, dressed only in his white pants and in the process of pulling a shirt down over his head. "Good, you're back." He padded closer on bare feet. "We need to talk. Come, take a seat by the blaze."

I plonked down and folded my legs beneath me on the cushions we'd scattered in front of the blaze while Father paced in front of the fireplace like a guard dog. Those earlier knots in my gut surfaced. "What's going on?"

His grimace darkened. "I want you to win the boon for us."

"What for?" Sure, I contemplated winning the boon for myself, but that was for Aisha and me to break free of his ridiculous mating plans.

His stomping quickened, and his posture tilted forward as if burdened with the world on his shoulders. "The moon goddess influenced your sister to put your name in the challenge for a reason."

"What are you talking about?" I shifted in my seat, unsure I liked where his words were leading.

"Once you win the boon, you will claim the Hungarian land for Turkish rulership."

I jolted to my feet. "Are you insane? If you've ever wanted to give Levin a reason to declare war on us, that's it right there. He won't hold back his retaliation."

He shook his head, yet the frown splitting his mouth covered me in goose bumps. "We'll use it as a bargaining chip."

I collapsed back onto my cushion, alarm bells ringing in my head. "For what?" He stopped in front of me, and his voice lowered. "This stays between us."

I nodded, too terrified to take another breath.

"Levin intends to kill us after the battle of innocence. He plans to win the boon himself, claim our land to get back at us for disrespecting him at the council on our first day."

My whole body shook, and every sensation deadened. It was my fault for suggesting the stupid challenge in the first place. "Are you sure?" The words shook.

"Yes. I've had my guards spying from the moment we arrived. And the only way to keep our heads intact is for you to win, claim his land, and we use it in exchange for our lives. Your win will be public, in front of his council, and by Varlac laws, he will have no choice but to let us walk away with the win. If not, he'd have every Varlac leader from around the world on his doorstep, ready to rip him apart. But it doesn't mean he won't then turn his fury to our family. And we'll be ready by the time he attacks."

"What about Marcin ... and me?"

"I made a horrible mistake thinking this could help settle the war between us. Levin has no intention of peace, and I can't leave you with this barbarian. We go home and strengthen our family with the eastern and northern lands."

"What does that mean? War?"

A scowl twisted his mouth. "What would you have me do? I doubt my bargaining chip with Levin will last once we go home, so I have to do what I can to protect us. And if that means strengthening our allegiances with neighboring Varlac packs by mating you and Aisha, then we'll do what it takes. Right now, Levin's number across Europe outmatches us four to one. He'll butcher us all."

I could barely feel my legs, and I stumbled toward the window. The tranquility outside was a ruse, promising freedom, yet it lay in the lands of a ruthless dictator, and everyone trembled under his reign. Now we were also trapped in his cage.

"Then let's go home."

He shook his head. "Levin's guards are watching us. How do we sneak away with all of us, the guards, the servants, and not draw attention? If we do escape, they'd be right on us, and in attack mode." He lifted his chin. "What we need is time to escape, and that means winning the boon. Until then, we act as their guests, pretend you'll still mate with Marcin, and don't raise suspicions."

"But I have to first win the boon against Marcin."

Father stepped closer. "We're one step ahead. He's injured, and it will slow him down."

"But Levin's waiting for Marcin to heal first." Not to mention I'd just given Marcin a healing brew I got from Barka that should help him with his wound. I was torn between the guilt of telling Father the truth and my wolf side insisting we had to come to Marcin's aid.

Father took me by the shoulders "We'll survive. Trust me. I will push Levin to start the tournament earlier, convince him you are no challenge for Marcin, even in his injured state."

The door to the main room creaked open, and we both jerked around to face the intruder.

Aisha strolled in, her huge smile deflating the moment her sight landed on us. "Geez, who died?"

Father's voice boomed in her direction. "You are never to leave the room alone again.

I've told you this before."

She frowned but lifted her head. "Fine, I'll ask Zeki to go with me." "No. You won't leave this room unless it's for meals."

Aisha marched closer, throwing her hands in the air. "What am I going to do all day?"

"Play with the dracwulves." Father stomped into his room and slammed the door behind him.

Aisha stared my way with a raised eyebrow.

I shrugged, not sure telling Aisha about our situation was the best decision. With her free-spirited and flighty attitude, she might confront Levin.

Aisha traipsed to her bedroom.

Silence fell over the room, and the air grew heavy. My pulse galloped. We were prisoners in Hungary, and now our survival lay on my shoulders. I had no option but to win the battle of innocence to save my family, leaving Hungary behind forever.

But the reality of walking away from Marcin left me paralyzed and heartbroken.

CHAPTER 15

MARCIN

"Fuck, heal already." I hobbled toward my bed, wincing each time my foot touched the floor. It had taken me half an hour to climb out of the bathtub and get dressed with this damned leg. The hot water and herbs helped with the swelling, but not the pinch traveling up my thigh every few seconds. Sweat beaded my brow.

A deep sigh followed, and my wolf whined, sounding like a tortured animal. Yeah, he felt the pain. Nothing I could do about it. Wulfkin healing worked fast, but not so fast when a leg had been butchered by a bear trap.

Knowing Father, if I didn't heal fast enough, he'd just as likely put someone else in my place to win him that boon. Then Enre might never be set free. He'd lose his home in Transylvania and have Father breathing down his back for life. Not to mention his new pack would be added to Father's army. Then there would be no stopping him.

An inferno seized my insides, and on my next step, my knees buckled. I collapsed and half twisted, dropping onto the bed. What the shit was going on with me?

When someone knocked on my door, I pushed myself to my feet again, ignoring the fierce pulsing from my wound. "Come in."

Vincent strolled in and shut the door behind him. "You're not looking too great." "Thanks for the update. I feel like shit." Fire seemed to cover my flesh, and I wiped

the sweat collecting on my upper lip. "How's the pack?"

"Good." Dressed in jeans, riding boots to his knees, and a bomber jacket, he strolled toward the fireplace and turned his back to the blaze. "A few have asked to come and see you. They're worried since they saw you lose so much blood once you crossed the finish line." He rubbed his arms.

"Anytime, you know that."

"Yeah, well, the guards outside are limiting who can visit you, so I had to ask if you'd welcome visitors."

I hopped over to the window and leaned against the frame. "Give me a couple days, and I'll be back." I slapped a hand to my thigh and winced, regretting my decision instantly.

"If not, you can count on me to step in for you."

Vincent was my go-to guy, and I trusted him unconditionally. But I couldn't burden him with the task of defying Father when it came to claiming the prize for the boon on my behalf, then landing himself a permanent spot on Father's target practice radar. My risk to take. "Appreciate it."

He moved closer, his lips pinched to one side. "You've got a great opportunity here." The embers glowed around him. "What have you decided on for the boon?"

"Father's been on my case about it nonstop with his own demand list."

He nodded quickly as if his mind were elsewhere, and my response barely registered. "This could help us deal with your father once and for all. But it has to be the right move to avoid him wriggling out of it."

Vincent had his head in the right spot, and like me, he acknowledged that the great Varlac of Europe had to step down from his position. Maybe I was being selfish, preparing to use my boon to safeguard Enre and his pack, rather than looking at protecting every wulfkin.

The window rattled against my back from the breeze outside.

Vincent stood there with hands on his hips, staring at me.

"We can't demand you replace him, but we could ask for all territories to fall under your ruling. Levin will be locked in place with no land to his name. To gain anything else, he'd have to challenge another alpha. His territories currently have other alphas living there, so they would automatically fall under your jurisdiction by default. In the meantime, we work on poaching members of his pack into ours. Then you make the move to claim his position with or without the council because he'll be powerless."

I cocked my head, staring at Vincent, the seriousness behind his gaze. He always put the wulfkin first, protecting them against Father. "I like your thinking. I'll have to give it some thought."

But Vincent's brow furrowed. Obviously, he wasn't finished on the topic. In all honesty, with the slicing pain around my ankle feeling like my leg had been hacked off, I didn't have the mindset for political espionage today. So, I changed the topic.

"How are our injured wulfkin from the venery doing?" He shook his head. "Most are healed."

"Good." I shifted in my seat on the windowsill, putting more weight on one side. It didn't help.

Vincent crossed the room and leaned against my bed. "You're on everyone's lips." "As suspected. I did win."

He shook his head. "About how you won. Many are saying your win is a fluke and owed to Selena."

I tensed but refused to give in to drama or gossip. People reveled in it. "They can say what they want. It doesn't change the fact that I won."

He ran a hand through his hair. "Some are saying your win was unfair, and you don't deserve the spot."

"Let me guess who's leading the charges? The losers from the venery? Father's pack?"

A smirk curled up the sides of his mouth. "You got it."

"There were no rules about how you could win. Cross the line with the stag. That's what I did."

He shrugged. "Figured you ought to know." "Appreciate it."

"And what about you and Selena? Are you two hitting if off?"

Since her arrival, it was hard enough working around my own messed up emotions, let alone hers.

"I'll tell you once I know." I broke into a chuckle, and goddess, it felt amazing to laugh for a change. "Anyway, how's the vixen you're dating? She's from Croatia, right?"

Vincent pushed to his feet, his mouth a straight line. "Turned out she had another two wulfkin on the side. That's why I'll no longer endorse long distance relationships. And get this, my mom contacted me about a lonely female in her pack. She thinks this one will be a perfect match for me. Geez, now I'm being set up on dates by my parents."

"Just like my father's doing to me."

Vincent nodded, smirking. He was beyond suave with the ladies and was rarely without one on his arm, so it wouldn't be long before he was hooked up again.

"Well, I gotta go. We're running a mock hunt with the newbies today."

"Wish I could join you." More than anything, I craved to run wild in the woods. "You will soon." He clapped my shoulder and retreated from the room.

Should have guessed the rumor mill would kick in, but in the grander scheme of the situation, I didn't give a fuck what anyone said.

Another knock at the door had me flinching. "Enter."

Tibor, the head council member, strolled in. His long coat bopped around his shins, and his cane tapped the floor as he hurried closer.

"Marcin, you're up and about. Fantastic."

Instead of getting up to greet him properly, I sat there like an invalid. I swallowed my pride and said, "Still got more healing to do. So, have you given my proposal about Father any more consideration?"

"That's why I'm here."

I squared my shoulders and shuffled to the edge of the window seat, my hands gripping the frame.

He halted a few paces in front of me and rubbed his mouth

with one hand. "The council and I want you to use the boon you'll win to set things right."

"What? That's not what I had in mind."

"The moon goddess has given us a new opportunity to tackle our problem. You simply claim half the wulfkin packs in Europe, making you an equal to him. Every decision he makes will need your approval." He leaned closer and lowered his voice. "You inevitably strip him of creating his own rules."

I stared at the old wulfkin's gray hair receding at the temples, the wrinkles pulling at the edge of his eyes. "You're afraid to go against Father. I get it. But your proposal leaves him as emperor. What makes you think he won't block any rule changes I want to make? That's not the answer."

Tibor's cheeks reddened as his grasp tightened around the black cane. When he spoke, his voice was clipped. "What would you rather do with the boon then?

"I'm working on that. And I appreciate your offer, but I suggest you and the council rethink your approach. After the challenge, I will call for you to band together and face Father alongside me."

Tibor paused, staring at the snowy scenery behind me. "Aggression isn't always the answer. I'd think you of all wulfkin would know this." He tottered from the room without another word.

Fucking hell. Anyone else lining up outside with their ideas on how I should use the boon? I couldn't take it, and in that moment, the room pressed down around me. Fresh air was a must. I climbed to my feet, using the wall for balance, and stumbled toward the door.

Except, Barka, the pack medic, waltzed in with fresh bandages draped over her arm and a bucket of water. Her silver hair was pulled into a disheveled bun, the permanent crease on her brow somehow comforting because it never changed. "Come, we'll make this quick, boy. Roza's in labor."

"I'm fine, really. Go tend to the wulfkin about to give birth. That's more important."

Barka had the blackest eyes, and when I stared into them, it felt as if I'd fallen into the abyss. At ninety-six, she should have retired, but Father kept her close for her medicinal knowledge and concoctions with herbs. "No son of the emperor will die under my watch. Now sit."

I hobbled to the bed, and Barka pulled a seat alongside me. "How's Roza doing?" I asked.

"Fine. She's terrified to have the baby after hearing a tale about wulfkin not being able to shift after pregnancy. No truth in it." She shook her head, loosening more strands from her bun. "If that were to happen, I'd easily conjure her up medicine to help."

"You can do that?"

Her gaze lifted, the multitude of lines around her mouth deepening. "It's in her head, boy. Now, lift your leg on the bed."

I lay back and pushed all thoughts out of my mind. After this, I was definitely heading outside.

Even if it took me an hour to get downstairs, I had to change the scenery and get my mind focused on something else.

<hr>

The sun warmed my cheeks as I slouched on the bench in the courtyard as Zeki crossed the yard, offering me a curt nod before vanishing indoors. Alone. Just me, the snow, and the potted plant Selena had dragged outside. Bell-shaped flowers swung in the breeze, delicate and vulnerable, a lot like Selena. Beyond those first impressions, she was strong, stubborn, and independent. Just how I remembered her and all the reasons I was attracted to her in the first place.

Despite the chill in the air, I was burning up as if I had a fever. I peeled off my coat and set it down on the bench.

I caught movement to my right, someone emerging from the door near the well. Purple fabric flapped around Aisha's legs. She pulled the shawl around her shoulders tight.

Without a glance my way, she ran across the yard to the doors of the foyer and vanished inside, in the same direction Zeki went.

What was she running away from? If I had a functioning leg, I might have followed her out of pure curiosity. Instead, I might ask Vincent to keep an extra eye on her.

A few seconds later, the door near the well creaked open again, but this time, Selena appeared, still dressed in her black ninja gear. Her gaze swept the yard until it landed on me. The slight flinch in her posture gave away her surprise to see me.

"Not who you were expecting?" I asked.

She scanned the area one more time before strolling my way, her hands by her side, her hips swinging deliciously. "Why aren't you still in the bath?"

"I was pickled and ready to come out. Anyway, you never returned."

Her attention dropped to her feet. "Yeah, sorry. Thought I saw Aisha in trouble in the courtyard. Sorry for running away before."

"Was she all right?"

Selena nodded, but the lack of emotion in her voice told me she lied. What would it take to make her trust me?

"Anyway, how are you feeling?" When her gaze lifted, sunlight framed her green eyes, set against her tanned skin and dark hair flowing over her shoulders.

My wolf roused inside me. We both agreed that getting lost in her beauty might be the best for all involved. I somehow suspected this vixen wouldn't so easily agree to run away with me again.

"The swelling's gone down, which is good," I said. "It still hurts to put my weight on the foot."

She stared at me, her gaze narrowed, then she reached over and placed a hand on my forehead. "You're clammy and hot. You've got a fever and probably shouldn't be out here."

"The room was suffocating me."

"Know the feeling. I keep looking out into the woods from my room and wondering what it would be like to leave everything behind and go out there. To run free, chase my meals, and forget everything. Wolves have it so much easier than us."

"Yep. They get to be at one with nature. We try to balance ours with humanity.

Sometimes it seems as if I don't belong in either world."

We exchanged glances, and for those few seconds, we were back in Turkey, sitting on a log in the woods near her place, planning our escape. She spoke of the cabin in the forest where the only rules imposed were those dictated by the universe and her body.

Me, I wanted to be anywhere she went, to protect her, love her, and make her smile every day.

Selena leaned against the wall with her hands curled in her lap. "Do you ever wonder how things would have turned out if we had been successful running away?"

"More times than I'd like to admit."

She nudged me with an elbow. "Still afraid to show your emotions?" "Not afraid. I prefer to save it for those moments when it really counts."

Her head cocked to the side, checking me out in a way that screamed disbelief. "And what if you're so busy overanalyzing whether a situation deserves your emotions, that you miss a perfect opportunity?"

"Well," I reached a hand over and grazed her cheek with the back of my fingers, "I'm willing to take that risk."

"Your loss." She leaned her head into my hand, her eyes closing momentarily.

I shuffled closer on the seat and slid my fingers through her hair to the back of her head, drawing her closer. Her hair was like silken strands against my fingers. Even velvet wasn't as smooth.

Her eyes opened. We were inches apart. Our breaths merging into one.

"Every day, I regret us not escaping." I kissed her, inhaling her response because in those few seconds, only this moment mattered. Her hands glided around the back of my neck, pulling me closer. Our tongues dueled, and I sucked on her lower lip as she mewled. My wolf responded instantly, prodding to get closer, wanting to lift her in my arms and take her away from this world, to start afresh.

She leaned into me, her mouth passionate and hungry. Unlike the kiss back in the woods, this one was real and full of raw desire. If she kissed me with such savagery, then maybe all was not lost between us.

I wrapped her in my embrace and left a trail of pecks along the edge of her ear. "I've missed you."

She didn't respond at first, but remained in my arms. I closed my eyes and let myself believe we were anywhere but here, just the two of us.

Then, as if reality made a presence, she untangled herself and pulled away.

A chill replaced where she'd been seconds earlier. Had I said something wrong?

"I'm sorry. I shouldn't ..." Up on her feet, she hugged herself, and her cheeks blushed pink. "I ... I have to go." She glanced around the yard for a moment.

"Your sister went that way." I pointed to the door leading to the foyer.

Selena glanced back at me momentarily, her mouth partly open, ready to speak, her eyes begging for acceptance. Instead, she rushed to the door, vanishing as her sister had minutes earlier.

I was alone once again, Selena's honeysuckle scent floating around me, my lips tingling from her touch, and yet I couldn't work out what I'd done wrong. For someone set to mate with me, and given our history, the only reason she'd run away and hold such distraught feelings behind her words was because she had no plans on going through with the ritual. And just like that, the one good thing in my life felt as if it were being ripped away.

CHAPTER 16

Two days had passed since I'd last seen Marcin. Nearly forty-eight hours since we shared a kiss, and I'd gone cold turkey on him.

This morning, I woke up with him still in my dreams, the memory of his lips on mine, and my wolf buzzing with desperation to return to his side. But didn't she realize that was out of the question now? The only way to stop myself from going insane with grief was to practice fighting every minute of the day and avoid the endless banquet dinners with the Hungarians. Still, my wolf pined endlessly. But deluding myself with fantasies had been a grave mistake on my part. After Father's confession about Levin's intention to murder us, I had no option but to focus on the upcoming battle of innocence. And to wipe Marcin from my heart because our future was never meant to be. Especially since Father now planned to mate us to other Varlac clans to strengthen his army.

My wolf shuddered—she craved freedom—and my chest was close to splitting in half, but our hands were tied. *Forget Marcin.* Telling myself that a hundred times a day didn't change a thing.

Goddess help me, but I couldn't stop picturing myself in his arms, drowning in his kisses. I kept seeing him naked in the bathtub. His torso, his devilish smirk, and ... I gulped. His hardness. Not even at full alertness, he looked huge. Part of me had toyed with the idea of reaching over and stroking him. Considering how things turned out, maybe I should have. And by the sexy gleam in his eyes, I suspected he'd have welcomed it.

Anyway, from now on, my focus was on winning the boon to save the lives of my family and Turkish wulfkin everywhere. Along with Daciana. No more fluttering about after Marcin like a love-struck schoolgirl. My priority should be on uncovering exactly what challenge Levin was setting for the final tournament because I didn't put it past him to make it impossible to win.

I ran shaky fingers through my hair, drawing strands off my face and into a ponytail, and I wiped my cheeks dry.

Aisha ran into the guest quarters, her eyes wide, and grabbed my wrist.

"Something's wrong with Marcin. He looks like a walking zombie."

"What are you talking about?" I pulled my hand free and scanned the room for my coat.

"He looked terrible over breakfast, all pasty and sick. Someone had to escort him out.

Something's happened to him."

"Are you sure?" A quiver coiled through my belly. She nodded quickly, her hands fisted against her chest.

My body went rigid, and my arms trembled. Without another word, I sprinted out of the room, making a beeline for Marcin's room across the castle. At his door, I knocked in haste, my stomach crackling with torment.

"Yeah?" Marcin's voice was soft, wary.

"It's me." I didn't wait for a response but pushed inside.

Marcin sat on the edge of his bed, shoulders drooped, hands on knees as he gasped for air. When he glanced up, his face was pasty and shiny with sweat. Dark patches gathered beneath his glassy eyes. "Took you a while to come see me." His voice was croaky.

A sudden coldness hit my core, and I rushed to him. I should have visited earlier, should have checked that the healing brew helped him, should have made an effort. "What's going on?" I drew his hand in mine. "Come, sit by the fire."

"No. I'm burning up."

I placed a hand to his brow. His clammy skin was an inferno. A heavy sensation spiraled out of control inside me. "How's the leg?"

"Completely healed. The wound's closed up too. Thanks to the brew you got from Barka, there's no more pain. Except for this damn fever that's getting worse. It's draining me. My head spins out of control when I stand up."

I placed a hand on his neck, focusing on his galloping pulse as if he'd just run a marathon.

"What have you been taking?"

"Barka prescribed plenty of liquids and herbal tea. I'll be fine, don't fuss over me."

Perspiration bubbled on his upper lip as his gaze swept behind him, to an oversized backpack propped up against the bed, and then I really studied Marcin, dressed in knee- length boots, jeans, and a black snow jacket. At first, I thought it was due to his fever, but when he climbed to his feet and reached over for his bag, I realized my mistake.

"Where are you going?" I asked.

"Won't be long." He brushed past me, but I grabbed his wrist. "Is someone going with you?"

He pulled away, and our hands pulled apart. "Like I said, I won't be long." "Then I'm coming with you."

He laughed but broke into a cough. "You don't even know where I'm going." "Doesn't matter." I buttoned up my long coat. "Let's go."

For a long moment, he studied me with a narrowed gaze. "You're stubborn, you know that, right?"

"What's really going on with you?" My voice cracked.

"I think the bacteria from the rusted bear trap has given me blood poisoning. I searched the symptoms online."

"So you'd rather use Internet suggestions than a real doc?" Why was he being so pigheaded?

"You know I can't go to a human hospital. Our medic put it down to a cold."

"I saw a wulfkin with sepsis die within a week because he left it untreated." Dread clung to my insides.

"You're not making me feel very confident."

"Just saying, if you do have blood poisoning, why didn't you come and see me or tell someone else?"

He threaded his arms into the backpack straps. "Lots of chickweed grows in a nearby cave. It's a weed with extraordinary healing properties, and it's used as a blood cleanser. It has healed me before from injuries. Just need to mush it up with a few other ingredients, and it should do the trick. Our medic's run out of chickweed, so I'm making a small trip into the forest."

"A cave?" After getting stuck in the dungeon back home for two days straight, I never wanted to be in a dark, confined place again. "Ask one of your pack or guards to go retrieve it."

He cocked an eyebrow. "No. I'm doing this myself."

While Father would encourage me not to get involved, not to help Marcin, and to focus on bettering my chances at the challenge, I could never live with myself if I sat back and let Marcin die.

"Tell me where this cave is. I'll go collect it."

"I'm coming with you." He headed toward the door. "Stop being a hero. You can't stand straight."

"The cave is deep in the woods, and I don't know how to describe the location. But I know where I'm going."

"This is madness, Marcin, even for you." I weaved in front of him. "You're getting worse and need to take it easy. Maybe someone else knows the area and can come with me? Don't waste your energy."

Marcin shook his head and took my hands in his, his touch burning hot against mine. "Nobody knows about the cave. Only me." He leaned in and kissed me on the nose before heading for the door, his steps wavering sideways for a moment. "If you're that insistent, then meet me near the shed behind the castle in fifteen minutes while I shake off the guards outside. Bring a snow jacket and hat."

He was completely insane, but if it meant healing him, I'd do anything it took, no matter how psychotic he was acting.

---

*B*ehind the castle stood a one-story brick building with no windows. Trees shrouded the backside of the structure that could easily be mistaken for a tool shed. This had to be the place Marcin mentioned. Everything else was contained within the walls of the castle.

The roller door on the building was pulled up, and inside sat five snowmobiles, all in red. A smile slid across my lips—best way to trek through the snow, rather than on foot.

Inside, a shadow moved about amid the vehicles. "Marcin?"

"Good. You're here." He stepped out of the corner, rigged up in a snow jacket and goggles over his eyes. As he stepped closer, his chest worked hard for each rapid inhale, and his skin glistened with perspiration.

"For fuck's sake. Tell me where this place is, and you can go back to bed."

He shook his head. "You'll get lost." He handed me gloves and goggles. Then he studied me and smiled. "You look cute in that hat."

I adjusted the beanie over my ears and couldn't stop the fire burning my cheeks. Okay, we were on a rescue-style mission, not getting all hot and geeky over Marcin.

Geared up, I retreated as Marcin climbed onto the middle snowmobile, kick-started the motor, and reversed out of the building. He patted the seat behind him. "Climb on."

"Why don't you want anyone to know about your secret cave?"

He gazed back momentarily. "You know that lookout we discovered in Turkey?" "Yeah." During a long walk through the woods back home, Marcin and I had stepped

out onto a ledge no larger than a small hatchback car. It

overlooked the Black Sea in the distance, the sun was rising, and the world was silent. I wanted to believe we were the first to ever uncover that spot, the first to take in the view from that angle, the first to share a kiss on the lookout. And we made a promise to keep that location our little getaway. Our place to visit when the real world got too much.

"Well." Marcin's voice sliced through my memory, and he was now facing the front, gripping the handlebars. "This cave is my haven."

A warm tingling spread through me. This location was his special place for escape, and I understood perfectly well why he wouldn't want to share it with anyone else.

"Thanks for letting me join you." I climbed on. "Let's get this done before Father puts out a search party."

The seat beneath me purred and vibrated. Marcin reached back and grabbed my arms, wrapping them around his waist. "Hold on."

He revved the engine, and we drove away from the shed. The wind tugged on my clothes, but with my snow jacket, only my legs felt the chill. I ducked behind Marcin to stop the biting cold from hitting my face.

We powered down a hill, my body pressing tight against Marcin's back. Despite the layer of clothing between us, my wolf still reacted, shoving me forward, insistent we sidle up closer to him. Well, only way that would happen was if we were naked. But I wasn't going there.

I stared at the trees we passed, a deer a few trees away, and the white plume behind us.

The snow sparkled like a million stars in the night sky. For those few moments, I let myself pretend we weren't rushing to find a miracle cure to save Marcin's life, my family wasn't in mortal danger from Levin, and Father wouldn't mate me off with someone else purely to secure himself a bigger army. Those gargantuan problems were an anaconda around my chest, squeezing the life out of me, making breathing a chore. I wasn't asking too much and just wanted to enjoy a ride through the woods with my soul wolf without the world on my back.

An hour later, my legs were numb from the vibration, and my insides were shaken up from the bumps and mounts we'd raced over. We pulled over near a monster pine, its trunk twice my width. It loomed over us like Father might do if he found out I helped Marcin.

"We walk from here. It's not far."

I removed my goggles and swung my leg over the seat, but the stiffness in my back had me tripping sideways as I caught myself. A thick wall of trees formed a barricade in front of us, and a steep hill rose beyond them. "How did you find this place?"

"Exploring." He opened a compartment on the side of the snowmobile and wobbled on his feet, but held on to the machine for balance.

"Shit. This was a mistake."

He didn't stop and pulled out his backpack. "Let's go."

I tracked alongside him, going at a slower pace than usual. He wheezed, and we stopped every few steps. At this pace, we might reach the cave by morning. As much as I detested the idea of going into a dark enclosure, for Marcin, I'd do anything. Weaving around a cluster of trunks, we commenced our climb, my boots sinking into snow to my ankles.

Marcin wavered a few times, and I stayed close in case he fell or slipped. If he collapsed now, we were in deep shit, stuck in the middle of nowhere. Could I even find my way back? The fresh snow covered our tracks, and then what? Worse yet, what if someone followed us? The assassin maybe or that Hooked Nose guy from the woods who looked ready to rip me apart.

Marcin used trees to pull himself up and spoke without looking my way. "You," he inhaled deeply, "have been gone two days."

I was unsure how to respond. So I went for part truth. "Been busy. Plus, didn't want to bug you while you weren't feeling well." The lie burned my throat on the way out.

The stare he cut me as he stopped for a moment was filled with disbelief. "Don't lie to save my feelings. I can take it."

I continued walking, using a low-hanging branch to stop

myself from tumbling. Snow slapped me in the face from the tree. That was the universe punishing me for lying.

"You okay?" he asked.

"Yeah, thanks. Listen, let's just focus on getting up this freakin' mountain and not worry about anything else. Couldn't your haven be somewhere easier to reach?" My foot skidded out from under me again, and I landed on all fours. Calling on wolf strength, I pushed myself to my feet and slugged it higher, passing Marcin. I offered him my hand. "Let's go."

He might be staring at me as if he'd never accept in a million years, but his body wasn't cooperating, so I reached over and snatched his hand and drew him behind me. *I could do this.*

Two hours later, we reached the crest, and we were both exhausted. I was on my knees, while Marcin leaned against a tree, wheezing heavily. Why had I agreed to this insane trek anyway?

Behind us lay an ocean of snow-topped trees. The castle was a tiny spec. "Let's take a break."

As if my words were a challenge, he straightened his back. "We're almost there." He pointed down the other side of the hill we'd scaled and into a valley of pines.

"I don't see a cave." "It's there."

I took his hand and placed it over my shoulders, taking some of his weight, thankful to be going downhill. Then he stopped in the valley and dropped to his knees alongside a massive boulder sticking out of the ground. Behind it, the mountain rose sharply with trees growing at a steep angle.

Marcin scooped armfuls of snow, shoveling them aside. I fell down alongside him and did the same, quicker so he'd get the hint and back off.

On our next scraping, we exposed a layer of thick branches. I rolled them aside, revealing more rock and a gaping hole in the side of the mountain.

"Y ... You ..." My lunged seized up. Darkness swallowed everything in the pit. Goddess help me, I hated dark, confined places. "That's no bigger than a rabbit's warren." I trembled at the notion of going in there, but I kept telling myself this was for Marcin.

It could barely fit Marcin if he went in feet first. He stood and kicked his foot into the fanglike icicles hanging over the mouth of the cave. He glanced over his shoulder at me, an eyebrow arched. "Are you all right?"

My voice spiked. "This isn't a cave. It's a freakin' hole in the ground. A grave." Every time I inhaled, it rattled on the way down.

"It's okay. I'll go. You stay here and wait."

His legs wavered, and he collapsed back down onto his knees. I jumped up and took his elbow, helping him to his feet. "You can't even stand up, how are you going to do this alone? I'll do it."

Then my sights returned to the opening in the ground, along with the way the land dipped inward. My skin rippled with pinpricks at the notion of going down there. An invisible hand squeezed my heart.

But staring at a frail Marcin, he somehow looked smaller. Or maybe it was his drooped shoulders, the life fading from his eyes. Goddess, I was insane for even considering this.

"How far in are these plants?"

"It's not too far. Just down the tunnel."

I released a long exhale. Why hadn't I asked more questions about this place? I could have gotten Zeki or even Aisha to join us. My sister was a spider when it came to climbing.

"Seems I've discovered a small chink in your armor." The corner of his mouth curled upward in a sexy way that should have had my knees weak, but the dread clinging to my skin had me locked in place.

His words were broken by a sudden explosion of coughs, and he stumbled on his feet.

"Shit, Marcin." I pushed one leg closer. My hands fisted in my pockets, heat collecting across the nape of my neck. *Just get it done.*

Marcin's life was on the line. The reality struck like a

hammer to the chest. My words vanished, and my sight fastened on the black hole, seemingly calling my name.

Fire slinked up my legs, and I was overheating. My clothes suffocated me, and my focus kept dipping to the hole behind him.

Just get this done.

Marcin was right behind me. He'd gone down this hole before and survived; plus he called it a haven. But what haven looked like a pit? Maybe looks were deceiving. And Marcin didn't seem like the daredevil type. Surely, this seemed worse than it was. I remembered the potted plant hidden in a dark corner inside the castle, and somehow it survived. It pulled through. Maybe I would survive this too.

I lowered myself to my butt, the cold seeping through my clothes, and shuffled closer.

My legs sunk into the darkness. Beneath them, the stone floor plunged downward.

Beyond that, the inky darkness was a curtain. Black, just like the prison I'd been locked in back home. Closing in around me. Constricting my airway. *Goddess, I'm going to die.*

"You'll land on a ledge. It's safe."

Okay, don't overthink it, don't ... I held my breath and shimmied forward, lowering my body slightly. I was in the hole up to my elbows. I crunched my eyes tight and shuffled even closer.

I can do this. I can do this.

A warm kiss landed on my brow. I opened my eyes to find Marcin's face inches from mine, his exhale caressing my cheeks. "You're doing wonderfully. Just a bit more."

His smile had this calming effect on my nerves. If I didn't do this, Marcin might pass out in the tunnels, and I'd have no way of finding him. I inched deeper, the gaping mouth of the cave now reaching my neck.

Then my feet skidded on a slick section of the stone. My body lurched downward, hands jutted out for leverage. I found none and fell. Screams echoed as the cave swallowed me whole. Darkness engulfed me, compressing me. Wind rushed up around me, ripping my clothes, pulling my hair.

My heart banged behind my breastbone. Why had I agreed to this? Stupid Marcin. Stupid me.

The flush of cold wind slapped me in the face as I flew through the air and landed with a thud on my side, my body rolling in momentum. When I came to a dead stop, goddess knows where, my heart was scaling my throat. I could have crashed into a wall or fallen off a ledge or landed in the lap of a bear or viper or ... I had to get out.

Ten feet above me, the entrance to the hole blared with light. Lucky I hadn't broken a bone or my neck on the way down. A figure blocked the light. Marcin. I climbed to my feet. He better not be coming down here.

Then his large figure rushed downward. A loud thud sounded, and Marcin was already staggering to his feet, groaning with pain. I pulled him to his feet by his arm.

"Are you insane? Why did you come down? How the shit are we going to get you back up?"

"I never said I wasn't coming."

My body shook with fire racing through my veins. "And you said we'd land on a ledge."

His flashlight switched on, pointing to the ground. "It's a ledge."

I was pacing and couldn't even remember starting. "This was a mistake. We have to get out. I'm serious." On either side of me, darkness leached closer, encasing the walls, the path, everything. A few paces away, the ledge we stood on turned pitch black, vanishing into a sheer drop off. *Oh, my goddess.* "We could have died."

Marcin stepped in my path and gripped my shoulders. "We're still alive."

Each inhale hiccupped on the way down. Get it together. Marcin was the one on death's door, not me. I pushed back my shoulders and took the flashlight from him.

"Okay, which way? We'll do this quickly." I lifted the light and pointed it down a passage. The tunnel was, at least, seven feet in height and wide enough for several people to walk alongside each other.

I pushed one foot in front of the other, then another, and soon we were walking deeper into the mountain where the land sloped downward, mustiness permeated the air, and the dripping sound of water echoed around us.

"How are we meant to climb back out by the way?"

"With a bit of hard work, but it should be doable." He kept bumping into me, unable to walk straight. I wrapped my arm around his, drew him closer, and we plodded along slowly.

"What do you mean, should be?"

He glanced over, smirking.

Oh goddess, I'd definitely entered a cave with a maniac. Surely, I could scale that

entrance. But what about Marcin? He was getting weaker by the moment, and no way could I lug him up with me.

CHAPTER 17

MARCIN

Fear crippled anyone who let it into their heads, so it surprised me that someone as strong as Selena carried such a phobia. But she faced her demons, one step at a time. I'd guided several newbie pack members who were too scared to run alone in the woods or insisted they could only hunt alone. One time, a wulfkin broke into a cold sweat each time he had to transform into his wild side. The poor guy associated the change with losing control as he had when a child. They were afflictions of the mind caused by a traumatic event, but mostly treatable with time and persistence. Some wulfkin could never completely get over their trauma.

Selena gripped my arm against her, leading me forward. My legs ached like hell, and each step resembled walking on nails. Perspiration rolled down my spine, and my vision kept blurring. But if Selena could face her fear, I could do this. The idea of not joining her had crossed my mind, but what sort of wulfkin would I be if I let her go alone in a strange cave?

A loud splintering echoed overhead.

Her voice trembled. "What was that?"

"The land moves all the time. It's normal."

"Yeah, but being down here isn't."

I wanted to laugh, but it hurt too much, and in all honesty, focusing on Selena took away from the gravity of what was coming my way. Death if we didn't get there in time. I focused on each excruciating step and inhale. We had to make it.

"Maybe we should leave." Her soft voice called to me. She kept the beam and her attention on the path ahead of us, not on the crevasses in the walls we passed, or the narrow tunnels filled with darkness.

"We'll be quick."

When we reached a three-way passage, Selena halted. "Which way?"

"Down the middle."

She took the lead, and while my inner wolf nudged me to take charge, my energy was spent. My feet dragged behind me with my mind wandering to the notion of dying, here in a cave, next to Selena. Not how I intended it to happen, and of all the things to take me down—a stupid bear trap.

"Talk to me," I said, needing to change my thoughts. "Anything."

"Hmm. Remember that time you flipped out because one of my cousins refused to give you access to their room in Turkey?" She arched an imperious brow.

"He stole my boots."

"What?" She cut me a glare that could freeze fire. "As if he'd want your boots. Come on, Marcin. You were cocky back then and refused to accept that poor Murat hated anyone going into his room. You intended to prove a point."

"Bull. He took my boots." On my first day at their mansion, the little bastard had whispered that by the end of the day my boots would be on his feet. And then he stole them. I resisted the urge to break down his door and rip his legs off. "I climbed to his window and saw him lying on his bed, wearing them."

Her eyes widened. "And this whole time, I figured you strolled around barefoot for a few days just to prove your point."

It killed me knowing he'd stolen what belonged to me. Later in the week, I broke into his room, retrieved my boots and took every pair Murat owned, and tossed them over a cliff. Not a proud moment. What guy owned sixteen pairs of shoes anyway?

Selena stopped. "Dead end." The ball of light from her flashlight bounced across the stone wall at the end of the tunnel. "We must have missed a passage." Her attention dipped to the heap of loose rocks piled into tiny mounds near the walls.

I took her hand in mine and guided the beam toward a thin breach in the wall.

Shadows galloped across her pale cheeks. Not a word fell from her tight lips, but the way her shoulders slumped, the fear behind her gaze blazed awake. "You're completely and utterly insane."

"It's just on the other side of his wall." I let myself lean into the rock divider, each punishing breath shallow and raspy. Had one lung given out already?

She pulled me up and took off the knapsack, clasping it with her other hand. "Fine, but I'm not one bit happy."

Protesting words scraped against the front of my mind, but with no strength to argue, I let Selena assist me toward the breach in the wall.

Sidestepping into the crevice, I shuffled alongside her, our hands linked. My chest and back scraped against the stone. I'd done this dozens of times, so why was my gut tight as concrete?

Darkness closed in around us as the beam of the flashlight pooled on the ground.

The air grew mustier, and loose rubble scraped beneath my feet with each agonizing sideward step. The crevice was tight. I gasped, trying to suck in more air. *Don't focus on that. Keep moving.*

"What made you ever decide to go through this tunnel in the first place?"

"I hid here from my father after he beat me up for helping Enre run away." Selena didn't say a word. Her thumb caressed the back of mine. "That's horrible. Sorry."

The reflection from her flashlight was enough to reveal the glistening in her eyes. But

I didn't need her pity. We'd both had fucked up lives, and that was what drew us together all those years ago. In all honestly, I wasn't sure I'd forgo the opportunity to meet her or those heart-felt connections for anything.

Her mouth opened, but instead of her words, a loud groan rippled overhead. The ground shook beneath my feet. Tiny rocks hit our heads from above.

"Shit." Selena's voice climbed.

A shudder ran through me. In all the years I'd trekked here, there had never been so much as a tremble. We were more than halfway through the passage. "Go, go."

Selena squeezed my hand and hurried her shuffle, me behind her. "Why did I listen to you?"

My legs moved faster. No time for pain. When my head spun, I stumbled and my shoulders grated against stone.

The cave shook around us, and the wall behind me shifted slightly. Then a great roar erupted. Rubble rained down on us, and a huge plume of dust rushed up behind me like a tsunami.

Selena hurried. Each step was like wading through mud, my vision dancing.

The fine dirt strangled my throat. My knees weakened, and I tumbled against her.

She placed an arm around my shoulders and dragged me out. I pushed against the wall to help take some weight off her.

Dust filled my nostrils, my ears, my mouth. Surely, I was coughing up a lung.

While we finally emerged from the fissure in the wall, I tripped out of Selena's arms, landing on my knees, my throat raw as the hacking dissipated. Selena rasped but already pulled me to my feet, away from the hole and near a wall. I slumped against it. A haze blurred my mind, which pounded worse than before.

When I glanced up, Selena stood there, staring at me, dread flooded her expression. Dust covered her face and clothes.

If anything had happened to her, I would never have forgiven myself. The pulsing urgency to protect her rose and fell through me, but right now, I couldn't even lift an arm, let alone save myself.

Her gaze kept dancing between me and the dust pouring out of the breach. "We could have both died, but now we're stuck in here."

Then she studied me as a doctor might do, scrutinizing every inch before making a final assessment.

She grabbed the backpack she'd dropped and dug inside for the bottle of water and lifted it to my lips. "Drink."

The cold liquid was refreshing. She drank some too.

"So is this the place?"

I nodded as my heart pounded so hard in my chest I was convinced these were my last moments. But it only accentuated the banging in my head.

She faced the rest of the cavern. "Whoa."

In front of us lay a room that easily rivaled the great hall back home in size. A bumpy and rough surface covered the cave, icicles suspended from the ceiling as if we'd entered a frozen fairy tale, but the real showpiece was the frozen waterfall against the back wall. The once cascading water was frozen midmovement, and now a rainbow of colors shimmied against the ice from the light streaming through the tiny holes in the ceiling.

Selena wandered farther into the expanse, her gaze whipping across the room, from the side wall with round holes to the iced-over river beneath the waterfall, and then across to the patches of greenery clawing a meager existence in the light like stunted plants.

"That's the chickweed," I said.

She rushed to them.

My muscles quivered with urgency for her to hurry. I was tapped out, gone.

Selena ran back, a small bundle of white flowers and green leaves in her tiny fist. "Are you sure these are the chickweeds you were talking about?"

I nodded, too exhausted to talk.

She crouched alongside me and placed a hand to my brow. "You're burning up." With the plants set on a flat rock surface, she retrieved her blade.

"Spices." I pointed to the bag. My voice was barely a croak.

She unzipped the bag and dug inside, plucking out a small plastic bag filled with a brown powder. The moment she opened it, I inhaled the ginger, cayenne, and kelp powder. She chopped the chickweed, and I watched the way she cut with precision. Within seconds, she had the plants chopped finer than any machine. Using the side of the blade, she combined the powders into the plant, mixing them together. Then she scooped them with the knife. She trickled the green paste into the water, screwed the lid back on, and shook it vigorously.

"I'm really hoping this helps you."

She pressed it to my lips and lifted the base of the bottle.

I drank it down in small sips, finishing it. The grittiness stuck to my teeth and coated my tongue; the taste was a combination of dirt with a hint of sourness.

A wave of drowsiness washed through me, but I couldn't work out if it was the plant or the blood poisoning.

"How do you feel?" Her loud voice resonated around us.

I stifled a yawn. A hazy blur coated my vision. I rubbed my throbbing temples.

She reached an arm toward me. Her touch was an ice cube.

Lethargy wiped through me, worse than before, to the point where my head weighed more than my entire body. I forced my eyelids open.

Selena was in my face.

Gray patches danced in my vision, and I shook my head, but my eyes hurt to keep them open. Selena's mouth was moving, but I couldn't hear a word.

So fucking heavy. Maybe just a second to shut my eyes, a fleeting moment to rest a bit. Then darkness pounded through my mind, my vision blanked, and I fell into its abyss.

CHAPTER 18

SELENA

Marcin slumped against the wall, his head drooped, long hair cascading over his face. For years, I'd prayed to the moon goddess for Marcin to come to Turkey, to admit the arrow in my shoulder was a misunderstanding, so we could run away as we'd originally intended. But I had been deluding myself and learned to accept that my future did not include Marcin. Yet this visit burst open those emotional floodgates I'd nailed shut.

The thing was, now that he'd been dangled in front of me, I wasn't so sure I could tuck him into the recesses of my mind again or have my heart shattered a second time.

"Moon goddess, if you're listening, please heal Marcin. Let the chickweed do its trick."

I wiped the blade clean across my pants and tucked the weapon back into my boot, then grabbed Marcin's flashlight and swept the beam across the cave.

Tiny streaks of light from overhead gave the room a faint glow. We were closed in here, no exit. The cave-in made sure of it. A tight ball looped in my chest. But I refused to believe we were stuck, and getting all freaked out wasn't the answer. Father always said to keep a cool head in times of trouble. So, I'd follow his advice.

I pulled out my phone. No reception, of course.

Once Marcin woke up, he'd have limited energy and require plenty of rest and food. Lying in a freezing cold cave wasn't conducive to healing.

In hindsight, I should have told someone we were coming out here, though in reality I had no idea where here was. Marcin intended to keep this place to himself, so I doubted he told anyone either. We were fucked ... to put it politely.

I released a long breath and circled the perimeter of the cave, studying the jagged walls, the clusters of chickweed, and the hanging icicles. Beautiful, if they weren't blades hanging above our heads. Goddess, I had to get out. I paced around the area, remembering Marcin's words from when we'd landed inside. *We're still alive.* Well, I hadn't died yet, and look how long I'd been in this blasted death tomb.

My attention returned to the rainbow across the waterfall. Then I glanced up at the streaks of light coming in from the ceiling. Two of them were right above the structure and shined on the ice. But the closer I got, the more it became clear there was no way two tiny beams could create that much light. I curved around the frozen pond and climbed up on a ledge alongside the waterfall.

A faint glow came from behind the sheet of ice. What if ...?

I grabbed a stone the size of my head and smashed it into the glasslike wall repeatedly. Fragments flung free, and a crack snaked upward.

Excellent. I continued whacking the ice. A shard the size of my hand fell away, and a light breeze fluttered out, gingerly caressing my cheeks. I didn't stop working until I'd created a large enough hole for me to slip through.

Inside, I crouched low and squeezed through a tunnel studded with miniature icicles as if I were stuck in an iron maiden.

Don't focus on the low ceiling or the walls pressing in around you. Just ahead.

I shuddered but kept inching onward. Around the next bend,

a bright light appeared and warmth spread through me, excitement pushing my legs faster. I hurried through the curving burrow, emerging into the woods. The earlier dread clinging to my flesh washed away on the breeze.

"Yes!" My voice echoed, and a breeze swished through my hair. I strolled toward the fringe of pines in the distance, contemplating the idea of catching a small snack. A rabbit or two would help Marcin when he woke up. Maybe luck was finally on our side.

The sudden whipping of wind brought a new scent—wolf, raw and animalistic.

I stood still.

From behind a tree to my right, a gray wolf trotted out. My next inhale confirmed him to be a normal wolf, not a shifter. More of them emerged, branching out into a semicircle, about fifteen feet away. Nine sets of eyes on me.

My muscles seized. On my own, I'd stand no chance against this pack of wolves. Maybe with Marcin, but not in his current state. I calmed my pulse, visualizing an aura field traveling up my body.

No one made a move, and I lowered my head and gaze, to appear less of a threat. The alpha with a white ear inched closer. Even if I transformed, they'd be on me in no time. Hungry wolves ate anything, even loners of their own kind if desperate enough.

I backed away in slow motion, never turning my back to them. They'd interpret that as a challenge, and once they got me, they'd sniff out Marcin and finish him.

A snarl reverberated from the alpha's chest as sunlight gleamed off his gray coat.

Goddess, I didn't need this now.

I reached a shaky hand toward him.

He slinked forward, sniffed the air, and released a low rumble.

"I'm not going to hurt you." My scent always calmed animals. Otherwise, I'd be a fool to ever offer my hand to a wild wolf.

Perspiration trickled down my spine. I held tight and broke into a soft humming lullaby, hoping my voice would have the same effect.

His black eyes rolled upward in a hypnotized state, only the whites showing. Exactly how I'd expected him to react. Docile and calm.

A second wolf trotted closer and growled, and immediately the others followed.

I cringed.

The alpha snapped back to attention, his eyes on full alert, fur bristled down his back.

This wasn't going to work with such a large pack. His lips peeled back, ears flat against his head.

I threw my hands into the air to look as big as possible. "Get out of here. I'm not your meal. Shoo."

Seizing a thick branch near my feet, I hurled the weapon at them. My intention wasn't to scare them. That tactic would never work, except to give me time to escape. Quick sidesteps took me toward the cave, my gaze never leaving the encroaching danger.

Calling to my wolf, I released a thunderous growl. I moved faster, but my foot hit a rock in the snow, and I fell to my knees.

The wolves pounced, flanking me from all sides. Hot breaths streamed from their mouth, their ears flattened against to their heads.

A meal. That's what I was to them. I jumped up and bolted. The entry lay ten feet away. Too far. The crunch of snow closed in.

Never run from a wolf, but here I was sprinting through ankle deep snow. Because that was how my day was going.

The hairs on my neck shifted, alert, and my skin rippled.

Teeth snagged on my upper arm. A guttural threat in my ear. Flesh and fabric tore. I shoved my elbow backward, connecting to soft tissue, throwing him off me.

I lunged into the cave's mouth, my shoulders scraping the walls.

Claws snapped against rock right behind me, heavy exhalation a drum in my ear.

I swerved through the passage and dove through the hole in the waterfall, then grabbed a rock and tossed it at the entrance. It barely missed the gray wolf. He whined and jumped backward. The tight entry allowed only one to push through at a time.

And right now, the alpha had his head poking through the ice wall, teeth bared, nose creased.

In no time, I ripped off my jacket, ready to transform, but the wolf hopped through the frozen waterfall hole, surveying the surroundings, his sight set on Marcin.

"No fuckin' way. He's mine."

I grabbed more rocks and threw them at him, hitting the side, driving him back up the ledge and outside.

A quick glance behind me confirmed Marcin still lay there without a clue in the world of what danger lay at his feet.

Time to get this handled. I leapt up onto the ledge, and screamed in the predator's direction, trying to intimidate him.

He bit back just as fast, inches from my face, in fact, a few strands of my hair caught in his teeth.

Enough of this crap, and definitely no time to transform. I reached down for more rocks.

But he attacked again, his mouth latching onto my side by my arm, throwing me off my feet and onto my side. The bite was a blade slicing flesh. A silent whimper gurgled in my throat as he dragged me through the waterfall hole. *Push past the pain.*

I punched his face, over and over.

He lost his grip and stumbled backward. Before he attacked, I hurled more rocks near my feet, my shoulder screaming with pain. He whimpered and retreated a bit farther away. A second wolf shoved in behind him, but the limited space meant he couldn't attack.

No time to waste. I retreated and grabbed a large stone nearby, throwing it into the passage.

The wolves scampered a few steps back, but their growls told me they weren't giving up that easily. Neither was I.

I rushed with one stone after another, until I'd blocked up the place enough to stop them from coming through. My pulse was in a frenzy. Now I prayed they moved on to find an easier meal.

Through the gaps of the stone wall, the gray wolf stared at me, not making a sound. Then he retreated, the clack of claws on stone. Was he giving up or biding his time?

I pulled back and stood there for a few moments, waiting for a reshow or something. The sting lanced down my arm from the bite. Looking around, I spotted Marcin's backpack.

Running across the room, I tripped over a tuft of chickweed, just catching my balance before I landed face first onto the stone surface. My chest was pumping with adrenaline. What I wouldn't give to have a calm day for a change.

The warm trickle of blood stung my arm, so I tipped all the bag contents out. Another bottle of water, jerky, a blanket, and a shirt. That would do the trick. I grabbed the black top and folded the fabric as best as I could into a layered bandage, pressing it under my torn sleeves and placing it against my wound. I'd heal soon enough, but first I had to stop the bleeding.

Back alongside Marcin, I draped the blanket over his body and grabbed one of the jerky sticks. I crossed my legs and sat next to him, figuring we weren't going anywhere soon, so I might as well get comfortable and heal.

A feather-soft touch caressed my cheek, the kind that loosened my muscles. I curled my body and rolled away, but something kept poking into my side.

When someone coughed, my eyes fluttered open.

Marcin stared down at me with the softest bedroom eyes, the ones I'd imagined waking up next to for years. Except, we weren't in a bed, and he wasn't snuggling me. He sat beside me, knees bent, arms draped over them. We were in alone in a cave, a light dusting of snow filtering down from the cracks overhead, and instead of guarding Marcin, I'd dozed off.

"How are you feeling?" he asked.

I sat up and wiped my mouth. "Shouldn't I be asking you that?"

"My strength is back, even if my head still spins. I'm more rejuvenated now than I've been these past few days." His attention shifted between me with my bulging shoulder and his shirt tucked under my jacket. His focus changed to the backpack on the floor with all the contents spilled out. He sniffed the air.

"What happened? Did you get injured making that hole in the waterfall?"

"Fought a pack of wild wolves, got bit in the process, and I used your shirt to stop the bleeding." I reached in beneath my snow jacket and lifted up the makeshift bandage. The wound had closed up, despite the dried up blood caked around the bite mark. I pulled back the shirt stuck to my skin with dried blood and winced.

"Here, let me clean that. It's the least I can do." He grabbed the corner of the blanket and soaked it in water from the bottle.

Considering the worry swimming behind his eyes, I figured it'd be easier to accept his help than argue the point. I unzipped my jacket, slipped it off, and pushed the shirt over my shoulder.

"Maybe you should took take it off."

I cut him a side stare, but he held on to his stoic expression, obviously intent on proving me wrong. "You'd like that, wouldn't you?"

"You bet." He couldn't hold back his smile, and my heart fluttered at the way his lips parted. For those few seconds, my mind danced with the possibility of leaning in and tasting them. Letting myself fall into his arms, demanding he take me, and forgetting the pile of crap waiting for us back at the castle was a brief, but wonderful, thought. In all honestly, all our problems would be solved if we simply ran away now. And hand on heart, if it weren't for Aisha, I would do it. The temptation swirled in the pit of my stomach, but the real world quickly flattened that dream.

Marcin patted the damp fabric across my shoulder, gently

rubbing the dried blood around the wound. "So, a pack of wolves, you say?"

I nodded. "Nine of them."

He leaned in closer, wiping clean my injury, revealing the bite mark. "Did you get hurt anywhere else?" His voice lowered, and an underlying tone of worry coated his words, even if my first interpretation of his words shifted into flirty gear. The thing was, with him so close, his breaths were a siren's song, and my own wolf fluttered through me in sex-starvation mode.

"Thanks for protecting me and finding us a way out." He set down the blanket and skimmed the back of his fingers across my cheek. "That's the second time you've saved me. You're giving me a complex."

My response wouldn't come at first. It was jammed inside my libido, too consumed by the temptation to have my way with Marcin. Alone in a cavern. No family nearby. Yet, the truth of the upcoming battle of innocence, and me having to go back home afterward, sat on my mind like an unmovable mountain. I wanted it gone.

"Well, I hope me saving you doesn't make you feel emasculated."

His hand slipped a strand of hair behind my ear, his touch sending goose bumps down my back. "Never. If anything, I was wondering how I could ever repay you." A devilish grin split his mouth.

A tingle spread below my stomach. The kind of repayment I had in mind might make even Marcin blush, though considering the mischievousness behind his eyes, I somehow doubted it. Still, it went against everything I'd been telling myself to do. Keeping my distance from Marcin, not encouraging him, and making it clear I wasn't interested had been the plan. Sticking to that idea would hurt less when the time came for me to break our mating agreement. With Levin's threat to attack our family, I had no choice but to return home with my father. Just thinking the words had my chest constricting, my eyes stinging. So, was it so wrong to release those worries for a while?

Our foreheads touched.

My voice was barely a whisper. "Can we pretend none of the shit between us has happened, and we're back in Turkey when the world seemed filled with possibilities? Even only for now?" Because in truth, that was what I'd wanted for so long—to rewind time.

"For you, anything." His voice was a whisper, soothing my insides in all the right ways.

I brushed my lips against his, closing my eyes. He returned the passion threefold, his mouth hungry against mine, our tongues meeting like long-lost lovers. And beneath his kiss, I softened as if I were snow on the first day of spring.

His hands skipped down my arms, along my waist, and to my hips. He drew me closer and guided me across his lap. A blaze ripped through my body, every nerve sensitive. His fingers eased under my shirt, digging into flesh. I pressed closer, desperate for more.

We'd never gone beyond heavy petting when we were younger, but now the temptation of finally having sex with Marcin tingled through my body.

Breaking away, he left a trail of kisses down my chin and along my neck, his voice gravelly and beyond sexy. "I've missed you so much."

"Me too." My response came quick, no hesitation because I longed for him terribly; the way trees craved rain, the way earth drank in the sun, the way oxygen gave life. That was Marcin for me. A lifeline I thought I'd lost.

I pulled off my top and flung it somewhere behind me.

His lips found my collarbone as he unfastened my bra. It fell between us, and at once, his mouth latched on to a breast, sucking, his hand on the other, kneading.

My whole body trembled with ecstasy and anticipation of more.

I mewled at the way his tongue grazed my nipple, the fire for Marcin flared awake with the intensity of a thunderstorm. Breaths sped up, and my hips rocked back and forth across his hardness. I leaned back slightly, giving him easier access. "Harder."

He complied, his teeth gently gnawing on my tight bud.

His fingers fiddled with the zipper on my pants, pulling the fabric down. Releasing the hold, his eyes opened, and the sexiness behind his gaze made a ripple of euphoria zip through me. He stared at me with the same look I'd craved all these years, the ravenous desire in his parted lips, desperation in his touch.

Marcin cradled my face in his hands and crushed his mouth against mine, so intense my legs threatened to give out. No man could ever sate the hole that Marcin had left in my heart. Desire surged through me. Damn, Marcin could melt an iceberg with that tongue.

"Pants off. Now." He smirked. Goddess, right now I'd do anything he asked of me. Anything.

I climbed to my feet, as did Marcin.

The apex between my legs was ready to implode as he took me in fully in with his roaming stare. I shivered as he pulled my pants and panties down. By the time I stepped out of them, his fingers were already on me, gliding along my silkiness. My insides trembled uncontrollably.

"I adore how your body responds to me." After licking his fingers and an elated expression captured his gaze, he peeled off his jacket and shirt in one go, toed his boots off, then dropped his pants. Commando. Just how I liked it, but ... goddess. Thick and alert. And all mine.

"Come here, my little wolf." He grabbed my hand and drew me against him, his cock scorching hot against my lower stomach. "The first time I fuck you, I want to watch every bit of your pleasure on your face. Then I'm taking you from behind."

His husky voice had my insides pulsing, and I struggled to find my words, so I simply nodded.

He smiled, then placed the blanket and his coat on the ground before lying on his back. His hand reached for me and drew me closer. "First, I'm going to fully taste you because I've wanted to tongue fuck you from the first moment I laid eyes on you in Hungary. Take a seat."

Kneeling alongside his shoulders, I straddled over him, and he quickly shimmied lower. His hands gripped my hips and drew me lower, his face now buried between my legs. His mouth latched on and sucked, lightly pulling at my inner folds.

My moan spilled out, loud and wavering with pleasure. I moved in rhythm with his flicking tongue. Faster. Quicker. "Fuck. Oh, fuck."

His hands swept around my ass, prying my cheeks apart, and his fingers skimmed the length of my butt, the tantalizing sensation creating a deeper level of excitement, building up by the second. My head was fogged in rapture as Marcin devoured me.

A scream ripped past my mouth as an orgasm convulsed. Marcin never ceased his tongue fucking. He groaned his approval, and his eyes remained open, studying me.

Every part of me tingled. I burst into giggles and pulled up, but Marcin wasn't releasing his grip, holding me down as he licked ferociously.

Oh, goddess. My giggles morphed into mewls of delight, and his hands caressed up my body, taking hold of my tight nipples, squeezing them as his mouth greedily lapped me up as if I were a slippery peach. And within seconds, I floated through the second round of excitement rapturing all the way through me.

Marcin finally released me and guided me up on my knees. And while the urge to beg him for more lingered on my mind, a part of me was relieved to catch my breath. He shuffled upward through my legs until his cock hit my fire. He sat in front of me and licked his lips. "If I could, I'd be buried in you forever."

"Goddess, yes." Positioning myself over his cock, I rubbed the slickness across his tip, then lowered myself in slow motion. His girth stretched me wide—hell, he was huge— hurting me in all the right ways and filling me completely. I slid farther down on him, and Marcin's eyes rolled back, as did his head. A powerful moan rumbled from his chest, echoing in the cavern.

Then I rode him fast and furious, rodeo style. One hand in the air, the other gripping his shoulder, I pumped up and down, the slapping sound bliss to my ears.

His eyes opened, and the sexiest grin widened his mouth as his eyes settled on my bouncing breasts.

"Fuck me, babe, fuck me hard."

His hips bucked with each thrust, deepening the sensation, his cock hitting the back of my wall. Our hearts and lungs raced in unison, the purr in the back of my throat deepening. He stroked my inner walls in a way that had me teetering on the edge of cloud nine.

And Marcin studied me the whole time, his expression lost in euphoria.

He clasped my hips, bringing me to a halt, sliding himself out, and I already missed him. "Turn over and show me that sexy ass of yours."

My thighs trembled, but I did as he asked, flipping over on hands and knees, parting my legs, ready for more. The cool breeze hit my inferno.

Marcin grasped my butt and squeezed. Then his cock was at my entrance, pushing in ever so slightly, spreading me.

"Let me know if I hurt you."

"Fuck me already." My words stumbled over one another.

He rammed into me, and I screamed from the forcefulness of his thrust. Damn his strength was exhilarating. He pulled back out and jackhammered back inside over and over, stretching me, driving me insane, and then he fell into a steady rhythm, rocking back and forth.

His fingers coasted around my waist and lower and found my sensitive folds, rubbing them in a circular motion. "Come for me," he moaned, and I felt him tense. "Now."

My body responded, fully under his hypnotic sex command, and I shivered with my third orgasm. At the same time, Marcin pumped inside me, groaning so loud it would have scared off the pack of wolves outside.

"You're so beautiful." He pulled out and lay down alongside me, drawing me into his arms, against his chest, one leg curled over mine in a protective manner. "Once the shit with the battle of innocence is over, this is how I plan to spend every second with you."

My voice refused to come. All the warmth in my body had drained away. I wasn't ready to face the hard facts yet—that Levin would attack my family no matter how much Marcin protested—that I had no choice but to help my father and mate with another alpha—or that I didn't see how a future between Marcin and me could ever exist. I buried my head into his chest, the pain, the tears, everything that reminded me of the shitty life being forced on me.

CHAPTER 19

MARCIN

*L*ong shadows swept across the woods as the sun slipped behind the mountains. When we found no wolves waiting to make a snack of us outside the cave, we made a mad rush for the snowmobile.

After a speedy fifty minutes on the vehicle, we broke cover and merged onto the flat terrain behind the stone castle—my home, my prison. Grand stone towers crowned with pointy thatched roofs stood like giants overlooking the land. Crenellations ran the length of the walls, keeping enemies at bay. For me, the biggest enemies lay within the walls.

Flickering lights illuminated several of the rooms in the main building of the castle, but the windows to the great hall remained black. No late night meetings tonight, meaning no panic or problems had arisen.

Selena's soft skin still tingled under my fingers, her taste on my tongue, and her sweet smell still dancing in my head. A part of me contemplated dragging her back to the cave and never resurfacing. That could be a problem.

Her arms were wrapped around my waist as I drove the snowmobile over a slope, gunning the engine. She hadn't said a word since we left the icy waterfall palace. She snuggled tighter against my back, and I felt her warmth and breasts pressed into me.

Soon enough, we rounded the castle and pulled up in front of the shed. Selena climbed off, and I killed the engine. Swinging my leg over, I sat on the snowmobile, not ready to leave behind the day I'd spent with her.

She glanced over her shoulder at the looming castle, then back my way.

Before she could run away, I reached for her hands and drew her between my legs, embracing her with my body. "There's no rush to go inside yet."

She wrapped her arms around me, tucking her face against the side of my neck, and released a long sigh.

"What's worrying you so much?" I rubbed her arms and kissed the top of her head. "You're making this so much harder."

I pulled her back from me by the shoulders so I could see her expression. "What are you talking about?"

She licked her lips, and I couldn't deny how gorgeous she was with the last remnants of the afternoon golden sun sparkling against her tanned skin and dark hair. I ached to touch her again in a way that filled her expression with desire, to hold her perfect breasts with the ruby nipples, calling me, torturing me.

"Today was everything I'd wanted for so long," she said. "Everything our future should have been."

"And you'll have it. We'll mate, and I'll give you the world."

A slight frown creased her brow. I reached over and smoothed it with a thumb. She kissed my palm, and that simple act had my heart aching to carry her to my room right this moment, to insist on the mating ritual, to be certain she would be mine for good.

"You can trust me with anything, you know that?"

"Of course." Her response shot out a bit too fast, making me question her sincerity.

What was holding her back? In the cave, the way she cared for my wound, responded to my body ... proved her caring nature. Even the way she now held on to my hand showed I meant something to her.

Pushing her to open up about her problems wouldn't work.

If she'd intended to tell me, she'd have done so already. I had to show her how trustworthy I was, so I changed topics. "Are you excited about the battle of innocence?"

Her eyebrow cocked as if deciphering a hidden message behind my words. "I'm going to give it my best attempt and help prove Daciana's innocence since I'm representing her." She fell silent and simply watched the snow around us.

Her simple response had my instincts on high alert for so many reasons—her matter- of-fact voice sounding as if she were convincing herself rather than me, and this was her first mention to me about saving Daciana. Selena was hypercompetitive, yet she made no hint of kicking my butt or getting the boon for herself. And that simple overlook revealed her true intent.

Then Father's words came to mind about the sultan intending to claim the Hungarian land for himself. Was that the reason she now looked ready to bolt in the opposite direction?

But I couldn't let her win, not when so much was at stake. Winning the boon would not only help me finally deal with my father, but it would protect Selena and her family from certain death.

Broaching the topic could turn ugly, not to mention Selena pulling further away. Nope. I had to keep her close and make her see why me gaining the boon was best for everyone. But I had to tread carefully.

"Maybe we can work together during the challenge? Help each other?"

She shrugged. "Do you know what the battle of innocence will involve?"

"Not yet, but I'll ask Father. Though I'm guessing it might be a similar challenge to the venery."

"Hunting down another animal? Unlikely. He'll want to make this one difficult. What if he sends someone to hunt us?" Her breathing grew rapid, and she chewed on her lower lip, worry creasing her perfect brow.

"I doubt we'll be hunted. Maybe he'll have us retrieve a hidden object in the woods? Who knows with Father. The last time he set a challenge for a wulfkin, it involved trekking through the woods in search of an elusive white fox. It's not always brawn with my father, but stamina and using your head."

"Oh." The worry refused to leave her eyes.

Before I could stop myself, I leaned in and stole a kiss. "It will be all right. Don't worry." The way she responded, her hands gliding through my hair, her mouth mashing against mine, it was obvious she wrestled with her desire too. And her wolf was there again, a shiver rippling through me as mine rumbled, acknowledging we were meant to be one.

I broke our kiss, our faces remaining inches apart. "Maybe we can continue this in my room?"

She left a peck on my chin, then pulled free from my arms. "Father'll be wondering where I've been all day. Better return before he calls for a search party." She retreated, but I refused to release her hand.

"Thanks for helping me with the blood poisoning. Not many people would do that, especially the one person who was in the same challenge for a boon." Despite my intention to keep my mouth shut, I couldn't part ways without first discovering where she stood on the whole prize situation. Too much to risk on a whim.

Her expression didn't shift, but the long pause meant I'd caught her off guard. When she did speak, a soft undertone caressed her words as if whispering them made her confession less real. "I couldn't let you suffer. That would make me a horrible person."

My thumb rubbed the back of her hand, coaxing her to continue sharing. "Horrible would never be an adjective used to describe you. But you're definitely beautiful, strong, and loyal."

"Loyal?" She arched a dubious brow.

"To your family. It's an attribute I wished more wulfkin in Father's pack held." She slipped her hand away from mine. "Yeah, well, sometimes loyalty isn't all it's cracked up to be."

I studied her downturned mouth, the way the scattering of snowflakes gave her an innocent look. "Is there something you want to tell me?"

Her gaze lifted to meet mine, her lips parting and desperation behind her eyes, and for those few seconds, I was certain she'd speak up. She pushed her shoulders back and simply said, "Nothing to tell. Anyway, gotta go. See you later." She spun and took hurried steps around the corner of the stone wall, arms tucked into her pockets, head forward as she vanished from sight.

If there was ever a time to worry, her lack of conversation said it all. But I had a few more days before the final battle to get Selena to trust me and hopefully tell me what was going on with the sultan. If he was set to claim our land, it would lead to a disastrous rift between our packs with blood spilled on both sides. We'd never merge again. Any chances I had of mating Selena would vanish. Dry air rushed to my lungs as I inhaled, icing my insides.

Getting closer to Selena was a necessity, whether she liked it or not. I pushed off the snowmobile and headed to the shed to unlock the doors.

Half an hour later, I was at the top of the steps to my quarters, noticing no guards stationed near my door or anywhere along the hallway. Maybe Father finally realized I'd be fine on my own, or worse. What if he assumed I'd been kidnapped and took his army to search for me? As if that would happen, unless his intention was to use it as an excuse to begin a war.

As I reached for the door handle to my room, an escalating whizzing as quiet as a mosquito raced up behind me.

I threw myself sideways, spinning around in a crouching position, and my hands fisted.

A dagger whacked into the doorframe with a dull thud.

I plucked the object and pounced down the staircase, stuffing the weapon into my back pocket. The assassin had been there this whole time, and I hadn't sensed him or her at all. I sniffed the air. The same bitter scent hit me as on the first dagger from the poison, along with a pungent, muddy stink used to conceal the real culprit. Someone was watching me, waiting for my return.

At the landing, I scanned the passage on either side. Empty. One led directly to the dungeon, the other toward the main part of the building where the majority of wulfkin lived. If it were me, I'd steer clear of an audience and go for the quiet path with no one to spot me. So, I swung toward the dungeon where the back door headed behind the castle for quick escape.

I swung left to the back exit but found the door locked. Only a few people in the castle had keys: several of Father's guards and head council members. The assassin hadn't left this way. I spun and raced down the steps to the dungeon. No one around. With no prisoners to restrain, there was no need for guards.

Taking the steps two at a time, I headed to the door curving toward the courtyard but found it locked too, meaning the assassin had gone into the main part of the castle.

I grabbed the dagger from my pocket and noted the moon crescent etched into the hilt. The same one I'd seen on the Turkish flag in the dining hall.

An invisible hammer slammed into me. The ground swayed beneath me as a tremble clawed up my spine, and a primitive instinct, like that of a savage dracwulf, took me over. The one that demanded I charge to the sultan's room, pin him to the wall by his ears, and force him to reveal the truth.

It all came together. Selena acting strange, refusing to admit she aimed to win the boon, the sultan apparently claiming our land if he got the boon, and the attempts on my life. Had I been blind this whole time?

Back in the war room, after the first assassination attempt, she must have concealed the dagger. My insides frosted. But fuck, why the hell did she save me in the venery? If she wanted me dead, why go to such lengths to help me with the sepsis?

I sprinted down the corridor, past the stairs to my wing, and farther along another corridor lit by torches. The courtyard lay empty, so I pushed through the door to the stairway leading to the Turkish guest wing.

Upstairs, no guards, but a belly dancing song with heavy bass reverberated from the room. I knocked on the door. No response, and without thinking, I pushed the handle open, the wave of music colliding into me. A life or death situation, and I refused to wait another second if it meant confirming Selena was indeed involved.

"Hello? Anyone here?" The floor vibrated beneath my feet from the beats booming from the speakers against the far wall. Clothes were strewn across the floor. Why hadn't the Turkish servants fixed this up?

A loud thump came from the room to my right, where the door was slightly ajar.

I stalked closer and peered inside. Yeah, me spying was wrong on every plane of existence, but so was the concept of someone trying to kill me.

I peeked through the gap between the door and the frame.

Selena had her back to me as she fiddled with a black box on the bed. She opened it as if it were a suitcase. Then I saw them.

All my thoughts evaporated. A line of black daggers matching the one in my hand. The evidence was right before my eyes. I was the biggest joke in the world. Acid-like pain radiated through me and ripped at my heart.

I shifted on the spot, and the floor beneath me creaked.

Selena spun around, gripping a dagger in her hand. Her fingers curled around it. She stuffed it back into the case, slamming it shut.

"What are you doing here?" When she faced me again, her face had turned pale. "Have you never heard of privacy?"

I pushed the door open and walked inside. "What's in the case?"

"None of your business. Now leave." She stepped in front of the box, blocking it from my view.

"Not until you tell me what's going on." I stuck my hand out and opened my fist.

Her jaw dropped open as she gawked at the dagger in my palm. "Marcin." She cupped her mouth, covering a gasp. "W ... where did you get that?" Her voice broke. She wrapped her arms around her stomach, and if this were any other moment, I'd be convinced she was about to hurl.

"It barely missed me near my room. Just like the one that almost got me on your first night here." I gritted my teeth. "And this whole time, I trusted you. You lied about the weapon. You took it before I could see it, didn't you?" My words boomed, overshadowing the music. "Did you try to kill me?"

"Never. Look, I know this looks bad, but ... I can explain."

"Did you take the dagger from the weapons room?" My voice deepened.

"Yes. But it's not what you think."

While her downturned mouth called to me, I couldn't move my legs. Was this part of her act, or was it sincerity? I wasn't sure anymore. Who exactly was Selena? "So, you deny trying to have me killed?"

"I would never hurt you." Her attention dropped to the floor. "It's complicated."

"You're not convincing me. Or would you prefer I called my father? I doubt he'd be so willing to give you a chance to explain." I had zero intention of getting Father involved, unless, and that was a gigantic unless, my suspicions were true and all our lives were in danger.

"Wasn't us. I took the dagger because if anyone found it, we'd be killed without question. We hid it to avoid war. But someone stole two daggers from our box. We think it was taken as soon as we first arrived, when the servants took our bags to the room." The sorrow behind her expression was so real, and I almost fell for it.

"Convenient excuse." Blaming someone else was a guilty person's first go-to reaction.

She moved closer. "One of your wulfkin is trying to assassinate you and frame us. But killing you is the last thing on our mind. My father simply wants to stop the war between our clans." Her tone wavered, and she swallowed hard. "You have to believe me." Her soft tone implored that I listen, but everything in my head was screaming the opposite.

My head hurt. My father lied—I'd accepted that for a long time, and so did most of his pack—but I honestly considered Selena different. Had I been wrong in my judgment?

She licked her lips and squared her shoulders. "I never told you because I thought you'd tell Levin."

"So you don't trust me."

Her gaze drilled into me. "Come on, Marcin. After all the crap from our past, don't give me some bullshit that you trust me one hundred percent."

"From the first night with the dagger, I suspected you were hiding something. Now you're telling me it's someone else, and he or she is after me." My hands curled into fists.

"But you still haven't told me why your father would bring such weapons into our home when he was invited as a guest. Or why you pretend not to care about winning the boon in the battle of innocence when I've heard your father intends to claim our land for himself."

A crease formed across the bridge of her nose, but her feigning innocence wasn't fooling me. "That's—"

"Did you ever intend to mate with me, or was I an excuse?" I stepped closer, and she recoiled.

Her body shook. "Don't you dare try to blame all this on me. I've saved your life twice since we arrived. If I wanted you dead, why would I bother? Besides, I sure as hell wouldn't use poison. I'd cut your head straight off." Fierceness snapped across her expression, the kind I'd expect from a killer. "And yes, I do plan to win the boon, because that's the only fucking way I can protect my family from your monster of a father who has sworn to kill us once the challenge is over. You wouldn't understand, living here under his protection. Maybe your little haven isn't so perfect after all because someone from inside is trying to kill you. You're searching for blame in the wrong area."

So the sultan was aware of my father's threat, and yet he didn't run away. He chose to fight. The Turks were brave but stupid. Winning wouldn't achieve anything but to delay the inevitable attack Father would plan against them. I looked down at the dagger in my hand, inhaling its bitter scent. I'd smelled it before. Was it the poison locals used on arrows when hunting animals? If so, the Turks could have gained help from inside our ranks to get some. "Where did you get the poison from?"

Her eyebrows squished together. "What are you talking about?"

"Stop playing games with me. Tell me the truth."

She gave me a blank look, so either she had no idea, or she was the world's greatest

liar.

"We didn't do anything wrong."

Maybe her father organized the poison, which explained why she seemed baffled.

"You should leave." Her tone was uncertain. "But if you ever felt a morsel of love for me, then you won't tell your father about the daggers. Otherwise, you might as well kill me yourself right now." She stared at me without blinking, daring me to take her life. I'd rather die first.

My body deadened. "And will I be safe?"

She nodded, running a shaking hand through her hair. "There are no other missing daggers."

I glanced out the window at the night blanketing the mountain caps as Selena picked up the box of daggers and stuffed them into a duffle bag near the wall.

Silence was a straitjacket around us, and each breath rattled on the way down. What was I supposed to believe now when all the evidence pointed at the Turkish clan? And Selena's caring nature, was that her trying to deal with the guilt of what was coming my way?

She brushed past me, and I followed her into the main room. But then the door opened, and the sultan waltzed in. I wrapped a fist around the dagger still in my hand.

He froze the moment he saw me. "Marcin, I wasn't expecting you here." His attention shifted to Selena. "You should have told me we were expecting a guest. I would have made sure a guard was with you."

The sultan's words were strangled. My presence wasn't a welcome sight, so I headed toward the exit. "Well, I better leave you. Selena, we'll speak later."

She simply nodded and returned her attention to the sultan.

With the door shut, I stood outside in the dimly lit corridor for a moment, trying to fight off the grenade settling under my heart.

CHAPTER 20

I slumped against the window frame in our guest room, the glass at my back icy from the night.

What have I done?

My stomach ached in the way it always did when I was about to get blamed for a mistake, but me blurting the truth to Marcin was a mountain of a blunder. I'd told Marcin everything, gone against Father's wishes, and now our lives were in Marcin's hands. His accusatory stare refused to leave my mind, along with the torment behind his voice, just as it had been years ago in Turkey, after I'd been shot with an arrow. Since arriving in Hungary, my attraction to him had intensified, my wolf insisted he was ours, but I never should have let myself get close. Would he now hate me forever?

"Selena? Are you even listening to me?" Father's voice pierced my thoughts as he marched toward his room. "Let's talk in here. Less chance of anyone hearing us."

I stumbled through the fog in my head and followed. Once inside, he shut the door behind me, and I glanced at the indent in the bed where his box of daggers had been minutes earlier. The ones Marcin had seen, but that wasn't the problem, him almost being killed was an issue. He'd been the target all along as I suspected, but now he was well aware the weapons belonged to us.

Before I told my father anything, I had to be convinced Marcin wouldn't confess to Levin. Otherwise, our packs back home were as good as dead once Levin declared war and attacked us. Father would probably murder me. Thank the moon I had a couple more days before the challenge to convince Marcin of our innocence. I rubbed my temples from the banging inside my skull. My heart beat so fast the tears were welling behind my eyes because I couldn't think of a way to make Marcin remain part of my future. I shouldn't care because I'd be forced to return home after this, but damn it, I cared. I'd let him into my life again, and now it killed me that so much drama was driving us apart.

"I've done it." Father patted down his jacket and lifted his chin, wearing a proud expression. "I got Levin to agree to the challenge being tomorrow morning."

"What?" No! My knees quivered, and I sagged on the edge of the bed, ready for the world to swallow me whole. I couldn't handle any more surprises.

"Aren't you happy?" He patted my shoulder. "Marcin should still be slow from his injury, giving you the perfect opportunity to win the boon."

The smile radiating from Father made me feel like the worst person in the world. I couldn't bring myself to tell him the truth. I was too gutless to see his fallen expression, to have him accuse me of killing our family and our packs.

"What's wrong?" His brow creased. "This is what we need."

My response was stuck to the roof of my mouth, sticky and too thick to spit out, so I nodded. I'd never feel happiness again, not when my insides were twisted into a knot. All I could think about was collapsing in on myself and hiding. This new revelation meant only one thing. Speak with Marcin and get this sorted, even if it took all night. I'd make him see our situation. Going into the battle of innocence with us feuding wasn't the answer, especially without knowing where he stood or what he'd told Levin.

"Anyway," Father continued. "Where have you been? Was Aisha with you?"

I shrugged. "No, you were keeping an eye on her."

"She told me she was with you." The way he stared at me had me leaning in close, and then his voice boomed. "Where in the moon is she?"

I shook my head, convinced she was somewhere taking more photos of her hands and feet.

"I'll go search the castle. I'll find her." Up on my feet, I hurried from the room.

"Bring her to me. Immediately."

I sighed and bolted into the hallway, not needing this crap right now. Though, a detour to Marcin's room wouldn't hurt. Quickly, I moved through the stone corridors where candles painted disfigured silhouettes across the walls.

Outside his door, I halted. My stomach stirred. Had he told his father about the daggers? If he had, he'd have double the protection watching over him, but there wasn't a guard in sight.

I knocked on the door with urgency. "Marcin, it's me."

No response.

I banged my fist louder. When he didn't answer, I tried the door handle. Locked. I sprinted down the steps and headed straight for Levin's wing. Sure, it'd be swarming with guards, but I only intended to walk past and try to spot Marcin. Once I reached Levin's quarters, only a handful of guards were there. I strolled past them casually, their gazes cutting into me. No panic in their expressions and no loud voices behind the closed door to their backs.

Okay, maybe I overreacted, so I followed the circular corridor that made a loop through the castle. Time to find my sister and get my father to chill.

"Selena?" a man's voice called from the passage behind me.

I glanced over my shoulder and saw Father's guard, Rafa, running toward me, his face grim.

"What's going on?"

"Your father asked me to fetch you." He panted. "Something's happened to Aisha."

Dread rippled through me. "W ... What happened?" Had Levin taken her for hostage?

Had someone hurt her? I pushed past Rafa and bolted toward our wing, ignoring the frowning wulfkin I passed, and barged inside to find Father pacing back and forth, his eyes rubbed raw.

"Where's Aisha?" My words blurted out as I ran to our room, shoving the dracwulves back inside when I didn't find her.

Father faced me, his cheeks blotchy with redness, the same look he gave me when he seethed. "She's gone."

"What do you mean, gone?" A chilling menace burrowed deeper under my flesh, savaging my nerves.

He huffed and shook his head, sending strands of white hair across his head. His voice morphed to a murmur. "Rafa told me he spoke with a Hungarian guard who saw her leaving the grounds earlier today but didn't think anything of it."

"Maybe she went exploring?"

"The nearest town is hours away on foot."

I swept the room, noting the mess of clothes on the floor. Aisha trying to find an outfit to wear in a rush. More garments had been strewn all over her room too. "She's left too many clothes behind to run away. She'll be back." This wasn't like her one bit, yet the anxiety bubbling in my chest said otherwise. "Let's wait a while before we panic." I chewed on my lower lip, then fished out my cell and called her. After five rings, it went to message.

"Hey, it's me. Call me back ASAP." I followed it with a text.

Father paced the length of the room and back, one hand holding the side of his face. "If Levin has hurt Aisha, I'll rip him apart with my bare hands." His voice trembled with rage.

With no response on my cell, which was unlike Aisha since she had the phone glued to her palm, I tapped open Twitter and typed in her handle. Her last post was a few minutes ago. No words, just an image of her hand, stretched out and covered in swirly henna patterns. The background was blurred, but I could sort of make out a building and a sign. I enlarged the photo, but it only pixelated it worse. Next to her was a blur of someone standing close, but not much else. Well, she clearly wasn't in danger.

"What is it?" Father glanced over my shoulder.

In the right hand corner of the photo, bright spotlights revealed a set of train tracks fading into the distance, and then it hit me like a battle-ax to the stomach. "She's at a train station."

"Where the bastard is she going?"

"I'll get her back."

"I'm coming too, so I can wring her neck. If she's posting photos, then she's not in any trouble. At least not until I get through with her." He headed for the door. "I'm sure Levin wouldn't mind lending us a car."

Father's presence would quickly turn the situation from bad to terrible, and if Aisha was running away, he was the last person she'd want to confront. I had to first discover what was going on. "Better if I go on alone. How would it look to Levin if you left the grounds in a rush? Let's not draw attention to ourselves." *Yep, put attention on Levin's suspicions instead.*

His mouth warped into a frown. "Fine, but be quick. And keep me posted." "Of course." It seemed I couldn't catch a break today.

I slammed the door to the green Volvo and sprinted across the train station parking lot, streetlights illuminating the night. A frozen wind blasted against me. Walking past a cluster of young boys, talking loudly, and an elderly woman with a walking stick, I finally made it onto the platform. People dotted the area, and I pushed past another woman. Why were so many people out tonight? Scanning the area ahead and behind me showed no Aisha.

I'd only found one train station on phone maps nearby, so it had to be this one. Unless I'd missed a train and she'd already left.

Then Father would go AWOL and ... I couldn't ponder the consequences. I brushed past more people, their perspiration smells filling my senses. Still no sign of Aisha. I pulled my phone out and dialed her number again. She might not be answering, but if she was in the vicinity, I might hear her phone ring.

I lowered the phone, listening. Nothing at first, then the beat of a belly dancing tune echoed from across the train tracks, on the other platform. I sidestepped a young couple for a better vantage and spotted my sister staring at her phone, then tucking it into her pocket.

A guy stepped up alongside her, wrapping an arm around her waist, drawing her closer.

Zeki!

Lifting her chin, she pressed her lips to his. My legs weakened beneath me at the sight of her with Father's captain of the guards. How could I not have known they were an item? Actually, the signs were there, always together, whispering, laughing. Even back in Turkey, they'd been inseparable. I put it down to her having a crush on a wulfkin eight years her elder. I thought back to my spotting Zeki handing a parcel to a Hungarian guard —I was wrong about thinking he was betraying us. He'd probably paid for transport into town.

Father would kill them both if he knew. That would explain why they ran away, but this couldn't have come at a worse possible time. And most likely in their eyes, the most opportune one.

I raced toward the steps leading to an overhead bridge and the other platform. Then a hoot blared and a rattling train approached on Aisha's side. She and Zeki were hurrying forward with the rest of the crowd.

Fuck no.

I shoved past a guy and sprinted up the steps as the train screeched to a halt. The conductor's Hungarian words blared from the speakers. I shot across the bridge and flew down the stairs as everyone streamed inside the train cars, Aisha and Zeki included.

"Aisha," I called out, but she didn't hear me.

Jumping down on the platform with a thump, the heavy odor of oil and rotten stench of train brakes filled my nostrils. I hurled myself into their train car. The doors slammed shut behind me.

Pressed against bodies, I held on to the handle overhead as

the train lurched forward before I ended up in someone's lap. Then I lifted myself on tiptoes and surveyed the area. There in the corner, I spotted Zeki's dark, sweeping hair, and heard Aisha's giggles.

I shoved through the muddle of bodies and stepped out near the back of the car where Aisha snuggled into Zeki's chest, her arms wrapped around his waist. He had one hand around her back, the other holding the pole to keep them upright.

Zeki spotted me first, and an incredulous stare skimmed across his eyes. "Selena."

Aisha's head jolted in my direction, her eyes wide, her body flinching away from Zeki as if she'd been electrocuted.

"What are you doing here?" she asked. The intensity behind her eyes was painful. Her posture was stiff, and her words flew free. "You can't make me go back. I refuse to be mated. I want to be with Zeki."

"Why didn't you speak to me first? I could have helped you. Now Father's freaking out about you running away."

She huffed and pinched her lips.

"And what about you, Zeki? You're abandoning us at a time Father depends on you the most."

He swallowed hard and lowered his gaze to Aisha, then back at me. "This was our only chance to escape and for no one to find us again. Once we go home, she'd be sold off, but I won't let anyone hurt her. You of all people should understand."

Everything I'd done recently was to protect Aisha from Father, so how could I not sense their urgency for freedom.

Aisha glued herself against Zeki, her arms holding on to him with such desperation that my throat choked. I remember feeling that much in love once with Marcin in Turkey. Heck, I felt it earlier today. It seemed as if the world could pass us by, but as long as we were together, nothing else mattered. And I wanted that back too.

"Goddess, of course, I understand." I collapsed into an empty seat behind Aisha. How the shit was I going to fix this? Technically, the Hungarians wouldn't be asking too many questions if they didn't see Aisha again, but Zeki was a different matter since he was always by father's side when in the company of Levin.

Aisha squeezed in alongside me and whispered, "Zeki is my soul wolf. We've mated without anyone knowing. Our wolves are connected. Please, Selena, just tell Father you didn't find us. I'll find a way to contact you once we settle down."

I lowered my voice. "News will get back to Father. Where will you hide?"

"There are remote packs with a few members in the forests across Europe. I'm sure we can join them. Plus, Zeki is an amazing warrior." Her smile beamed as she glanced over at him, the fighter who wore a grim expression.

"Father doesn't know you've left," I said, staring at Zeki, his shoulders slouched. Regardless of what Aisha said, no pack welcomed new members easily, and most would attack before asking questions.

"When I find a safe place for Aisha, I'll return to help the sultan, say my farewell, and take my pack with me to start a new life with Aisha by my side."

"He'll put two and two together before that. Come back with me. I can help you with a more sensible plan."

"No." Aisha shook her head, her bottom lip between her teeth. "I'd rather die before I go be sold off."

"You tell her, girl. Never be forced into anything," an older woman with wild, gray hair a few seats down chimed in. Wonderful, we had an interactive audience.

"Aisha, the battle of innocence is tomorrow." I wanted to say I couldn't do it without her support, but that was me being selfish. "Father will need Zeki there when the challenge is over. We can't appear weak. Don't give Levin any more reason to turn against us."

"But how are we meant to leave then?" Her expression crumbled when her gaze swept to Zeki.

I took her hand in mine. "You have my word that I'll help you leave once the challenge is over. I'll distract him. I don't know how, but I promise." How could I not? If someone had offered me this opportunity when Marcin and I intended to run away, I would have jumped at it within a heartbeat. Maybe it wasn't too late for Aisha to have what I couldn't.

Aisha leaned against me. "Yes, I trust you." She took Zeki's hand, drawing him closer. "What do you think?"

He rubbed his mouth, taking a long pause before responding. "Okay, we go back, but the moment the challenge is over, we leave."

"All right," I said, my response quick, because all I could take was one problem at a time. Getting the boon was priority. Well, maybe speaking to Marcin tonight. Then I'd deal with Aisha and Zeki.

The lady listening to us sighed loudly. "Girl, if I were you, I wouldn't go back." Aisha leaned to face her. "Yeah, well, I'll do anything for my sister."

CHAPTER 21

MARCIN

Snow squished beneath my boots as I marched toward the shed outside the castle walls. Clearing my head was crucial. I yearned to release my wolf and run through the forest, but I needed to reserve energy for tomorrow, so the snowmobile was the next best thing to getting away from everyone and all the fuckin' hell going on here.

A tornado thundered through my veins, and every rational thought had fled, replaced by a sense of betrayal. Selena's story made sense, but her excuse wasn't sitting right with me. The Turkish daggers, the second assassination attempt on me, they all supported her argument, yet I couldn't bring myself to believe her. And if I hadn't caught her today, would she have ever told me the truth, or was I the poor sucker who was being used? All I wanted was the truth.

Outside the shed, the night was too silent, and the invisible noose around my neck hardened. The trees didn't stir, a heavy moon hung overhead, and silver dots speckled the heavens like bullets. Instead of a gorgeous night, it should be blasting down with hail and denting everything in its wake. My life sure was fucked. Tomorrow was the battle of innocence. Father had said the sultan insisted we bring it forward, and if it weren't for Selena helping me with my injury, I'd stand no chance of winning. Obviously, the sultan intended for me to participate while still wounded, giving Selena every chance to win the boon.

Maybe Father was right all along. The sultan intended to use the boon to claim our land as his, so was Selena trying to stop it by helping me heal? Or was it her guilt assisting me?

If she won, Father would open up all-out war. Wulfkin would die. He'd target the sultan and his daughters first, and I'd stand no chance at protecting them. Why would they be so stupid to claim this land?

I only saw one solution. Win the boon, no matter the cost. Firstly, I'd set my brother and Daciana free on their own land. Then I'd challenge my father on the basis that he was unfit to continue leading with his insistence of wulfkin paying for their alpha's actions. The council would be forced to make a move instead of hiding in the shadows like cowards.

Options were running out, and so was my patience. Enough of everyone jerking me around. This shit ended now. But I had no idea what Father was planning tomorrow. Each time I'd broached the topic with him, he brushed me off. For the first time, I realized what a mistake it was that I hadn't pushed the topic. If I intended to win, I should know what was coming my way. *Idiot.*

I reached for the lock on the shed door when male voices reached me. They came from around the back entrance to the castle.

Unable to decipher the words or who spoke them, I listened anyway. With the absence of wind, their scent remained concealed, so I crept toward the castle through the fresh bed of snow. I glanced around the corner and spotted Father and the sultan talking beneath a spotlight near the metal doors leading into the castle.

They turned in my direction in unison.

"Stop skulking, Marcin." Father's voice was loud and filled with sarcasm.

I stepped out and approached the Varlac leaders.

"Then it's agreed." The sultan held out his hand, and Father accepted his handshake.

"Agreed."

The sultan glanced my way as he broke the handshake, tightness pulled beneath his eyes, and his twisted lips screamed regret. "Good night, Marcin."

Once the sultan had returned to the castle, I turned to Father, the hairs on my arms standing on end. "What's going on?"

"Nothing to bother yourself with." He slapped my shoulder and guided me toward the castle. "You focus on winning tomorrow."

"What were you and the sultan talking about just then?"

"When you're a father one day, you'll understand that sometimes sacrifices must be made, even if your family will hate you for it."

I stopped in my tracks, a few paces from the door, and faced him. "What have you done?"

He broke into a deep chuckle and patted my shoulder again as if I were his loyal dog.

"Absolutely nothing. I'm simply helping out another father."

I came up short on what the sultan could possibly have done that required Father's help. Whatever it was, it had my nerves jumping because when Varlac leaders agreed on something, it couldn't be beneficial for anyone else.

"Well, you and the sultan are getting along now. Maybe there'll be no problems if, let's say, Selena wins the boon." I held my breath, watching for his response.

He cut me a caustic look, the kind that promised death, and his voice dipped into a guttural growl. "I did not raise you to be a defeatist, or have you let that bitch get into your head?"

Oh, there was my real father, the one who tainted everything he touched with spite.

"I'm just saying it would benefit both clans if you and the sultan collaborate instead of fight."

His cold-pebbled eyes didn't flinch. "I can see what you're doing. Stop fishing and focus on gaining the boon so you don't force me to give special treatment to Selena." His tone swelled with a scathing inflexion when he said the words *special treat-*

ment, and the way the corners of his thin lips curled upward when he mentioned Selena left my arms covered in pinpricks.

CHAPTER 22

Outside our guest room window, the morning sun rose from behind the mountains, the snow glinting beneath its glow, and not a single cloud marred the sky. Considering the battle of innocence was today, everything felt surreal, too picture perfect for such an occasion.

"Our lives rest with you, Selena." A dark tone underlined Father's words, the kind he used when he readied to attack an enemy. No emotions, just taking action and ready to die if that was what it took. Was I ready to do the same?

"I've had to pull massive strings to change the challenge to today and give you an advantage over Marcin. Don't waste my efforts."

When I turned to face Father, my throat morphed into a desert. He would be shattered to uncover that I had no such advantage, that I'd insisted to Barka to create an antidote brew for Marcin or, worse yet, had told him about the poisonous daggers. Following last night's mix-up with Aisha running away, I spent hours defending her to Father, who exploded and ranted nonstop. We didn't mention Zeki's involvement as that would only piss off Father worse. But no matter what I said, he wasn't calming down or letting me leave the room. So much for my plan to speak with Marcin to coax him into understanding that we had nothing to do with the assassination attempts against him. That idea went to shit as I remained locked in my room with Aisha.

So, I was going blindly into battle.

Father patted my shoulder and nudged me toward the door. "We should head downstairs. They'll be waiting." He glanced over at Aisha, who remained sheepishly silent, kneeling in front of the fireplace. Whatever happened today, I had to help her with Zeki. Images of the way she clung tight to him on the train lodged in my thoughts, along with the similarity of my situation nine years ago. Me. Marcin. The untamable beat of my heart, the anticipation swirling in the pit of my stomach, gripping Marcin's hand so hard it hurt ... none of it mattered. Fate had different intentions for me; maybe it wasn't too late for Aisha to have a fairy-tale ending.

Father opened the door, and Aisha got up.

Okay, time to do this. I marched past him into the corridor.

"Aisha," he said, "I'd like you to remain here."

"What? No way!"

"Zeki," Father called out. "Make sure she doesn't leave the room. Assign two guards, then join us downstairs."

I stepped back, but Father blocked my passage, shaking his head and giving me a look that insisted we leave my sister behind.

"Baba, please don't leave me here. I'm sorry about yesterday. I want to support Selena."

I caught her gaze above Father's shoulder, but the moment Zeki stepped into the room, he shut the door behind him.

"Selena, let's go." Father waited for me to start moving.

Soon enough, we were downstairs. We strolled the hallway in silence at first, and the morning icy breeze circled around us from the open doorway farther ahead.

"What didn't you want Aisha to see?"

"Selena," Father's voice filtered from behind me.

He paused and rubbed a hand across his mouth. "Sometimes we have to do things that we don't want, but it's about the greater good. Protecting our family. No matter what you see when we head outside, remember that, please."

"What did you do?"

"What I had to. And you need to act like a Varlac's daughter, not an emotional child." Father took me into an embrace. His warmth washed away the coldness from outside, although doubt, and now fear, kept badgering me. What was going to happen outside? I shut my eyes and, for those few seconds, pretended we were back home on the balcony overlooking the sea and feeling like nothing could ever touch us. Father's protection would keep away the dark, the monsters, the hurt.

He broke away first. "Let's show them what we're made of."

My voice vanished, so I resumed our long trek down the dim corridor. Before long, we emerged into the courtyard, and I squinted until my eyes adjusted to the brightness.

We crossed the snowy yard and headed straight for the grand iron doors leading us outside the castle grounds. Shivers ran down my arms, my insides looping into knots.

Father glanced over and nodded. "Stay strong, always."

A cluster of wulfkin, maybe eighty or more, huddled closer to the line of trees to our left, their chatter as ear piercing as cicadas. Upon our approach, the crowd parted. Ahead, Levin stood on a wide stump. Several feet away, Marcin was in deep conversation with his second-in-command.

I passed Irmak, his eyes almost apologetic, and he dropped his gaze. Was he the assassin, or was he simply disgruntled for being left here by Father? Mental note to ask Father to take him home after the challenge, but right now, I struggled with the immense presage that all our days here were short lived. I offered him a smile and kept going.

Once we broke free from the group of spectators, my sights swept to Marcin. He had his back to us. His stiff posture and fisted hands by his side had goose bumps littering my arms. Why was he so upset? The past week had drawn us closer, but when he glanced my way, it suddenly seemed as if he were miles away, on another continent. I wasn't sure if the distance was because of him or me.

A guttural howl sliced through the air from behind me.

I snapped around, my gaze landing on Klaus and Grit about twenty feet away, each chained to a monstrous pine tree.

My heart rattled. I'd forgotten how to breathe.

Our pets tugged against the restraints around their necks, snarling in our direction, frothing at the mouths. My insides convulsed as Klaus's nose creased, his fangs exposed, staring our way. He released a thunderous growl, and Grit followed suit. Our childhood pets, the animals we'd spent years playing and running in the woods with, now fought restraints, the chains clanging, the grating of iron against wood a distressed sound.

The fire burning through my insides could ignite the entire Hungarian forest. Father's words about staying strong flooded my mind, and how he was forced into this. Not to mention keeping Aisha at bay. Because they were using our pets for the battle of innocence. Was it because Aisha ran away yesterday?

Fur spurred down Grit's spine, and he paced back and forth, his chains clanging. The tree shook with each thrust. The only way they'd behave this way was if they were drugged.

The world in front of me blurred, and Marcin was now by my side. When had he moved? "I'm so sorry." His tone crackled. "I tried to stop him this morning."

I pushed past Marcin and approached my father. "How could you?" I yelled. "You said Klaus and Grit were in another room as punishment for Aisha's actions."

He raised his chin as if showing emotions in front of the Hungarians would make him appear less of a Varlac leader. Well, in that moment, I'd just lost a father.

Gripping my arm, he lowered his voice. "Stay strong. Don't give him a show."

Levin chuckled softly in the distance. Obviously, our agony was his amusement, and right then, I wished I had one of the poisoned daggers because I'd drive it into his heart with my bare hands.

Marcin marched toward Levin. His voice resonated, but his words were lost in the darkness spiraling inside my head.

Father's words were barely a whisper in my ear. "It was the trade-off to stop Levin from imposing the full law against us for bringing dracwulves onto his territory even though he gave his approval, and to get the challenge brought forward. Our lives are at stake."

Wulfkin surrounded us in a semicircle, and I bet my life if Levin gave the word, they'd attack us without hesitation. The reality of our grim situation hammered into me. We were cornered, no escape. All I could picture was me fighting for our lives, wondering who'd take my side. Marcin?

I stared at Levin, who stood with a conceited expression stretching his lips. Chin lifted and head back, he wore a cocky smile I'd gladly rip off his face.

Everything rested with me, and I had to make Marcin realize that me winning was the only way for my family to survive.

"Hello and welcome." Levin's voice boomed across the wide clearing. Even the dracwulves silenced. The monster from my nightmares stood on top of his tree stump, inspecting everyone with his beady eyes. Marcin inched closer to his second-in-command, hushing his whispers.

Just the sound of Levin's voice had loathing leeching through my veins, and with each passing second, I contemplated finishing him before I left for Turkey. He was a horrendous wulfkin who had no right to lead anyone, let alone take another gulp of air.

"Today is a ceremonial day to remember. We're holding the battle of innocence, as suggested by our reputable guest, Varlac Sultan Boran." Levin didn't even attempt to conceal the hatred in his voice.

Yep, a full out war had commenced under the guise of fake politeness and rules that apparently meant jack when it came to the European Varlac.

"I call on our two champions. Marcin and Selena."

My body kept shaking, but I forced one leg out in front of the other. Soon, I stood alongside Levin. Marcin was on his other side. The great expanse of wulfkin in front of us wore a cocktail of expressions from confusion to pity to anger. They had no idea who the real me was, only what they'd heard from the lips of a liar, and yet they apparently judged me.

At the edge of the group, Father glanced my way with a slight nod, the one that said to keep following the rules, to keep being a puppet. But an inferno roared out of control through my chest, and every molecule of my body trembled with the temptation to drag Levin from his platform and rip his heart out.

The dracwulves' snarls bled into the breeze. I fisted my hands. *I can do this. I can do this. Don't give Levin the satisfaction.*

"The rules are simple," he continued. "These abominations, the dracwulves, will be released into the wild for our champions to hunt and bring back, preferably dead. Their heads will suffice." I heard the smirk in his voice.

"Are you mentally ill?" I couldn't hold back my tongue as I faced Levin. "You're purposefully releasing two drugged dracwulves into your woods. They'll kill everything in their paths. Humans included, if they reach the nearest town."

He didn't even glance my way but spoke louder. "Marcin will represent Enre. Selena will stand for Daciana. Come back with a dracwulf, and the wulfkin you represent will be innocent. Fail and they will face death. And remember, the first champion to bring back a dracwulf will claim the boon." He clapped loudly. "Nice and simple. Oh, and the dracwulves have been given a shot to help bring out their true nature."

Bastard. My insides battled between the terror of facing a wild dracwulf and not harming my pets.

"Releasing wild dracwulves into the woods goes against your own rules," Marcin said. "You have to stop this now."

Levin waved at a handful of guards, dressed in long, black coats with the iron wolf emblem on their upper sleeve. They approached the dracwulves. One of them lifted a rifle and released a round into the air.

Klaus and Grit scampered behind their trees, the chains holding them back from bolting.

The mass of wulfkin stepped farther away, almost in unison. I stopped myself from charging the guards and using the weapons on them instead.

My insides were wrapped and broken at the shots.

Another round was released, the thud echoing around us like an erupting volcano, spitting embers and lava into the air.

The group of guards closed in on the dracwulves as they pulled against their restraints. Two wulfkin crept closer and fiddled with the large iron locks, unlatching them. The guards stood in a semicircle, a barricade between us and my former pets.

Several spectators retreated toward the castle in a wild rush.

Three more shots were fired into the air.

Grit scampered the quickest, the chains unraveling from around his neck as he sprinted

away. My pet, Klaus, was free too, but he didn't move. He stood motionless, his gaze finding me between two guards. A silent chill crept along my spine, the subtle benediction of fear.

Wild dracwulves were notorious hunters and never forgot who harmed them. In this case, I'd let them down and allowed Levin to chain them up like beasts. Dracwulves always returned for vengeance. Always. But I prayed our pets were different and remembered me, even under the influence of drugs.

Klaus released a blood-curdling howl, the kind that raised the hairs on my arms. I took a step backward.

He turned and bolted deep into the woods, blending into the shadows.

Goddess, please have him remember the good times we'd spent, the treats I'd given him, when he'd slept on my bed, or I'd soon be hunted for letting him down and allowing someone to hurt him.

My lungs contracted painfully. Each exhale escaped in gasps.

No one else said a word.

"Well, I did say today was going to be a momentous day." Levin laughed as only a madman who'd just unleashed demons into the world could. "But right now, this challenge is a bit too easy for our challengers."

It was? What was he on?

"Father, what are you doing?" Marcin's protest was ignored, along with any common sense it seemed.

"Marcin and Selena will be given a serum, making it impossible to transform into their wolf forms for the next three days."

My father stepped out from the crowd. "You've gone too far now, Emperor. I won't abide by this."

"This wasn't part of the rules," I blurted.

"Tsk, tsk. Let me finish." Levin wiggled a finger at me.

I was inches from reaching out and snapping it in half.

"As I was saying—"

"Enough," my father boomed. "No more will be said. This is a hard enough challenge.

You will not impose additional rules."

Levin huffed. "Those dracwulves are still young, and what fun would this be if we made it too easy for our entrants?" He raised his head and continued. "One more thing— "Bullshit," Marcin's voice exploded. "We are here to help prove innocence, not be judged ourselves. You've gone too far."

Levin waved a hand, and several guards stepped closer. "Enough fuckin' interruptions.

These are my rules, and you will listen. The champions have three days to capture their dracwulves. Otherwise, their representatives will be found guilty, along with the champions. All will be punished accordingly."

My father started pacing. "I don't accept these terms. You should have discussed this with me first."

Levin jumped down from his pedestal and stalked closed. "Dear Sultan, this is my land and my laws. Besides, you requested an early challenge. What's wrong with upping the stakes a bit? Surely, your ancestors would have approved. Or have you grown weak in your old age?"

Father's face reddened, but Zeki stepped alongside him. "We should've been aware of the punishment before the challenge."

"Does it matter?" Levin asked. "I want to make sure everyone participating takes it seriously." He approached Marcin and clapped a hard hand to his back. "Isn't that right, son?"

Then he turned to the crowd. "And may the best wulfkin win the boon."

CHAPTER 23

MARCIN

Fuck control. Releasing my wolf and lunging for Father would give me the ultimate satisfaction. He'd gone too far. Everything he touched always turned to shit, and this had become fuckin' absurd. Pacing back and forth between two trees wasn't helping my charging adrenaline or my wolf who shoved against my insides, demanding release and retribution.

"Marcin." Barka, our medic, motioned me toward her with a curt wave of her hand. I trotted closer, my pulse bouncing beneath my veins, and everything around me blurred from the rage pumping through me. Baka had been practicing the art of treating wulfkin since before my birth, but her methods weren't always the best, like the misdiagnosis of my blood poisoning. Yet when it came to potions, she was a magician. Maybe she'd entered the wrong profession.

A guard approached and patted me down, each touch a hard strike.

I caught his sinister grin, snatched his wrist, and shoved him away. "Enough. I'm not hiding anything."

He shouted, "Marcin's clean."

What the fuck was I going to sneak into the race?

Barka rolled up my sleeve, and I felt the piercing syringe sliding into my arm—a concoction of the blood they'd taken from me minutes earlier and a serum to temporarily pacify my wolf. A buzz zipped through me, deadening the sensation in my chest, in my stomach. My pulse halted, and a surge of panic gripped me. I couldn't breathe. My lungs seized. I smacked a fist into my chest and recoiled, convinced I would die from suffocation before the tournament even started. Was this Father's plan? Then as if a window had been opened, a gush of air flooded me, and I gulped for the next inhale.

The warmth and strength of my wolf were gone, replaced by emptiness. Darkness. And suddenly I felt less of a wulfkin. *Only three days*, I kept reminding myself.

Ten feet away, Father smirked my way, but behind his dead eyes was a clear threat. My suspicions darted to the council. Had Tibor or another told Father of my plans? I searched the field behind the castle—wulfkin were conversing in quiet whispers, a few exchanging what I guessed was money. The gamble on who would win had commenced.

Selena approached Barka and received her injection. The tightness at the corners of her mouth had zero to do with the pain, especially with the death glare she hurled toward my father. Her lips were flat lines, and I worried what state of mind she embraced. Losing it now wasn't a smart decision, though I suspected it was Father's intention. Throw us off our game, especially Selena.

I reached over and took her hand in mine. "Don't let him get to you."

She nodded, obviously not trusting her voice, trembling against my touch. Her tight- set jaw revealed how close to the edge of flipping out she was, similar to the wulfkin I'd trained, the ones I'd pushed to breaking point until they revealed their true nature—fight or flight.

I squeezed her hand lightly, giving her something else to focus on rather than the anger that overwhelmed us both. "Prove my father wrong. Show him how amazing you are."

Her brow twisted into a tangle of lines; then she slipped her hand free. Selena's mouth parted, but no words came. She dropped her gaze, catching her breath.

All the encouraging words in the world meant crap if she wasn't ready to accept them. And I couldn't blame her. Without her wolf, her old hip injury slowed her down, as I'd seen back in the venery. Add her internal struggle about hunting her own pets, and she'd make rash decisions. When Father had killed Enre's pet fox, Enre withdrew and had never been the same. Father's actions had snapped his mind. And Selena didn't deserve to live with such torture and resentment.

"Selena," I whispered. "We're in this together."

She turned to face me, the edges of her mouth curling upward. Behind her, I spotted Tibor, the head councilman, watching the circus theatrics taking place. He wouldn't meet my gaze, but rather shook his head and vanished into the horde of wulfkin.

I stepped around Selena to chase after him and make him face the consequences of his passivity, but a firm hand pressed down on my shoulder from behind, drawing me back.

"Marcin, it's time." Father nudged me to face him, then drew me away from the group by an elbow to a small patch of woods with no one in earshot.

When he spoke, his words were barely audible. "I know you don't trust me, but sometimes," he said, glancing at the wulfkin in the distance, then at me, "trust is all we have. I believe you will do the right thing, and you need to know I'm doing the right thing too. Even if it doesn't seem so."

Placing my faith in Father was as idiotic as believing a wild dracwulf wouldn't rip my heart out. His rules were to slow down Selena, to ensure I won, to give him his victory. That was what mattered.

Fuck him. I wasn't playing his game now or ever, and once this ridiculous carnival was over, I would thrust him aside, even if it meant using my fists and teeth. His reign would end. But first I had to protect Selena and ensure her family was safe, along with my brother and Daciana, I needed to win the boon. I had to show the council, the sultan, my father, everyone ... that I could play by the rules when it mattered.

Father brushed past me and called out, "Let the games start."

His announcement sparked a frenzy of wulfkin closing in behind us in a semicircle. Conversations and whispers escalated like a plague of locusts.

Selena was by my side, and despite the nerves biting into my calmness, I knew there would be no going back.

We were guided to a band of trees where shadows shifted and dark patches could easily conceal a dracwulf. Shivers wrapped around my spine, twisting and pulling. Snow cascaded quickly now. I inhaled, but the depth of my smelling sense was gone. Pine scents tickled my nostrils. I couldn't sniff out the dracwulves. I didn't have my wolf's strength, but I'd trained in human form for years. I'd use that experience to my advantage. Whatever it took, I'd win the boon. Not for Father, but to protect those who meant the world to me, to make up for my mistakes in the past.

A guard pushed a backpack into my hands and shoved one toward Selena. "Water, a blade, a cigarette lighter, snacks, and blanket."

Next to me, Selena's focus was straight ahead, lost in the zone. Exactly where I had to be. *Get it together, man.*

I shook myself, stomped the ground with my boots to drive away the cold. The dracwulves had bolted dead straight, but my plan was to stay close to Selena. These were her pets, and she would be more familiar with their behavior than anyone. Besides, I suspected they might seek her out, especially with the way the larger dracwulf had stared at her in disbelief. And I planned to be there for my chance to win.

Show time.

The piercing trumpet blared, and Selena took off. I lunged after her, my legs pumping furiously, snow grinding beneath my boots. The explosion of cheers and voices faded behind me. None of it mattered. Not when I had a dracwulf to hunt.

The cold wind and snowflakes slammed against me.

Save Selena. Save her family. Save my brother and Daciana. Save all wulfkin. Nothing like having the world on my shoulders. If not me, who else would accept the challenge and confront Father?

I careened around an enormous tree, jumped over the roots sticking out of the snow like giants' knees, and bolted behind Selena. No stopping. If Selena hadn't helped me with my leg and the blood poisoning, no way would I be able to keep up this momentum. Now I had enough energy to run circles around the world.

Paw prints dotted the soft snow around us. The dracwulves had definitely gone this way.

We'd sprinted for at least twenty minutes when Selena finally slowed her pace, her limp worsening. Then near an embankment, overlooking the great expanse of the snow coated forest, she came to a dead stop, hands on knees and gasping for air.

I skidded to a stop, noting the end of the prints. After retracing my steps a few paces, I found them again, but with the freshly falling snow, we were losing the tracks fast.

Sweat rolled down my back despite the freezing air as I marched toward Selena.

"Where would a dracwulf go?"

She reached into her backpack and grabbed her water bottle, taking several gulps.

"Why are you following me?"

"To stare at your cute butt."

Her cheeks glowed red and sweat bubbled across her brow, but behind her eyes, a fire was blazing. The last time I'd seen her this way, I was buried deep inside her. I'd prefer to relive that moment over anything else in this life.

"I'm guessing the dracwulves would stick together, so it only makes sense we do the same," I said. And pets or no, I would stay to protect her any way I could.

Selena stuffed the bottle into her bag and surveyed the terrain. "I have no idea where Klaus and Grit would go. They've never been in the wild." She headed right, along the top ridge of the hill.

I spotted white fur on a shrub and followed her. "So they're unpredictable. Even more reason for us to band together."

She spun to face me, her tone sober. "Don't waste your time. The boon is mine."

Despite her warped lips, my initial instinct insisted I drag her into my arms, kiss away the anger, and make her see that I wasn't going anywhere. Whether she accepted it or not, I planned to win the boon to save her life.

I marched alongside her and leapt over a dead log. "And how do you intend to take both dracwulves down on your own? I bet my life they're hunting together. Of course, I'd do everything in my power to avoid killing the animals, but it all depends on how the situation plays out. Our lives come first."

She spun around, cutting in front of my path, and headed back the way we came.

Okay, she had the same instincts as me—stay close to the castle. The dracwulves wouldn't go far, especially with the way the big one had eyed her. But she showed no sign of dread, and I recalled the way she had summoned the stags during the venery. Yep, she had an upper hand all right, which explained her cockiness.

I swung around a trunk and caught up with her. "So, you are okay with me killing one if the situation called for it?"

She halted, and for those few seconds of silence, her quivering chin said more than words ever could. But would she finally tell me her plans?

"Over my dead body."

Striding past her, I responded. "Well, if they attack me, I may have no other option. How else would I take down two wild animals and return them to the castle on my own?"

"Barbarian." Her hands gripped the backpack straps over her shoulders as she moved into my line of sight. "That's not what I expected from you."

"And what did you expect?" Curiosity poked a hole through my chest.

She shrugged. "For one of your pack members to meet you in the woods and to help you out."

"Now you're calling me a cheater."

"You said it."

"Well, you sure are showing your true colors. Like how you

never told me about the daggers." My voice lowered, her deceit still biting me.

Her nose pinched with a crease. "And give Levin a reason to slaughter my family if he found out?" She blocked my path and jabbed a finger to my chest. "Look, stop jabbering so much. If you plan to hunt with me, keep focused on the job and follow my direction. The first dracwulf we encounter is mine. Understand? That's the only way we'll hunt together."

She stormed away.

I sucked in the refreshing cold air, needing to keep my head in the game, to ignore her betrayal before it clouded my fighting ability.

Then she came to a standstill and turned around. "Did you tell your father about the daggers?"

"If I had, you wouldn't be here right now."

The tendons in her neck flexed. She didn't believe me.

"I would never put you in harm's way. Can't you see that, especially after everything we've been through?"

She dropped her gaze momentarily. "Just figured it explained your father's foul mood and sudden rule changes."

"He's like that every day. An unpredictable dick. You get used to it after a while." "I'd kill him before I accepted it."

"Quickest way to get yourself killed then," I said, and we continued our trek into the woods.

"Well, you've got more patience than me. I would have sliced his heart out in his sleep." No sarcasm layered her words.

"Everyone who's ever met him has had the same idea. Including me, at least once a day, but I couldn't bring myself to stoop that low, or I'd be no better than him."

We hiked, no words, and no sign of the dracwulves either. No footprints, fur on shrubs, no howls. We had nearly circled the castle when a twig snapped off to our right.

I froze and grabbed Selena's wrist, then waved toward the sound.

We listened. Waited.

Another crunch, this time closer, and coming from behind an

oversized cluster of undergrowth, easily reaching my hip. A dracwulf?

My gut was yelling to charge, to attack the wolf and get this done already. Take the dracwulf down now, claim the boon. End this.

I slipped the backpack off and plucked the knife out. Adrenaline fueled each of my precise steps.

Selena approached from a few paces away, no blade in her hand. She glanced over to my weapon for a smidgen of a second.

The closer we got, the louder my pulse thumped in my ears. I'd practiced for years in my human form. What difference did it make if I didn't have my wolf? The strength still came from within me. But this was a dracwulf! An animal I'd never fought.

More crunching. Louder this time.

Why wasn't it attacking?

Up ahead, the cluster of trees and shrubs created a halo of shadows, easily concealing the animal. Time to act.

A quick nod to Selena and we fanned out on either side of the spot. We leapt out behind the trunks, our knives poised, and my heart galloping.

A wild pig snorted and squealed, backing itself against a set of tangled roots, its eyes huge.

"Fuckin' shit," I blurted.

Night draped across the landscape of our first day. Two days left to catch the dracwulves and return to the castle.

Selena and I sat around a fire beneath a rock ridge that protected us from the snow. I salivated from the sweet smells of the roast pig on our makeshift spit.

"I don't get it." Selena bent her knees, hugging them. "Where can they be?"

"They could have simply bolted for the nearest town. But with our little piggy here, let's hope it draws them in our direction."

She glanced over to me, shadows dancing beneath her green eyes. Keeping a distance was her specialty today. Nothing I said got her to open up. Maybe that was for the best because we weren't at summer camp.

I swept a gaze across the dark curtain staring back at us from the woods. "After dinner, I'll take first turn standing guard."

I withdrew my blade from my boot and set it down beside me.

"Not sure I'll be able to sleep tonight. I'm happy to take first watch." She didn't even look my way as she spoke.

A laugh pressed hard on my throat. If she suspected me of backstabbing her, then that was perfectly fine because I wasn't so sure I trusted her either.

CHAPTER 24

SELENA

The cold froze my flesh, digging its claws in like an oversized paw. I shifted in bed, pressing myself against the warmth at my back, calling for sleep to sweep me away.

But when a hand squeezed around my waist, my eyes snapped open to a fizzling fire, its smoke a wisp, twirling on the breeze. Snowflakes drifted across the morning landscape, covering everything in its white dress. I wasn't in my bed. Oh, yeah. Wilderness.

Behind me, Marcin's breath wafted through my hair. I must have fallen asleep during my guard, and now we cuddled like lovebirds, instead of keeping watch for Klaus and Grit.

Time to get moving. Father had made it clear that Marcin wasn't to discover the syringe he'd slipped into my pocket after the guards had patted me down. The antidote would help reduce a dracwulf's aggression, and that meant getting to a dracwulf first. My eyes stung each time I thought about the anguish Father must have faced in deciding to give up our pets for our protection. I wouldn't let his actions be in vain.

I shimmied away in slow motion, but Marcin's arm slid across my shoulders, tightening his hold, drawing me closer. His forearm was inches below my mouth. My lips tingled with the temptation to lean back and kiss him. *Madness.* Goddess, any other time, and I'd gladly curl in his embrace, maybe even greet him a special morning hello, but that was me dreaming, and I had to stop fooling myself about anything happening between us.

"Where do you think you're going?" His sexy voice had my heart breaking into a sprint. My earlier determination to leave his side dissolved into a mess of melted snow.

After tracking down my voice, I managed to respond. "Time to hunt."

"I'd rather stay here a while longer." His hold wasn't loosening, and one of his legs shifted across mine, trapping them, our bodies plastered together, along with his morning hardness nestled against my butt. Any last strands of strength I had to push him away evaporated. Our time back in the cave flooded me with emotion and sweet memories. A tingle zipped down my belly and much lower.

"Just want to keep you warm."

His voice had that deep undertone that sent pin prickles across my skin and swelled my libido to a point of no return. "Y … you sure that's all it is?"

"I'll make it anything you want." His slightly hoarse whisper danced across my cheek.

Couldn't we be anywhere but in the woods hunting dracwulves? I peeled away his arm, much to my desperate ache to stay there, shuffled my legs free from his bind, and climbed to my feet.

Marcin hadn't shifted from his lounging position, lying there like a god, with dreamy bedroom eyes calling me back to his lips, to his embrace.

But he got to his feet, brushing the foliage from his pants, and zipped up his snow jacket. "If you keep staring at me like that, you won't be on your legs for much longer."

My cheeks were probably an explosion of red, and I reached for the water bottle. What was going on with me? My wolf wasn't inside me or pestering me that Marcin was ours, yet I craved him intensely. These feelings were mine—raw and animalistic. But with Levin threatening to kill us, me winning the boon was priority. Not my emotions for Marcin. Especially after I saw the hurt in his eyes yesterday when he mentioned the daggers.

He stuffed the blanket into his backpack, then proceeded to kick snow over the burnt- out fire. If there was ever a wulfkin I'd take as my soul wolf, Marcin was it. My beating heart agreed. His tenacity to confront Levin when the rest of the wulfkin in this pack said nothing made him a hero in my books. But maybe too much shit had gone down between us to ever move forward.

"Ready?" Marcin asked.

I brushed my hair back and grabbed my bag. "Yeah, let's do this." Before my resolve weakened.

---

*H*alf the day whizzed past without a sign of either dracwulf, so we now tracked through the woods on the west wing of the castle, heading down a steep slope. My feet slipped over the white powder, but I used the trees to hold myself upright.

My gaze locked on fresh marks in the snow. "Paw prints." We hurried closer, and I dropped to my knees alongside the indents with four toes and claws. Maybe a wolf, but they were too large.

Marcin stood near a skeletal bush, bare of leaves, and plucked white fur strands free. We exchanged hopeful glances.

"Grit."

"We keep moving." Marcin retrieved his blade.

Once I was back on my feet, we skulked along in slow motion. The wind blustered around us, shaking branches, their grating spiking my nerves. Every creak and snap had me flinching. How in the world did Levin think this would be a fair fight? Now I wished Father had given me two syringes, but I'd use my ability where I could ... if I could.

Marcin halted, his arm jolting against my stomach. "Do you smell that?"

I inhaled the crispness of the earthy forest, pines, before

taking another deep inhale. I caught it—the muddy, dog fur scent of a dracwulf.

This was real.

No matter what it took, I had to claim the boon. Even if it meant stealing the prize away from Marcin. He wasn't a wulfkin used to losing, though.

I cut a quick glance his way as he focused on the path amid the dense trees, his footsteps slow and precise.

Ignoring the darkness in my mind and in my chest, I pushed every other concern away and homed in on capturing a dracwulf.

Once we reached the valley, the sky darkened, and we both stopped, listening to a faint rumble of thunder reverberating in the distance. Ahead, I found indents in the snow and rushed to examine them. More paw prints. The dracwulf smell flittered on the wind, making it difficult to narrow down a specific location without my wolf abilities.

Fast steps, weaving amid trees, only revealed additional prints and fur tagged on brush, but no dracwulf.

Something red caught my attention from the corner of my eye. I moved closer, Marcin on my heels. At the base of a tree were the remains of animals, maybe a deer, several deer in fact, and even a boar. Bones, fur, skin, and blood were piled into a heap. Either this mess was their dumping ground or a snack for later.

A terrifying whisper trickled down my spine to my toes.

Retrieving the syringe played on my mind, but not here, not now. Maybe distance from Marcin was the answer.

"Let's split up," I suggested and retreated back toward the valley. "We might cover more area."

"Not a good idea. This is the dracwulf's stomping ground. We stick together and watch each other's backs." He headed farther along the valley, his gaze sweeping the woodlands.

Fine, we'd do this together, but one way or another, I'd get the first dracwulf. Klaus cascaded into my thoughts, along with the way he'd always stood by my side, guarded me. I remembered the time he was a tiny pup and slept on my chest. He and

Grit had been inseparable as pups. In the wild, wolves hunted together, though the prints belonged to one animal.

Farther ahead, a sheer rock wall jutted out of the ground, while the valley swung upward to the right. Around us, the entire forest seemed to sway. I was on edge.

A twig snapped behind us.

I jerked around. Lofty pines were draped in snow. Shadows shifted beneath them. A light dusting of white flakes drifted down around us, and the chill in my bones had zero to do with the weather.

"It's here," I whispered.

Another crunch. Louder. Closer. The distinct grunt I'd become all too accustomed to from Grit.

Marcin's gaze locked onto the woods behind me. He'd heard it too. "Stay close." He crept toward the sound, and I took that moment to reach inside the bag for my secret weapon. We'd finish this without hurting Grit too much. Or ourselves.

Movement to my left. A white blur charged me.

I recoiled, a yelp falling from my mouth.

Grit crashed into me, head first into my stomach.

I was flung back. My chest squeezed, and my hands grasped for leverage but found none. I hit the ground with a thud, knocking the wind out of me when my hip landed on a rock. An explosion of pulsing pain lanced through me.

Fear took over where determination had been only a moment before.

Grit was there, inches from me. His incisors on show. Blood matted the side of his face, and half an ear had been ripped off.

Marcin rushed toward us, brandishing a blade.

"Grit, it's me." As much as I tried to calm my voice, it shook. In slow motion, I dragged myself backward on my butt, the cold of the snow leaching through my clothes. My first attempt at a calm humming song came out as a growl, eliciting a threatening one from Grit.

He jerked his head around to Marcin, snarled and angled himself to my side, farther from the looming threat.

I broke into a hum, forcing a simple tune.

Grit's attention snapped to me, his eyes softening at once, pupils rolling back. I lifted a hand toward Marcin to stop moving. With my other hand, I still gripped the syringe and twisted myself on my side to rip the lid off with as little noise as possible. Every nerve was strained. My moment to tag a dracwulf and claim my boon.

A sudden crack of thunder erupted overhead, shaking the ground beneath us, roaring across the heavens.

The softness in Grit's eyes deadened, and his posture stiffened. My flesh rippled. Ice filled my veins.

Marcin's footsteps echoed. "Move."

I threw myself backward, turning away as Grit attacked.

Fangs latched onto my shoulder, sinking deep, hitting bone, hauling me through the snow.

I screamed. Dropping the syringe in the snow, my hands instinctually jutted out, punching Grit's face, hitting his teeth, his nose.

Marcin crashed into Grit's side, landing them both on the ground. I shuffled away, clasping my shoulder, and scrambled to my feet.

I grabbed the blade from inside my boot and scanned the ground. The syringe was gone, buried under snow somewhere. Shit!

Grit slipped out of Marcin's hold, kicking him in the gut as he sprinted toward me, his gaze locked onto my bleeding arm. Goddess, he saw me as a meal.

I bolted, but he slammed into my back, bringing me down, his teeth puncturing the back of my injured shoulder. Excruciating pain zapped through me, rising and spreading down my back.

His hot breath of coppery stink splashed over me.

But I was a wulfkin, not a meal, yet he wasn't releasing me. His jaws clamped down harder around my arm.

Nothing made sense, not the pain enveloping me, not my blurry vision, not the desperate cries coming from within. I lashed the knife at him, the blade biting Grit across the chin.

He whimpered. His hold softened, and I pulled free, rolling away.

Marcin was there, between us, releasing a guttural roar as close to a threat that any human could make, his hands in the air to make himself look bigger.

Grit wasn't buying it and lunged, his jaws going for Marcin's leg. Instead, Marcin swept sideways. Grit's head collided into his hip. Marcin dropped his blade, but swerved around and leapt onto the animal's back, an arm locked around his neck.

I hurried closer, my wounded arm limp by my side. Didn't matter, not now when Marcin wrestled a monster. Grit nipped at his face, his growls a deathly threat.

Grit bucked, tossing Marcin to the side as if he weighed nothing.

I gripped the knife, facing the dracwulf. His gaze danced between us, and finally rested on me because it saw me as the weaker opponent, the injured one.

Marcin pounced, delivering a fist to the animal's head, another to his side. Grit retreated but circled back in my direction.

I recoiled, the blade shaking in my fist.

Another rumble from overhead and the dark clouds shifted the afternoon sky into a shadowy netherworld ... complete with a hellhound ready to eat us.

"This way." Marcin grabbed my wrist and pulled me behind him. "Go. There's a cave in the stone wall. Run."

I sprinted, snow sliding beneath my feet. Behind me, footfalls erupted. The chase was on.

My body was numb. No time to stop. No time at all.

Ahead, the stone wall came into view, but no cave. I kept going. I spotted it and skidded sideways into the narrow breach in the wall, my clothes scraping against the rock, tugging on my jacket.

Grit seemed to be there, his jaws snagging my jacket, pulling me back outside. Before I could strike, Marcin bowled him over from his momentum and shoved me into the gap.

I stumbled inside a black cavern. Marcin was right there, thrusting himself in behind me.

Grit's head shoved through the gap inches behind him, teeth snapping.

I rushed to the closest boulder near the entrance and started pushing. Marcin was next to me.

"Fuck." He grunted, and the stone shifted, grating across the floor. The large rock rolled in front of the entrance. Grit retreated. Light spilled in from the tiny gap at the bottom and a sizable one above, but not big enough for a dracwulf to squeeze through. The light revealed a tiny area with other rocks along the walls.

We stared at each other, our breaths racing. Shadows crammed beneath Marcin's eyes. What were we going to do now?

Grit's growls echoed outside, as did the repetitive thump of his paws against snow. And I'd dropped the syringe. *Idiot.*

"Let me look at your shoulder," Marcin said, his voice strong and filled with adrenaline.

I glanced in that direction, blood smearing the fabric and dripping down my arm. With attention on my injury, the pain became agonizing as it spread across my chest. In haste, I unzipped my winter coat and covered the wound, my skin pinching. I held back a whine. With my shirt off, Marcin guided me to a rock near the entrance where the light beamed inside. Not once did his gaze dip to my bra.

Behind him, the enclosure appeared small; maybe it was just wide enough for ten people to stand. The sheer wall offered no escape through the back of the cave. Inside, the ground was littered with branches and dried foliage, tossed there by the wind. Half a dead log lay in here too. One end was clawed to death. Maybe the cavern was a bear's den. And now, we were trapped inside. On a bright note, I no longer felt dread of the small space. Probably because of the terror already consuming me about what waited on the other side of the boulder.

"What freakin' drugs did Levin give the dracwulves?"

"Let's focus on getting you patched up." Marcin retrieved the blanket. Using his blade, he cut two strips from an end. He soaked one corner with water and proceeded to wipe my wounds. "Without our wolf sides, I have no idea how long it will take you to heal, but stopping the bleeding is key."

Each touch sent a twinge of pain down my arm along with the sensation of ants swarming my skin. I stared at Marcin, who worked at cleaning my gashes. A slight crease pinched the bridge of his nose in concentration.

I reached across and wiped away the blood stain from his chin.

The expression behind his eyes was a blend of torture and fiery rage. "If I had stopped my father earlier, none of this would have happened." The dejection in his voice bled into me.

"It's not your fault. Your father's a monster."

He nodded. Soon enough, my arm resembled an Egyptian mummy, wrapped so tight my pulse barely pumped to my fingers. Once he stood, he used his foot to gather some of the foliage beneath his boots into a small pile, then crouched down. The flicking of the cigarette lighter echoed around us. Once the smell of smoke hit, he leaned over to blow against the rising flame. "Come closer to the fire to keep warm."

Unsure what to say to help our situation, I kept quiet. We might as well lay low for a while. I'd not only dropped my syringe outside but also my knife, leaving us with only one blade and one of my arms out of action. Yeah, we were in trouble. I joined him near the fire and sat with my legs crossed.

Neither of us was in a talking mood, but the stupid syringe plagued my thoughts. If only I'd removed the lid in time, I could have jabbed the needle into Grit.

Several hours later, the light had dimmed outside, and we slouched around the roaring fire. Marcin sat within arm's length of me, but he might as well be on another planet since he barely said a word. What was going on in his head?

Marcin picked up a thick log from against the back wall and set it across his lap. Using his blade, he stripped off some bark into one sheet. With the sheet on the ground, he hammered his knife along the length of it, breaking it into long strips about five millimeters wide. Hard to tell what exactly he was doing, but watching him work had a soothing effect on me. He grabbed a can of beef jerky from his backpack, pulled the lid open, and spilled the contents onto his bag.

He handed me one, then poured water into the can and set it on the edge of the flames. When he'd scrunched the stripped fibers into a ball, he submerged them into the heated water. Must be making cordage. Smart guy.

Marcin glanced over at me and handed me another jerky, which I accepted and devoured in three quick bites. Anything to take my mind off the searing cramping in my arm. *Please heal quickly.* "So what's your plan with the rope?" I asked.

"Might work as a lasso to capture the dracwulf. We aren't far from the castle. I'm thinking with your calming ability and the rope, maybe we can coax it back up the hill."

"So you don't plan to kill it?"

His brow bunched into a tangle of lines, and his voice lowered. "What do you take me for? My father?"

"No, I just thought ..."

My stomach clenched at the darkness clouding his eyes. The deep blue gleam I was used to seeing was gone.

"After everything we've gone through, you should have seen by now that I have no intention to hurt you, your pets, or your family. I want a better future for all wulfkin, one free of war and constant fear of punishment." He paused and shook his head. "I can't pin you down. I don't understand who you are anymore. For years, I felt as if I were drowning, losing my battle against Father. Then, after you came back into my life, you awoke something in my soul, providing me the strength to fight for myself too. I've been honest with you since you arrived, given you everything I have, but you still don't trust me. The secrets with the daggers and, outside, the syringe you tried to hide from me."

He turned away, sighing; his shoulders slumped as he used a stick to stoke the fire. "Maybe I don't know you as well as I once believed."

Guilt gnawed at my stomach, and ice threaded through my limbs. He'd seen the syringe but hadn't spoken a word.

I scooted closer and touched his arm, but he pulled away. "Father gave me the antidote for a dracwulf just before the contest but made me promise not to tell you. I'm sorry I didn't, and goddess, I wish I could take it all back. I'm so dizzy with all the crap happening to us that half the time, I don't know if I can even trust my own mind. Please know that I'm sorry for everything. For doubting you when I should have come to you the moment I found the dagger."

He said nothing, and we were thrown back into the murky embrace of silence. At that moment, the danger with Grit didn't compare to the threat of Marcin rejecting me. I'd been so consumed with protecting us from Levin, with doing what Father had told me, but never once asked the question of what Marcin needed.

I stared at him, the fiery glow reflecting off his stubbled jawline, the rawness in his gaze. A troubling tempest raked deep inside my gut, the harsh realization more than I could handle. I was a liar to everyone around me and, worst of all, to myself. But then again, my family had lied to me. Aisha's relationship with Zeki. Father blackmailing me into mating Marcin or he'd mate off Aisha. How could I have trusted anyone, especially someone like Marcin when he'd betrayed me in Turkey. Despite all the quicksand I was sinking in, I couldn't deny that I'd never be able to live without Marcin in my life. I'd fought so hard to save everyone except the one person who meant the world to me: Marcin.

MARCIN

I lay several feet away from Selena, who was fast asleep, her warmth a beacon calling to my freezing body, but I couldn't bring myself to move closer. Night engulfed the cave with only a few embers still grappling for life and not helping in the slightest with the chill. Sleep had refused to come last night after my conversation with Selena plummeted. Neither of us had said a word since. Before the battle of innocence, I started to believe her story about the dagger because the sultan wouldn't be so stupid as to use an engraved weapon against me, but it still irked me that she kept it a secret. And now, with Selena concealing a syringe, which I assumed was to reverse the anger in a dracwulf, her betrayal raged within me.

She probably didn't even understand that her winning the boon didn't guarantee security for Enre or Daciana, or for any European pack under Father's reign, or the Turkish from the onslaught coming their way if they had any intention of taking Hungary. If I won and claimed all the packs under my rule, it would work and strip Father of power. Everyone would be saved, including the Turks. As much as Selena would hate me for taking her boon, I prayed that one day she'd be able to see how my actions weren't to spite her. I wanted to help.

I climbed to my feet and crept around the fire, taking the

rope I'd twisted last night into a ball and heading for the boulder. The wind howled outside, trees rustled, and the chill whistled through the gaps.

Time to do this.

With my back to the adjacent wall, I set one foot against the boulder and pushed. It didn't move at first, so I took a steely breath and pushed again. This time, it slid, just slightly. Another thrust and it rolled enough for me to squeeze out, but not large enough for the dracwulf to get inside.

With one last glance at Selena, who slept peacefully—I studied how her eyes flitted behind her eyelids from a dream. The faint orange glow from the fire danced across her curled body, inviting me back to her side. I had to get moving.

Outside, the cold air snapped around me, and the waning gibbous moon draped the forest in a silvery hue. My steps slowed through the shin-deep fresh layer of snow as I scanned the landscape. Pines dressed in white engulfed the terrain, the featherlight patter of snowflakes cascaded on winds that carried a sharp bite. I pulled my snow jacket tight around my chin and headed in the same direction Grit had attacked from yesterday, fighting the blustery weather.

When I was barely a few feet away, a snarl droned from behind.

I stood motionless and carefully eased my hand to my back pocket for the rope, then glanced over my shoulder. From within the shadows of trees, Grit stalked in my direction, a blemish against the landscape. A stealthy hunter who'd obviously been waiting all night. Dread clung to my insides at his determination, remembering that when a dracwulf locked onto victims, it never gave up on taking them down.

He inched closer, the coat along his back an explosion of raised fur. As he passed the cave, he glanced at it, sniffing the air.

I whistled.

Grit's head swung in my direction, fangs on display.

"Come and get me."

As if he understood my words, he bolted my way.

Unraveling the lasso I'd created last night, I flung it. The loop snagged around Grit's head. I leapt out of his way. My hands tugged the cordage, tightening it around his neck, sending him into a jolting stumble.

He bucked, his back legs kicking out, his head thrashing. The rope slipped through my hands.

Grit already had an ear out of the loop and then the other. He was free. *Fuck.*

I retreated, never taking my sights off him, and grabbed the knife from my boot. In haste, I slashed the blade, nicking him on his good ear.

He halted, growling, then started circling me. I joined him in his war dance, my posture in a crouching stance. Weapons ready. Grit might be smaller than Klaus, but his ferociousness was insane.

The winds howled. I lifted my lasso, ready to toss it, but Grit's stare locked on my bleeding injury.

Change of plans.

I flung the rope directly at him, fast and hard, whipping him in the eyes.

He bounced back. His head shook.

Knife tight in my fist, I attacked. I careened around him and crashed into his side, bringing us both to the ground, him beneath me. My hands pushed down on his head to stop him from taking chunks of flesh out of me.

"Stop struggling and submit." The cordage was within arm's length behind him.

Shuffling my body across his, I stretched a hand near the homemade rope.

Grit thrashed against me, his snarls vibrating through my body.

My fingers reached out, inches from the rope. Almost there.

The moment I touched the lasso, Grit tugged free from under my hold. His jaws looped around, biting into my chest.

I cried out, and my body tensed. The pain sliced throughout my body.

Instinct kicked in, and I punched him in the head until he let go. With the rope in my grasp, I jolted to my feet and ran, stuffing the weapon into my back pocket, pressing a hand flat against the injury across my chest. No thinking. Nothing. Just bolting into the woods.

I glanced back. Grit leapt to his feet, rocking his head back and forth, then raced after me again.

The land sloped upward, and my thighs smarted with each leap, but it sure as hell didn't sting as much as the bite. Well, no hiding from the dracwulf now. He'd sniff me out in seconds.

At the crest, I swung left before looking back. Grit was only a few paces away. The snow slowed my pace, but the test of wills had become life or death to one of us.

Grit jumped onto my back, bringing me down again, face first into freezing white powder. I lost hold of the knife.

His fangs pierced the back of my neck. Excruciating daggers into my flesh. The metallic scent of blood filled my nostrils.

I drove an elbow backward, bucking him off and striking Grit's side.

Up on my feet, I struggled through the thick snow, my head wavering, my muscles seizing. No time to find the knife. More trees. My vision danced. *Keep going. Don't stop.*

Ahead, the castle loomed like a candle in the pit of hell. My legs pumped faster, taking longer strides. The soreness faded away as adrenaline propelled me.

Snapping at my heels, the dracwulf was right there, not falling back.

The clearing behind the castle came into view, along with the lanterns set up for our return.

I exploded from the woods, my sights on the empty field. Not a soul in sight.

Swinging around a large boulder, I turned to face Grit, my lungs gasping for air. The beast hopped onto the rock, his chest rising and falling. As was mine.

He lunged, hitting me square in the chest. Already soaked in blood, I stumbled as his momentum drove me to the ground.

Grit froze for a moment. He'd either heard or smelled something nearby.

His hesitation was just enough time for me to shove my hands into his shoulders, sending him teetering backward. I managed to get to my feet and threw myself onto Grit, my fists slamming into his head relentlessly.

The dracwulf whimpered, his body shaking. On my next hit, his head sunk and never lifted. His eyes rolled back, and within seconds, the muscles beneath my hands softened.

I straddled him, immobile, waiting. My breathing came too fast as I gulped for more air. When I pressed my hands on the pulse, I was surprised. He was still alive. Good. I retrieved the rope and tied his front legs together, and then his back, just in case he woke up.

I wiped at the blood oozing down my chest, feeling a sharp ache.

Footfalls to my left.

I flinched around.

Guards followed Father and the sultan from the back doors of the castle. Vincent and several of my wulfkin joined. As did Aisha, who ran ahead of them. Her glassy eyes fastened on Grit, and then the woods. My chest tightened into a knot. I had to return to rescue Selena.

Father reached me. His chest pumped out like a cocky rooster and the smile on his lips wider than I'd ever seen. The notion of him believing this win was for him, that he'd somehow won anything, had bile burning in my stomach. The tricky part hadn't been tackling the dracwulf, but dealing with the real monster—my father.

Behind him, the sultan wore a grim expression, the kind that cut through me. It sliced deeper as I imagined Selena waking up alone. Maybe I could return before sunrise.

Father blocked my view of the sultan.

He clapped a hand to the wound on my arm as I stumbled to my feet. I cringed on the inside. "Son, today you have made me proud."

Close to losing my footing from the first compliment he'd ever given, I reminded myself it had fuck all to do with me. In his mind, everything revolved around the boon. He grabbed my wrist with his frozen grip and lifted my arm into the air, his voice booming. "We have a champion. My son, Marcin Ulf." Instead of warmth, coldness seeped through my veins, and I ripped my hand from Father. "I'm going back to help Selena."

His face morphed into a horrendous beast, and for a split second, I swore he was transforming into his wolf side. Despite the shakes claiming his arms, he held it together.

"Then you forfeit your claim to prove Enre innocent."

My hands curled into fists until someone set a hand on my good shoulder.

"Come. Get your antiserum first." Vincent dragged me by an elbow.

Rage burned my insides, but I followed Vincent to Barka, the medic who was stood near a tree stump. Fuck Father and everything he stood for. Nothing he could do would stop me from going after Selena. Vincent was right. It made perfect sense to first resurrect my wolf side.

Barka pushed loose silver hair into her bun and picked up a syringe, twice as long as the one I'd received to deaden my wolf side. Needles didn't normally worry me, but this one appeared as if it might pierce all the way through my arm.

"Roll up your sleeve." Her words were strangled, and she kept glancing over to Father who was talking to his guards. Vincent had retreated behind us, so it was just the two of us, yet her demeanor seemed strange.

"Is everything all right?" I asked.

Barka wiped a spot on my arm with an antiseptic wipe and leaned in closer, her voice lowered to a soft whisper. "I sure hope that poor Turkish girl arrives back today." She removed the lid from the injection and flicked her finger against the barrel filled with red liquid.

"Why's that?"

She pressed the needle into my flesh, and I gritted my teeth.

Her voice lowered. "There was poison in the serum." Her

gaze wavered to Father and back before she jabbed deeper. "He made me do it, which is why you need the antiserum by the end of today. Otherwise, you'll die." She withdrew the needle from my arm.

"That's only two days into the challenge. He said three days to return the dracwulves."

The world beneath me swayed. Father had gambled with our lives, ready for us to die, for a goddamn chance to claim whatever fucked up scheme he'd made up in his head. And Selena was still out there. I was going to rip him to pieces.

Rage blurred my vision. Lava scorched my insides. I hurled myself toward my father, my fists striking his head and chest. Nothing would stop me.

He fell backward, but I fisted his coat tight and heaved him so close I could smell his pungent breath. "You fuckin' piece of shit." My insides shook uncontrollably, and before he responded, I head-butted him. He stumbled backward, his face bloody and his hands flaying outward as he collapsed onto his back.

Behind me, a cacophony. I glanced back to find Vincent with our pack in a semicircle around us, keeping Father's guards at bay. Several had transformed into wolf form, drooling like savage animals. "This is between father and son. Give them space," Vincent spat out.

My father lifted himself and broke into a chuckle. He wiped the blood from his mouth. "About time you manned up and acted like a real alpha."

The sultan appeared by our sides, clearly perplexed by the scene. "Tell him, Father." I shoved a hand into Father's chest. "Tell the sultan how the serum you gave us to restrain our wolf side was deadly. How it will kill Selena if she doesn't get the antiserum by the end of today. You gambled with our lives."

The sultan's face reddened. Four of his guards closed in behind him. When the sultan finally spoke, his voice trembled. "Is this true?"

Father's laugh died abruptly, and he dusted the snow from his long coat. "Sultan, you of all people can appreciate the importance of putting pressure on the contestants. This isn't a free-for-all, or we might as well turn this into a zoo and start selling popcorn. Last time I looked, we are wulfkin, not fucking pussies."

"My daughter is still out there. You have no right to play God. I would never endanger anyone in my pack in this manner. You're unfit to lead anyone."

The sultan came out and voiced what I'd been unable to say this whole time. I glanced around but saw no sign of Tibor or the council. Of course not.

"Watch your tongue, dear Sultan, because you are on my land. You're still subject to my rules."

The sultan shook his head, his mouth contorted into an angry line. He stepped closer. "You have no standing to impose your rules over me, a fellow Varlac alpha, after you've demonstrated what a wretched emperor you have become."

Father hardened his shoulders, standing his ground. "Enough of this bullshit. If you intend to keep your head, then shut your mouth. Anyone who dares to go help Selena will be punished by death. Along with those they hold dear. Now get the fuck out of my face. Marcin, meet me in my quarters."

I refused to budge from his path, not caring for the threat in his eyes. He would no longer impose his made-up barbarian bullshit. Especially after putting Selena and me in mortal danger.

"Father," I called out, loud enough for everyone to hear. "I'd like to claim my boon now."

He stared at me as a vulture might do when it spotted fresh road kill. Darkness skated across his face, and his eyes narrowed. "Be very careful, son."

"First, Enre is declared innocent and safe because I completed my challenge. The same applies to Daciana as Selena will arrive in time. My pack will release Enre and Daciana, then escort them to their home in Transylvania."

Father's posture shook, and his lips thinned, but before he could respond, I continued. "And under the very rules you imposed on every wulfkin in Europe, I call the council to hold you accountable for breaking the gravest of rules." I had no idea if Tibor would support me, but it didn't matter because I was going through with this now. And if he didn't back me, then I was taking him down too.

"What are you talking about?" His fake amusement didn't fool me. "You sound like a girl, making up stories."

I opened my mouth, but Tibor's voice echoed across the crowd. "Emperor Levin, for releasing two dracwulves into the wild where humans could've been endangered, for exposing these animals to humans, who could return to our land and search for the dracwulves, revealing our kind, you are charged and will be summarily punished."

Father's mouth gaped open, and for the first time, he was short of a comeback.

"Until then," Tibor continued, "the council no longer sees you fit in your role and has appointed Marcin to the position of Emperor, the Varlac alpha of Europe."

"This is preposterous. No one can touch me. No one!" He stormed past me, his shoulder knocking mine, aiming for Tibor.

Vincent stepped in front of Tibor.

Father's guards threaded toward him. Why the hell was Sanyi there? He was the same scum who preyed on young girls and guarded our dungeons. The wulfkin sidled up to Father and whispered in his ear as if they were best buddies.

And like a thunderstorm, the truth struck—the poison Barka mentioned in the serum, the poison on the stolen Turkish dagger with me being targeted. I'd never seen Father and Sanyi in the same room before, so who better to carry out evil deeds without it coming back to him.

My accusation surged loud and clear, claiming Father. "You had Sanyi steal the sultan's daggers, didn't you?" Father retreated, and Sanyi stepped in front of him. "And you tried to have me assassinated so the sultan could be blamed, giving you a reason to kill him."

His voice quivered. "Trust me, Marcin. You don't want to do this."

My mind whirred with hatred, the kind I'd never experienced for anyone. At that moment, my father deserved so much worse.

When Sanyi charged, I didn't hold back and threw a punch squarely on his nose. Someone else slammed into my back and grabbed my arms, pinning my shoulders.

Sanyi rolled his strikes into my gut and face. Each hit stung. I gasped. The sense of treachery consumed me, rage replacing any pain. Yes, my father was a leech, but to have him openly put me in harm's way was too much. Fury won out within me.

I kicked Sanyi in the groin, sending him reeling to the ground. When my head snapped back, it hit the wulfkin's nose behind me. My vision pulsed ... totally worth it. I swung around and laid a fist into the wulfkin at my back, then charged after Sanyi. Time to finish what we'd started.

Around us, Vincent and a handful of my pack were fighting Father's other guards. Enormous Turkish wulfkin joined my side. Half were wolves as they brawled. But Father was being protected by a small ring of his handpicked wulfkin. Coward.

Sanyi stood between us, his dark eyes narrowing. "You're a fool. We always had a cure for you from the daggers. But you spoiled everything." He shook himself and released his wolf side, clothes and fur a jumbled mess as a dark beast streamed out. This scum didn't deserve a pack, a family, or anything.

I crashed into Sanyi, knocking him over, and jumped on him, laying punches into his face. His back legs kicked me, pitching me aside. He rolled over and scrambled toward Father, who retreated with a circle of guards. They'd run away, hide, and not face charges.

Not under my watch.

Two of Father's guards eased away as interference. I stomped in their direction, striking one in the gut while the other wulfkin punched me in the ribs. I winced but stood my ground. "Get the fuck out of my way, under the command of your new emperor." Hell, those words sounded weird on my tongue.

They halted for an instant, but charged. I reeled out of the way before a third joined in, all three targeting me.

My head spun, and I gave just as good as I got, knocking one out with an elbow to the face. The others were relentless. Before I had another conscious thought, my wolf was there. Time to free him.

Behind his protection, Father was racing away. I shoved past a wulfkin, but someone tackled me, bringing me down. I reached a hand in Father's direction. "Stop him."

A wulfkin stomped on my hand, and I grimaced as the pain from bones cracking shot up my arm. Then my wolf steamed ahead, spilling past the dam of my human form. I welcomed the backup.

My wolf snarled, and I jabbed my jaws into the leg of the one holding my paw, tearing at the other hands on me. Before they could react, I raced past them. Just then, a blur whizzed from the side, a huge silver wolf going straight for Father—the sultan.

He pounced over a guard and lunged for Father, who turned around just as the assault collided into him.

Teeth wrapped around his jugular.

Father screamed.

By the time I reached Father's side, his vein dangled from the wolf's mouth. The sultan's mouth. Vincent dragged a kicking Sanyi away, but my sights remained fixed on the blood. The sultan released a bone-chilling howl, echoed by his guards. I watched in wonder as his body shimmied into human form, fur vanishing. A stocky man stood in front of me with my father's body sprawled at his feet.

Father was dead. His eyes were wide open, his mouth gaping with a horrified scream frozen on his expression. Goddess, it shouldn't have had to come to this, but even after all the chaos he'd caused, I wasn't sure I could have done it myself. He was my father and the only parent I had left. A small sting spread through my chest, and I prayed that the moon goddess take him to a place where love embraced him, eliminating hatred from his soul.

The sultan cleared his throat, and I glanced up. "Marcin, I hope you can forgive me for taking away your kill. I had a mistake to make up for in letting Levin use our dracwulves. After he poisoned you and Selena, enough was enough."

Right then, rational thinking was out of the question. I didn't have time to decide if it was from the sudden loss of my father, or Selena still out in the woods and in danger, or that the Varlac sultan, through killing Father, had just claimed the Hungarian land.

CHAPTER 26

SELENA

I kicked a pile of snow and pictured it as Marcin's head. The bastard skipped out on me during the night. Wasn't the first time he ditched me, but his backstabbing burned through me. He'd used me and stolen the boon from right under me. The dickhead tried to make me feel guilty about keeping secrets. On top of everything, he took his rope, and Grit was nowhere in sight. The tracks in the snow pointed to a scuffle that led up the hill toward the castle.

The firestorm thumping through my veins hadn't deflated as the afternoon sun sank behind the mountains. I'd discovered no signs of Klaus either. For the past hour, an ache continued through my limbs, slowing me, and it was joined by a banging inside my skull. Could be the lack of food or exhaustion. Each step grew heavier. I dragged myself to a boulder to rest.

Had Marcin claimed Klaus as well? Or had Klaus simply bolted? Maybe I misinterpreted his stare back at the castle as a threat when it could have been his farewell. He'd always been intelligent that way, detecting danger before I could. Sure, he had the drugs in him, but what if he simply used the angry energy to run as far from here as possible? The drugs would eventually leave his system.

The thing was, I wasn't worried for him because I couldn't see Marcin hurting Klaus if he had caught him. Though, I couldn't say the same for Marcin. Or for that matter, for myself when I returned without a dracwulf.

If Klaus had bolted deeper into the woods and stayed there, I wished him the best life. He'd been neutered as a pup, so breeding wasn't an issue. I just prayed he didn't attack any humans.

I shouldn't have fallen asleep last night. I shouldn't have hunted with Marcin, and most importantly, I never should have trusted him. He made me believe he cared for me. *Idiot.*

With every cell in my body, I'd fight and make him pay. The pressure behind my rib cage intensified, but it was the same ache I'd lived with for years after he left me in Turkey. Here I was again in the same predicament. I wasn't sure what hurt worse, the fact that Marcin used me or that I'd lost him forever.

I pushed myself up. Enough moping around. Time to take action.

Each step sent a twinge along my legs. Despite telling myself to move fast, my body wasn't listening. What was going on with me?

The tapping of wolf pads against snow sounded from behind me. I scanned the area and retrieved the syringe I'd found near the cave. Hopefully, it would be worth the hour of sifting through the snow to find it. No sign of my knife, though.

My thoughts dissolved as Marcin emerged from behind a tree fifteen feet away. He wore a grin and ran toward me. What the hell was he so happy about?

I tensed, my hackles flared. I would tell him exactly where he could stick that smile. But a gray blur sprinted from the woods to his side, rushing for him.

Klaus crashed against Marcin, bringing them both down. Serves him right for leaving me, but I didn't want him to die. I dragged myself closer, urging my legs to move faster, but my body slowed. *Come on, push past it.*

Marcin punched Klaus in the head, but the dracwulf wasn't releasing his hold on his arm. He hit him in the head again and wrenched himself free before grabbing a blade from his boot.

"Don't hurt him. I have the syringe to help him." I took the injection out and popped off the lid. Unsure why I should cooperate with Marcin, I had to stop him from harming Klaus.

Marcin charged toward the animal, sidestepped him at the last minute, but Klaus was too fast and whipped around, ripping into his thigh. Marcin cried in pain. Klaus retreated toward me, blood dripping from his mouth. He snarled as he glanced back at Marcin, who stumbled, a hand clasped to his bleeding leg. Pain capturing his scrunched-up face.

Klaus was protecting me!

My hand shook as it tightened around the syringe. Goddess, I never wanted Marcin harmed. While every instinct told me to jump toward Klaus and jab him with the antidote, my body faltered and barely stood upright. A wave of lethargy lapped through me.

If Klaus wanted me dead, he would have attacked me instead of Marcin. Maybe his drug had worn off, or goddess knows, it might be my link that halted his aggression toward me, though it hadn't worked with Grit.

I stared at Marcin, and each word came with a panted breath. "Why did you come back? To gloat?"

He swallowed past the obvious lump in his throat and dropped his gaze momentarily. "You have every right to be pissed at me."

"You bet your ass."

"Maybe first let's deal with the dracwulf who's staring at me as if I were a steak."

"Is one dracwulf and a boon not enough for your ego?" A fog spread through my head.

I stumbled a few steps away. *Keep it together.*

Klaus lunged for Marcin, but with the hilt end of the knife, he slammed it into Klaus's

head. The dracwulf shook his head and dropped.

Marcin stood his ground, his body waving as he clasped the blade, his gaze fixed on

Klaus who was attempting to climb to his feet.

I toppled next to a tree and fell against its strength.

Marcin's eyebrow arched. "I took Grit in because the boon would protect everyone,

including you and your family. But I haven't returned for Klaus. I'm here for you." "Bullshit." I landed on my knees, my hands in snow, the syringe still tight in my fist.

Klaus glanced in my direction and was still shaking his head, his body rocking on his legs.

Marcin limped sideways from his injury, but Klaus's gaze followed him, a snarl reverberating in his chest. "Listen to me," he said. "The serum we were given to stop our wolf side has poison in it. You're going to die if I don't give you the antidote."

I glared at Marcin. Lies. He was filled with them. "I don't believe you." He planned to claim Klaus for himself. Be the big hero.

Klaus's jaws snapped at him, but Marcin wasn't moving. He staggered sideways while blood stained the snow around his feet, and his face paled.

"You're feeling weak, sluggish, right? Can't you see? It's the poison. It was my father's way of controlling us, killing us if we didn't win."

"I'm just tired and hungry. Anyway, you're not looking too great yourself." I pushed myself to my feet, my knees trembling. Lack of sleep and hunger had never made me this lifeless.

"Please, Selena. If I don't give you this antidote, you'll die." He lifted a syringe in his hand covered in blood from his wound. "If this was for Klaus, I would have used it already."

I caught sight of a clump of silvery, dark fur on Marcin's jacket from another wolf. And the stretches on his face and neck indicated a brawl. Goddess, had he fought with Father? Was this his humane way of finishing me off because my father, Aisha, and everyone else I loved had already been butchered by Levin? My heart rebelled against the idea, but my mind pushed at the evidence in front of me.

A desperate urge to break past both of them and run to the castle pushed at my insides. My heart splintered. A blurry Marcin stood there, his face pleading with me as I swiped my eyes with the back of my hand.

I couldn't comprehend any of this. Could I trust him? He'd run away from me back in Turkey and did it again this morning. The boon was my lifeline, but he had ripped it away. I wasn't sure I could ever forgive him.

His voice climbed. "I'm sorry for not waking you this morning. I'm sorry for not believing you about the dagger. My father stole your daggers. I'm the idiot for letting our past dictate my behavior, my decisions. But don't let my stupidity sentence you to death." He lifted the syringe in his hand. "Please, Selena. I should have keep returning for you in Turkey, but I was foolish to believe my father that the arrow was meant for me. Fuck, I don't even know what really happened, but I don't care. It's the past, my mistake I'll fix. You mean the world to me, and I couldn't bear to lose you again. Now you're back in my life, you're mine, and I need you. I intend to keep you in my arms, safe and protected."

Marcin lifted his blade, ready to take on Klaus who approached from the side. The pain behind Marcin's gaze seemed genuine, but with my fuzzy head, maybe I was imagining it.

"Marcin ..." My words faltered, and my body quivered. I stumbled to my knees, my heartbeats had slowed.

An explosion of barks and snarls chilled my spine when I noticed Marcin and Klaus were back at it. Fur, flesh, and blood were knotted together.

My mouth opened, but no words came out. Goddess, I was so thirsty, I could drink an entire river right now. The world spun. What was happening? Was Marcin telling the truth about the poison? It seemed like something Levin would do.

I stuck a hand out with my syringe. Marcin was on his back, Klaus on top of him, chomping into his bent arm. *No!*

Steeling my nerves, I willed my muscles to move. *You can do it.* For Marcin. For Klaus. *Do it before they kill each other.* The past week had been a whirlwind of mistrusts and suspicions. Nothing made sense.

One sluggish knee after another, I dragged myself closer, my hands numb from the cold. I crawled toward them. "M ...

Marcin." His name was less than a whisper, an empty sound, but Marcin's head jerked my way, his eyes wide, his cheeks bathed in blood.

Several feet from him, I tossed the syringe and collapsed.

Each inhale was a rasp. The world slanted. Trees swayed in the breeze. My eyelids were heavy, and I gave in and closed them. The chill against my face was refreshing, calming, reassuring like a tender touch.

How much time had passed?

"Selena."

Was that the wind calling my name?

"Open your eyes. Please come back to me."

Nothing in my body responded, but everything had become so peaceful. A dark cloud hung overhead in my mind, promising me endless sleep, no more pain, no more anguish. I floated toward it.

CHAPTER 27

MARCIN

I flicked the lid off the syringe and jabbed it into Selena, driving the antiserum into her arm. "Don't leave me. Don't you dare." My voice crackled with desperation. I rolled her onto her back—eyes shut, inhales shallow.

My chest seemed to have turned to cement, and a sharp sting spread everywhere within me. I'd wasted hours tracking her down, her scent stolen by the winds when I should have moved faster. Instead of negotiating with her, I should have forced the cure into her system, ignoring her protest.

Now the pulsing beat of fear reprimanded me that I was too late, too slow. The fault was mine.

She lay in a cocoon of white snow, peaceful, as if nothing could touch her, yet she felt so far from my reach.

I'm here, Selena.

A few paces away, Klaus climbed to his feet, shaking snow off his coat. Gone was the rage in his eyes after I'd injected him with the antidote. Now he inched closer, sniffing Selena, whimpering. He collapsed onto his belly, his head resting on her stomach, his exhale a misty fog.

"She'll be fine. You'll see." The words hadn't convinced me, and kneeling in snow wasn't helping. "Come, let's take her home."

I stood on shaky legs, unsure how much blood I'd lost from

the injury in my thigh. No time for that now, or my busted lip, or the dozen bites and scratches littering my body. Nothing mattered right now, except Selena. With her cradled in my arms, I headed home, Klaus by my side.

Despite the drugs in his system, Klaus still remained loyal to Selena and had protected her. Had Father been wrong about dracwulves this whole time? Persecuting them because our ancestors didn't understand them?

Selena's body was limp in my grasp, and I kept glancing at the way her head was tucked against my arm, expecting her to open her eyes ... to hit me with one of her smart- ass comments. But it never came. By the time I reached the castle, frantic worry overtook all other thoughts. What if she never woke up? I hugged her closer, wanting to rewind time and protect her as I should have. If I'd only stopped her from getting the serum before the final race, or to have believed her about the daggers. If I had confronted my father earlier, maybe none of this would have happened.

I gasped, unsure of what to expect.

The sultan was there by the back doors to the castle. He ran toward us, his face white and his eyes screaming agony. Behind him, Aisha and the guards.

"Selena." The sultan's cry sliced my heart.

"Quickly, let me get her to a bed." It wasn't necessary, but if I stayed still a moment longer, I wouldn't be able to breathe again. I pushed past them and took her straight to my room.

After an hour of staring at Selena in my bed, still unconscious, I had to clear my head before I went insane with worry. The coil in the pit of my gut tightened the more I thought of her never waking up. *Fuck*, I had to stop thinking like that.

With the guards dismissed outside my brother's quarters, I pushed open the door and tottered inside on my injured leg.

Enre jumped off the bed and faced me, arms rigid by his side, hands curled into fists. He met my gaze squarely.

"Stand down," I said.

Daciana hurried from across the room, concern blanching her cheeks. "What's going on? No one will speak to us. We heard yelling and fighting."

"You're both free. Selena, a Turkish wulfkin, and I won the challenge. You've been proven innocent." The words were like a breath of fresh air on my lips.

Daciana released a strangled gasp.

Enre stood there, his eyes widening and his mouth falling open in disbelief. "You're bullshitting us."

"Why would I lie about that?" Time for Enre to open up his eyes and see the truth.

Light from the fireplace played over his confused features, and the irritation behind his stare waned as his gaze bounced between the open door and me.

Silence swept through the room, obviously the news stunning Enre and Daciana. "You're both free to return home. Transylvania is safe and Father will no longer be a burden."

Enre wiped his lips with the back of his hand and studied me. "Maybe I had you wrong all these years. Like what you said earlier about how you tried to help me when I was younger. Is it true?"

I smiled and broke into an explanation of how I distracted Father while Enre ran away, how I used to disobey Father's orders on purpose so he would take out his frustrations on me rather than Enre, plus a handful of other incidents.

Without another word, Enre moved closer and gave me a hug that could suffocate a bear. "Thank you." Shakiness underlined his words.

He pulled back and cleared his throat as a smile pulled the corners of his mouth up. "And Father? How is he taking the news?"

Probably rolling in his grave. "He's dead. The sultan killed him after he broke one too many rules."

Enre's gaze dipped momentarily as if he were offering Father a few seconds of silence. "So you're the new emperor, huh?" He clapped a hand on my shoulder. "Best news I've had in a while." His grip on my shoulder tightened. "But if you go power- raging crazy like Father did, I'll put you down myself."

"I'd expect nothing less."

Enre's smile broke, and the tension between us that had always been there since Enre was a young wulfkin eased.

Just seeing my brother content sent a beam of radiance through me. For years, I'd wanted the wall between us broken down, and this was a step forward.

Daciana was by my side, her hand on my shoulder. "I'm sorry for your loss."

I shook my head. "Thanks, but I lost my father a long time ago. Anyway, I sure could use support from both of you in the coming months, as not everyone will be happy with

Levin's death. Not to mention there were a lot of casualties in this tournament, and it will take some mending to heal what Father wrought." Then my thoughts took a dive as I remembered Selena was still unconscious, and it felt as if a snake were constricting my chest.

"Of course," Enre said. "We want to return to our families first, but we'll be back to help and bring reinforcements."

"Thanks. Look, I've got to go, but I want you both to feel at home. Please stay as long as you like. I've arranged for a few guards to give you anything you need. I'll see you shortly."

They both nodded in unison as if the news still hadn't taken hold.

A slight surge of pride filled me as I turned toward the door and hobbled out.

"The Hungarian land and every European pack falls under your reign, Marcin." The sultan stood several paces away, his chest proud, his words strong, and yet softness swept behind his eyes as they danced between Selena who remained unconscious in my bed and me. "You've proven your worth to take on such a role."

"Thank you." Shit yeah, I intended to rule over my family land and make things right.

He stepped closer, and I stood up on a shaky leg, in fact, my whole body was plastered in bandages, but my thigh was the only injury that ached with an incredible sharpness. I couldn't bear any weight on it. The sultan wrapped me in a hug and patted my back, his warmth a blanket. I clenched my teeth through the pain.

"I had no plans to take over this land," he said. "My claim of the boon was the only way out to save my daughters' lives, but with Levin gone, you are the rightful heir. I know you'll set things right." He broke our hug, and I sat back down, almost falling into the chair. "There should be no need for our clans to continue a war. You will now rule as the Varlac Emperor of Europe just as your father did."

"Yes and thank you for being the Varlac leader my father never could." I couldn't convey in words how much it meant to have this powerful Varlac alpha walk away from territory, to actually do the right thing for a change. Or maybe I'd never seen a wulfkin in such power put others first. I'd been wrong about him and his motivations and actions. This whole time, he'd only wanted peace, but I had allowed my father's hatred to seep into my mind. While I missed the idea of having a father, he'd died a long time ago in my heart. The ruler I'd lived with all these years was a shadow ... a demon.

"I'll ensure both our councils are aware of my decision," he said. "Now I better check on Aisha and make sure she doesn't vanish again." He left me alone with Selena, softly closing the door behind him.

I turned to Selena. The reflection of the blazing fire from the hearth brought shadows across the blanket and glinted against her dark hair sprawled across the pillow. I ran the back of my fingers along her cheek. She was warm to the touch, but her breathing remained shallow.

When I had received the antiserum, I sensed my change imme-diately, but maybe I reached Selena too late. Too damn slow, when I should have left the moment I learned about the poison in the serum. Cold regret filled my veins, along with images of her smile and her fighting words that wrapped around my heart, tightening their grip. But other regrets pushed to the foreground of my mind too. Those memories were a knife to my chest. With so much shit thrown our way, no wonder neither of us had a clue whether we were coming or going, who was to blame, who to trust.

Selena was my soul wolf. I'd known it from the first time we met in Turkey, but I was too blinded by political crap to see it clearly. Under no circumstance would I let her leave me again, unless it was her wish. No, we'd make this work.

I stared at her peaceful face, the rise and fall of her gorgeous lips. I lowered myself, the movement slow and soft, then I kissed them. "Please wake up."

Back on my feet, I limped to the window, staring out at the night and the silvery moon awakened over the land. My terri-tory. That fact still hadn't settled in. I'd been talking about it for years, planning it, and now that it became reality, I wasn't sure where to start. I had everything I wanted ... except Selena.

"Marcin!" Her croaky voice jarred through me.

My insides rattled as I stumbled to her side, pushing past the smarting twinge in my leg.

She sat up in bed, shoving the blanket off her legs. "Where's Aisha, my father—"

"It's okay." I took her arm to stop her from falling out of bed. "You need to rest, or you'll hurt yourself."

"Don't." She ripped her arm from me, scooting back away from me on the bed. Her eyes glistened, and her chin trembled. "Just tell me if they're still alive."

"Of course, they are." I perched on the edge of the bed to appear less threatening. "A lot has happened. Your family is safe. No one is going to harm them. In fact, the sultan just left the room to get some fresh air. Aisha was here before too, and now she's with Klaus and Grit. She's terrified and has been by your side for hours."

Her gaze bounced to the door and back, her hands fisting the silk sheets. "I don't believe you."

"Why would I lie?"

"Because you're a liar." Her words roared. "You stole the boon from me when I told you the first dracwulf was mine."

I hadn't intended on laughing, and in all honesty, I had no idea what made me, but I chuckled loudly at the insanity of how the events turned out. I probably sounded crazy, and the way Selena stared at me said as much.

"Look, Selena, let me catch you up on the details first. Then call me whatever you want."

Before she responded, I detailed everything she'd missed, from my father orchestrating the poisonous dagger, the deathly serum, why I took the boon from her, and also about the sultan killing my father. I explained that Enre and Daciana were now free. Lastly, I explained the generosity of the sultan handing over the Hungarian emperor position to me on the promise that I do a better job than my father. Not to mention, me still waiting for final confirmation that all Varlac alphas around the world agreed. I was confident it wouldn't be a problem, especially with the recommendation of a leader as respected as the sultan.

She sat there frozen. Her mouth gaped open, and her hands clutched to her chest. "Fuck."

"Yep. See all the fun you missed out on?"

Her eyebrows arched. "Levin's dead?" She paused for a moment, studying me with an inquisitive expression. When she spoke, her voice was a faint whisper. "Are you okay?"

"Hell, yeah. I mean he was my father, by blood, but he'd stopped acting like it when I was a child. I'm arranging for a proper burial to send him off to the moon goddess to face his final judgment."

She spread her fingers out in a fan against her breastbone, and her mouth fell open. "Wow ... not sure what else to say, but damn."

The door creaked open, and Aisha's head popped in. When her sights landed on Selena, she ran and hopped onto the bed, embracing her sister. "Oh, my goddess, you're awake."

Selena was shaking, her hands gripping Aisha's shoulders. "You're okay? Everyone's fine?"

"Yes!" Aisha's voice was high-pitched and her smile contagious. "Wait, I have to tell Baba. He's been worried sick." And just like that, she sprinted back out of the room.

Selena turned to me; her bottom lip caught between her teeth. "You were telling the truth."

I nodded and crawled my fingers across the bedsheets toward her, placing my hand on hers. "You're safe, as is your family."

"So, what do I call you now? Emperor? His majesty?"

"You can simply call me to your side."

She burst out laughing. "Lame, Marcin. Very lame even for you." But it didn't stop

her from inching closer to my side of the bed, staring at me with a newfound excitement gliding across her sinful grin.

Right then, Selena was my world, and I wanted to shout it from the rooftop. I cupped her face, then leaned closer, our foreheads touching, our lips inches apart. "Only one question remains."

"Yeah, and what's that?" Her words seemed to hitch as she forced them out.

"Are you still mine?"

Her wicked smile intensified. "Well, that depends."

The teasing minx had my pulse on a mouse wheel, racing insanely. "Oh, really. And what is this variable?"

"That you'll never lie to me or keep secrets again, and my family can visit anytime.

Maybe Aisha can move here with Zeki."

"Your father's captain of the guards?"

"It's a long story, but he and my sister have secretly mated. They may need somewhere to live until they get set up, in case they can't stay in Turkey."

Okay, I didn't see that coming, but it didn't bother me in the slightest. Who was I to turn away lovers in need? "Babe, if you want a mountain moved, I'd start working on it right now. Yes, it's fine. You'll be with me then?"

"For years, I've only fantasized about having you. So, yes, you're never leaving my side."

The warmth of a new summer day spread through me. I leaned in and kissed her, inhaling her scent, sensing her wolf stir, calling to mine. With her arms gliding over my neck, she drew me closer, her tongue surging with mine, her passion filling me with fire. Warm hands slid down my back.

The sudden knock at the door had us both springing apart as if we were teenagers again about to get busted for kissing. "Come in," I said.

Aisha ran in first, followed by the sultan. Their gazes locked onto Selena. Aisha jumped on the bed with us, her hands around Selena, squeezing her tighter than before.

The girls giggled, and Selena pushed past her sister and hugged the sultan.

"The goddess has blessed us with your recovery." He broke their embrace.

"Marcin has told me everything that's been going on. I'm shocked."

"As are we," the sultan said. "But you're okay, and that's the most important thing."

"What happens now?" Aisha said, her eyes fixed on Selena. "Do we head home?"

"Actually." I took Selena's hands in mine. "We have a mating ritual to organize first.

No one's going anywhere just yet."

Aisha squealed, and the sultan covered his ears.

I never thought I could ever experience such joy. For years, I believed the universe was against me, throwing everything in my path to stop Selena and me from being together.

But now, in hindsight, it was helping us shed our baggage, our doubts, our misunderstandings.

I glanced across at the love of my life, adoring the way her eyes smiled when she looked at me. Yep, this was the right path for us both.

*V*incent placed a careful hand to my back as I limped on a healing leg along a corridor toward the main foyer. "This is your turn to do your magic. Show the packs how a real leader operates."

Goddess yes, I was ready to change the rules for the better.

Sunlight poured in from the arched windows, lighting the passage, giving it a golden hue, matching my insides. A sense of calm swept through me at how quickly all the puzzle pieces were fitting together. Selena being by my side seemed beyond belief. She was now officially my soul wolf, though unofficially I'd already claimed her. The peace between the Hungarian and Turkish clans was guaranteed, and I had even received a heartening message from the Russian Varlac tsar with his congratulations. I wouldn't deny a part of me mourned Father. At the same time, I knew our world was better off without him. Enre and I were definitely better off. Especially with the handful of wulfkin loyal to Father now in the dungeon. A few weeks ought to make them rethink their priorities, and then Vincent would train them to our way. And he can be very convincing.

"Can't tell you how thrilled I am to finally help our wulfkin, to stop using fear as a way to control them. I want you there by my side the whole time, so don't get any ideas about running away with one of your dates." I nudged him in the shoulder.

Vincent huffed but grinned. "You couldn't get rid of me if you tried, even though I'm guessing Selena might want you to herself at times."

"You bet." I intended to oblige to her wishes because I couldn't get enough of her. Even now, her scent wafted through my head as her muskiness caressed my senses. My wolf responded.

"Oh, thought you should know the Turkish ward, Irmak, has been spotted in Northern Europe near a small pack in the Swiss Alps. He's run away."

Irmak, who'd been traded from the sultan for good fortune, didn't deserve what he received during his time here. "Is he okay?" With all the crap going on, I hadn't given it a second thought to ensure he felt more at home. I'd have to break the news to the sultan and Selena, but if he chose another pack, then I would support his decision.

Vincent nodded.

I rubbed my chin. "The alpha there is a friend of a friend. I'll contact him and send my blessings to embrace him into their family. He'll hopefully find peace there."

"Irmak will have a new start, and that's what matters," Vincent said.

I guess even with my father defeated, there were too many haunting memories for Irmak to have a new start here with us. Still, I wished him well.

"Anyway," Vincent began, "I was thinking about taking some time off to go home and visit my parents. It's been years since I returned."

I shoved his shoulder. "You sly dog, you're going to meet that girl your mom's setting you up with, aren't you?"

His mouth morphed into an overexaggerated frown. "No way. Are you insane? Those small pack girls come with strange baggage."

"Maybe you're just extra picky?"

His brows pinched together. "Hey, it ain't my fault I attract all the loonies."

"You said it, but someday you'll find the right one, don't worry." I pushed open the

doors to our welcome room.

Enre and Daciana stood in front of the fireplace, their bags waiting by the entry doors.

They glanced our way.

My brother stepped forward first and wore a huge smile, the one I'd wanted to see

from him for years. Maybe all wasn't lost between us.

"You're all ready to go?" I asked.

"Marcin, I'm ashamed to admit I didn't have faith in you saving us from Father. But

I'll gladly admit I was wrong."

Before I could respond, Enre had me in a hug—strong and warm. The kind I imagined

two brothers shared, but his embrace was a first for me. I never wanted it to end. My throat thickened, but I didn't do girly emotions, so I pushed out a response that sounded forced even to me. "Maybe you should have more faith in your older brother."

Enre stared at me with an eyebrow cocked. Instead of a response, he mock punched my shoulder. "You know it. And we need to catch up on lost time."

"Yes, we will, very soon."

Vincent opened the front doors as a black Volvo pulled out in front of the castle. "Your ride's here."

Enre gave me a knowing nod, the kind that offered me the promise of finally having my brother back. I approached Daciana and wrapped her into my arms, rubbing her back. "I can't apologize enough for the way you were treated. But from now on, you are family and welcome here anytime."

"Thanks, Marcin." She pulled back. "You will make an admirable Varlac emperor alpha and one that was long overdue to rule our packs. I'm proud to have you at our helm."

Her words were heartening. Hearing the deluge of positivity made my new role much easier to embrace. "Can't tell you how much that means to me."

"You'll do us proud." She headed for the door but turned and gave me a final wave before exiting. Once she and Enre drove away, I stood there, staring at the dark furniture Father had preferred.

Vincent's voice broke up my thoughts. "What are you thinking?"

"Well, for starters, we're getting rid of all the fuckin' candles in this place and installing recessed lighting and ducted heating."

CHAPTER 28

One Week Later

Father guided me outside into the castle courtyard where the night was speckled with stars and snow coated the ground, glimmering beneath the moonlight.

Aisha approached us from farther in the yard in a gorgeous cream gown with long sleeves and a corset, Zeki by her side, their fingers interlaced. Klaus and Grit emerged from behind them, both wearing white ribbons around their necks to match my white fur coat. Of course, I protested, but Aisha insisted.

Father's gaze fell on Aisha and then on their linked hands. A grumble rolled through his chest. "I haven't yet given my approval on this, so please don't flaunt it until we've had a proper talk."

"Come on, Baba, this is a special occasion. Mom just arrived and has already given her blessing. And you've agreed to us living here while Zeki trains his pack with Marcin's."

"Today is about Selena and Marcin, not everyone gossiping. Please, do this for me." He rubbed his temples.

Zeki broke their hold. "Of course."

Father sighed before turning to me. "You ready for this?"

The smirk I'd worn for the past week hurt my cheeks, but I didn't care. I pulled the fur coat tight around my body. "Yes!" I'd been ready for this moment ever since I first laid eyes on Marcin in Turkey, when we had our first kiss. Despite my turbulent time in Hungary, I'd discovered a new side to Marcin beyond the physical attraction. The depth of his loyalty to protecting the European packs from his father, commitment to helping his brother, and even how he never gave up on trying to make it work between us.

Aisha passed us with Zeki by her side, the two so close they might as well be touching.

With my arm curled around Father's, we headed for the open doors at the rear of the courtyard without a cascading snowflake in sight. The perfect night.

He nodded and patted my arm. "I'm proud of you. You know that, right?"

I leaned against his shoulder. "Yes, I do."

The full moon hung low in the heavens, glorious and enormous, its energy caressing my skin. We emerged through the doorway of the courtyard and onto a snowy path directing us toward a large group of wulfkin, at least 200. Their smiles beamed in our direction. Golden lanterns swung from the trees, creating a magical glow around the field for my mating ritual, a scenario I'd fantasized about for so long.

We passed Daciana in the arms of a handsome, blond human. I'd heard the tales of her human partner, how he'd embraced our race. But with his presence in Hungary, which was unusual to say the least, I couldn't help but believe maybe our packs were moving forward in the right direction if they accepted a human at the ceremony.

Next to them stood Enre, offering me a nod of approval, his dramatic blue eyes matching Marcin's. He leaned against a brunette. Her hand cradled on a small belly, rubbing it as she glanced my way with the sincerest eyes I'd ever seen. I gushed. They were pregnant, and I considered stopping to congratulate them. Definitely later. I smiled to everyone else, including Tibor and the council who gave their admiring smiles.

At the end of the crowd, I caught a glimpse at Marcin who stood in a fur coat similar to mine, but black. The sparkling in his eyes promised scorching kisses and wild nights. My pulse pounded in my ears.

Every ounce of strength was required to keep me from running to him and throwing myself into his arms. We'd been kept apart for the past three days—a Turkish custom— so a few more minutes wouldn't hurt.

Father guided me past him, and I stuck my tongue out to Marcin as he winked at me. My wolf brushed behind my chest for release. *Soon.*

Once we were clear of the crowd, we stopped at the forest's edge, and we turned to face our guests.

Last time I stood in this spot, Levin had appeared ready to tear me apart, but now, this scene couldn't be more opposite. I would never wish back those days with Levin. Marcin had buried him in the woods, and we said our farewell, but now was the time to focus on the future and a new life.

"Welcome, everyone, to this most blessed occasion," Father began. "To the final mating ritual for Selena and Marcin. It's not every day a sultan gets to give away his daughter to an emperor, but this is so much more. Selena and Marcin are soul wolves, meant to lead their lives together. I can't express how grateful and elated I am to bless their union." He glanced over at me, the corners of his eyes crinkling with joy.

Marcin stepped up on the other side of Father, keeping his distance as expected. Damn, I wasn't sure how much longer I could wait.

"You are most gracious, Sultan. I also have something to share."

My father nodded, and I was curious what Marcin would say.

"First, it's an honor to finally have the Hungarian clan as one pack, in union, and working together, not against one another. Additionally, we have now accepted the Turkish clan into our family. For that, I cannot express enough gratitude for how lucky we are to have them be a part of our lives. My brother,

Enre, is here with his mate and pack, so our family is a force to be reckoned with, but my aim is to bring all the packs into our circle as one unit." He paused and rubbed his lips. "Yet, there was one unfinished element from the recent battle of innocence that must be addressed."

I stared at him, as did Father, but he never once lowered his gaze from the spectators, well versed at keeping a large crowd hooked on his every word.

"I won the boon, but I never got a chance to claim my prize." This time, he looked at me with his sexy grin. "In front of everyone, I'd like to use the boon to elevate Selena to the status of Empress, a Varlac alpha, to rule alongside me with equal authority."

No one said a word, but my gasp probably echoed on the wind. Honored was too tame a word for the ripple of excitement zapping through me. I embraced it in a heartbeat.

"Selena, I promised you the world, and this is just the beginning."

Father clapped and laughed. "Yes, yes."

Words were stuck to the roof of my mouth. Marcin had bestowed me with a status I'd always craved. I was now an alpha, no longer under anyone else's command.

"May the ritual feast commence," Father shouted and waved a hand at someone in the distance.

A dozen guards emerged from the back doors to the castle, carrying tables, chairs, and barrels of blood wine. Plates of food piled high with marinated meat and steaks arrived.

"As is tradition back home." Father stepped toward the crowd. "We eat outside beneath the heaven and the moon goddess watching over us."

All the guests moved in a river toward the feast when Marcin took my wrist and pulled me aside, his other hand gliding across my lower back. "Come with me," he whispered.

"But ..." My gaze danced between the guests and the naughty smile capturing Marcin's lips. Then I noted Father looking our way, and he gave a small approving nod.

"In Hungarian tradition, the new couple must run free together. That's why you're wearing that fur coat."

He guided me toward the woods, the excitement bubbling deep in my gut. I peeled open the coat and pushed it off my shoulders. The cold snapped around me, but it wouldn't for long. A quick glance over at a naked Marcin warmed my heart as he blew hot air into his hands.

Naked, I pounced, calling to my wolf, and already I was shifting, stretching, sprouting fur. I landed on all fours and sprinted into the forest. Marcin was right there, alongside me.

The snowy ground flew beneath my strong paws as the breeze caressed my face. Faster. Quicker. I swerved right and purposefully nudged Marcin. He nipped at my ear in a playful gesture, and I snarled his direction. He played dirty. I sprang after him just as we used to do in Turkey. Wild. Free. Together.

He turned left, targeted the west wing, exactly where we had our showdown with Grit.

I swerved around trees, jumped over roots, and slid down the slope, snow cascading alongside me. In the valley, I careened right and headed for the cave where Marcin was headed.

He came to an abrupt stop, and I slammed into him, both of us landing head over tails. He released a goose bump–inducing howl, the kind I'd expect the Varlac Emperor of Europe to make. I rested my chin across the back of his neck, claiming him.

In no time, he shimmied into his human form and stretched out his hand for me. I shook the last remnants of my wolf side, then accepted it as he escorted me into the cave. The questions on my mind vanished the moment we stepped inside. The place had been cleaned. No foliage or branches or logs. The floor was covered in layers of creamy furs. Cushions lined the edges of the walls, and a fire burned in the far corner. In the back was a small table with bottles of blood wine.

"When did you do this?"

"Figured this could be our special getaway, just like the lookout back in Turkey. Now, enough talking. Come here." He curled a finger in my direction, a devilish smirk capturing his mouth.

I leapt into his embrace, wrapped my arms around his neck, and my legs snapped across his hips. At once, his hardness sprang to attention, rubbing against my butt. "I'm not going anywhere."

"Never." And his lips pressed to mine, powerful and starving. Tingles swept all over my skin and seeped through my body, filling me with a contentedness I'd never experienced before. Simply magical.

I accepted his tongue, sucking it, adoring the accompanying moans. His hands cupped and squeezed my ass as he stepped up against a tapestry-draped wall, pinning me in place.

"Fuck me hard," I said. "Make it hurt. No holding back."

"I love it when you talk dirty." He guided my hips over his cock and his tip teased at my entrance. I squirmed to lower myself, but he wasn't releasing me. "First, how much do you love me?" He licked his lips, his eyes transitioning into a sexiness that had me trembling with desire.

"And if I don't?" My words were barely a whisper.

"Well," he lightly slapped my butt, "then I'll have to stop."

"I love you more than the universe."

He smiled and kissed my nose. "I love you so much, I'd give up my life for yours." "It's not a competition."

And with that, he inched into me slowly, pushing inside, opening me up. I gasped for air, my fingers digging into his shoulders, holding his seductive gaze. My inner walls tensed, shivering from the sensation.

"Don't hold back, babe."

My response was a purr.

Then he thrust deeper. I screamed with pleasure, as he rocked back and forth, bouncing me on his cock. The sensation when he hit my back wall had my body shivering in ecstasy.

I tightened as an orgasm already curling inside me exploded. Everything fell from my mind and only the sensation of Marcin fucking me mattered. My stomach tightened as moans of pleasure filled the cave. When the excitement completely rippled through me, Marcin groaned, joining in on the song of pleasure.

Caught between him and the wall, I held on tight. Our

breathing sprinted, matching each other's, and our bodies glistened with sweat. "We're not going anywhere until I fuck you at least three more times tonight."

I laughed because his words alone had my whole body throbbing with the thrill and anticipation. When I leaned closer, licking the length of his ear, his saltiness blended with my arousal. "I wouldn't expect anything less."

Marcin carried me to the center of the room and crouched down, slowly lowering me onto my back as he climbed on top of me. His mouth leaned toward my lips. His kiss was hard, the way I'd envisioned it for so many years when I thought I'd lost him. Here and now ... wrapped in his embrace, his cock buried deep inside me ... I had no intention of releasing the wulfkin who was my life, my true mate, my everything.

Thanks for reading Shadow Shifters.

Reviews are super important to authors as it helps other reader make better decisions on books they will read. So if you have a moment, please do leave a review.

Find more Mila Young books.

Gods and Monsters
Apollo Is Mine
Poseidon Is Mine
Ares Is Mine
Hades Is Mine

Wicked Heat Series
Wicked Heat #1
Wicked Heat #2
Wicked Heat #3

Elemental Series
Taking Breath #1
Taking Breath #2

Fallen World Series Co-write with C.R. Jane
Bound
Broken
Betrayed

Broken Souls Series Co-write with C.R. Jane

School of Broken Souls
School of Broken Hearts

<u>School of Broken Dreams</u>

Haven Realm Series
Hunted (Little Red Riding Hood Retelling)
Cursed (Beauty and the Beast Retelling)
Entangled (Rapunzel Retelling)
Princess of Frost (Snow Queen Retelling)

Beautiful Beasts Co-write with Kim Faulks

Manicures and Mayhem
Diamonds and Demons
Hexes and Hounds
Secrets and Shadows
Passions and Protectors
Ancients and Anarchy

SPIRIT SERIES
Spirit of Christmas

ABOUT MILA YOUNG

Best-selling author, Mila Young tackles everything with the zeal and bravado of the fairytale heroes she grew up reading about. She slays monsters, real and imaginary, like there's no tomorrow. By day she rocks a keyboard as a marketing extraordinaire. At night she battles with her might pen-sword, creating fairytale retellings, and sexy ever after tales. In her spare time, she loves pretending she's a mighty warrior, walks on the beach with her dogs, cuddling up with her cats, and devouring every fantasy tale she can get her pinkies on.

Find me on: facebook.com/milayoungauthor

For more information...
milayoungarc@gmail.com